Ring
of
Truth

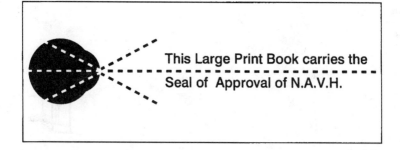

Ring
of
Truth

Nancy Pickard

Thorndike Press • Waterville, Maine

Published in 2002 by arrangement with Pocket Books, a division of Simon & Schuster, Inc.

Thorndike Press Large Print Basic Series.

The tree indicium is a trademark of Thorndike Press.

The text of this Large Print edition is unabridged. Other aspects of the book may vary from the original edition.

Set in 16 pt. Plantin by Minnie B. Raven.

Printed in the United States on permanent paper.

Library of Congress Cataloging-in-Publication Data

Pickard, Nancy.
    Ring of truth / Nancy Pickard.
      p. cm.
    ISBN 0-7862-3743-0 (lg. print : hc : alk. paper)
    1. Women detectives — Florida — Fiction. 2. Adultery — Fiction. 3. Florida — Fiction. 4. Large type books.
    I. Title.
PS3566.I274 R56 2002
  813'.54—dc21   2001054403

Special thanks to David E. Rovella,
criminal justice reporter for
The National Law Journal

Susanna

1

I'm Marie Lightfoot, or at least that's the name my publisher puts on the covers of the books I write about true crime. In classic "true crime" fashion, my latest one is titled *Anything to Be Together*. It's the tale of a murderous minister, the Reverend Robert F. Wing, who with his lover, Artemis McGregor, killed his wife, Susanna. Here's how it begins. This is the raw story that I am supposed to make you believe:

They were a matched pair: evil for evil, no holds barred. If the devil had split himself into male and female he could hardly have done a better job of creating two strands of a DNA for malevolence.

They felt their attraction instantaneously when they met.

It was easy to see, perfectly apparent to the only witness to their meeting.

As irresistibly as hydrogen bonds with oxygen, "like" attracted "like" that day in the church. But what did it really feel like, inside their bodies, the first time they saw each other? Did it pierce them like a knife? Did it jolt like electricity, shooting at light speed from their eyes to their breath, hearts, minds, groins? Or was it more subtle and delicate than that, more like a rare taste of something savory on their tongues? Was it love — or lust — at first sight? It looked that way to the church secretary who saw them meet. But what, precisely, did they see in each other at that moment that nobody else had ever seen?

Well, it is said that the devil knows his own. And her own. At a dark, submerged depth below the light of consciousness, they must have recognized each other. Lovers, twins, soul mates. Surely there was something ancient, wicked, and intimately familiar for each in the other's eyes. Before long, they knew they would do anything to be together, even murder — especially, and most deliciously, murder.

Too bad he already had a wife.

Too bad for the wife, that is.

That's what I wrote, so portentously that I have almost convinced myself that I believe it. It's overheated, isn't it? Sexy, steamy, as their lust is judged to be. It sounds as if the Reverend and the "other woman" were fated to meet, mate, murder. A jury believed part of it. They convicted him, freed her. Do you believe some of it, all of it? Ah, but you don't know the facts of the case yet, do you? I'm not sure that I do, either, and I wrote the book about it.

My book, if not their crimes, begins with innocence. There isn't even a hint of sex to begin with, except for the body of a naked woman abandoned to the subtropical vines, the snakes, the insects, and the putrefying heat. There is only the pure curiosity of childhood, betrayed in a decaying "Garden of Eden," on a stifling summer day in Florida.

Anything to Be Together

By Marie Lightfoot

CHAPTER 1

The suburbs look as if they're taking over Florida, but don't be fooled by appearances. Natives will tell you this state isn't what it seems. What it looks like is recent and skin deep; what it *really* is goes deep to porous limestone. Way down there, shellfish without eyes swim in water that Florida's famous sunshine has not warmed in centuries.

Live here long enough, and pay enough attention to its startling secrets, and you'll get the feeling it could revert to primordial ooze in the blink of a heron's eye. The Everglades could rise again and swamp the land, flooding new developments and turning them into ghost marshes. Hurricanes could topple every condominium on the beach and consume the last morsel of sand on reclaimed land. The gators could take over backyard pools, the panthers could prowl school grounds, and the bears that are confined to Ocala National Park could slip the fences and appear in town to ransack abandoned garbage pails.

It could happen, with only a subtle twist of the dial of fate: a bit to the left to get a monster hurricane season, or a bit to the right for global warming, and the whole state will disappear under water, just fall back into the sea. It wouldn't take that great a change in temperature or in the barometer to run the human beings off and turn Florida back to nature.

There are pockets of it, right now, where it looks as if it's happening.

Most people have no idea they're here, these pockets.

They're hidden in plain view, often behind KEEP OUT signs in dense, dark woody spots along a highway. You could drive by one so fast you'd think that momentary darkness out of the corner of your eye was a light pole flashing past. You could pass one every day on your way to take the kids to school and you'd never even wonder what was behind that dilapidated-looking fence.

"What's back in there?" one of your kids might ask.

"I don't know, but don't go there," you might say, without even thinking.

Of course, that would naturally get a kid to wondering.

Right in the middle of the most populous areas, there are hidden acres of snakes and Spanish moss, of gigantic looping ropes of vine. Poisonous frogs feast on insects that don't even have names. Tropical lizards disappear into the cracks of trees whose branches spread out as wide as their trunks climb high. This is the real Florida, as it was before people, and probably will be after us, too.

More kids know about those places than adults do.

When the grown-ups aren't paying attention, the children sneak in, on foot or bicycle, to roam the dangerous acres, and scare themselves silly trying to peek into deserted houses they call haunted.

On a steamy Tuesday in August of 1999, Jenny Carmichael egged Nikki Modesto into climbing over the padlocked gate of just such an abandoned property. Signs on the chain link fence warned NO TRESPASSING and KEEP OUT, but children don't seem to think such signs apply to them.

At least Jenny didn't. Nikki thought they did, or ought to.

"We shouldn't go in there," she protested.

They were ten years old, fifth-graders together at North Bahia Beach Elementary School, in Ms. Fran Baker's class. Jenny excels at soccer, specializing in a complex move called a "Maradona," which involves both feet going seemingly in four different directions at once. Nikki loves to read, but no horror stories, please. On sleep-overs, she always plugs her ears with her fingers and sings real loud if her friends start telling ghost stories. She was really really scared of this idea of Jenny's, but she didn't want to say that, so she tried to rely on legalisms.

"It's private property." Nikki pointed at a sign. "We'll get in trouble. There might be some man in there with a gun, and he'd shoot us."

"You're such a wimp," her best friend taunted.

Jenny, the daring one, is the fourth of five children. She is a red-haired, freckle-faced girl, always flaring into adventure and mischief, a bottle rocket of a child. But Nikki is an only child, quiet, and obedient. They're a natural pair of best friends, a perfect balance for their qualities of fire and ice, earth and air. The problem from reckless Jenny's point of view is that Nikki is a scaredy-cat. The problem from timid Nikki's point of view is that Jenny always wins their arguments, unless Nikki bursts into frustrated tears and runs away. Then Jenny comes back, shamefaced, to say she's sorry, and would Nikki like to bike around the block?

Nikki always would, if they don't ride too fast.

Jenny always rides too fast, and takes the hills — when she can find them, in flat Florida — like a racer.

They had propped their bikes against the chain-link fence around the property with the NO TRESPASSING and KEEP OUT signs. Federal Highway, one of the most heavily traveled thoroughfares in the state, buzzed right behind them. It's just "the big street" to them, which they aren't ever supposed to cross without a parent, but which they do cross, because their parents can't be with them every second of the day.

Nikki is the image of her Italian mom, with beautiful olive skin and big brown eyes and a shy smile that looks like an advertisement for innocence. She has a great giggle, and when it gets started, everybody around her starts laughing, too. Nikki has been known to set entire movie audiences into paroxysms of laughter.

It makes Jenny's day to get Nikki to

15

laugh, but that wasn't what she was attempting to get Nikki to do at this particular moment. Usually, it takes Jenny a long time to persuade Nikki to do something the first time; but the second time it's easier, and by the third, Nikki is trailing right along.

Jenny dared Nikki: "Don't you want to know what's in there?"

"No."

"There could be a cool old house, or a beach."

Behind the property was the Intracoastal Waterway, where they also were not supposed to go.

"I don't care what's in there."

"I do! I want to see. I'll go without you!"

"Go ahead."

Nikki didn't really mean that. Being left alone on the edge of the big street sounded almost as scary as going into the dark woods behind the fence.

"Okay, I will."

Jenny didn't really want to be alone, either, so she tried a new tack. "It'll be our secret hideout — wouldn't that be cool?"

That was an attractive prospect, all right, but to Nikki the patch of land looked as ominous as the darkness under her bed at night. Who knew what kind of scary creatures were lurking in there? Nikki is afraid of spiders, and snakes, and the dark, and almost anything that surprises her in any way. This makes it very challenging to be Jenny Carmichael's best friend, but there is nobody Nikki has ever known who can be so much fun as Jenny.

"Let's just go in a little, little ways," smart Jenny urged.

"How far?"

"One inch. Like, just over the fence. Watch this."

"Jenny, no!"

But Jenny was already scrambling over, and suddenly there she was on the other side, grinning at her friend. "See? I'm just standing here. Come on."

Well, that looked possible to Nikki, as long as they didn't go further.

She followed Jenny over, more awkwardly, because she isn't as nimble and athletic as her buddy is, but still she made it to the other side. Quick as a snake, Jenny grabbed one of Nikki's wrists and started dragging her deeper into the property, with Nikki fighting and screaming all the way. But Jenny is by far the stronger of the two, and before Nikki could stop her, she had them both into the shadows, already out of sight of the highway.

"I hate you!" Nikki screamed at her best friend.

They were bleeding a bit from scratches from tree limbs, and Jenny was trying not to look too victorious.

"It's cool in here!"

Cool it was, at least with regard to the temperature. But a sunny glade beckoned a few steps beyond, and it looked safe and cheerful to Nikki, so of her own volition she ran into it. And suddenly, as happened often with the two friends, it really did begin to seem like a grand adventure to her. She hated to confess it, because she *hated* it when Jenny fooled her, and trapped her into something scary, but . . .

"It's pretty," she admitted, looking up and around.

It didn't look so spooky in here, in this bit of sunshine.

They walked on, deeper, but only after Jenny *promised* she wouldn't make any sudden movements or the booga-booga sounds that Nikki hates. Jenny kept her promise pretty well, except for when she couldn't resist picking up a leaf and throwing it in Nikki's face and making her scream. Or faking a scream herself and shuffling the leaves at their feet, and yelling at the top of her lungs, "Oh, my god, it's

18

an anaconda snake!"

Nikki screamed and screamed at that one.

Jenny could laugh pretty hard, herself.

When they finally settled down, some of the fear seemed to have seeped out of Nikki, after she had screamed bloody murder at the phantom snake. She quieted down enough to follow Jenny deeper along a path that opened up between the huge trees with their greenery hanging down like enormous spiderwebs. And her eyes opened as wide as Jenny's when they spied the great big house at the heart of the property.

It was two floors high, though a tower at one end made it three stories at that point. Like the houses that the girls lived in, it looked "Mediterranean," complete with arched doorways and a red tile roof. But the similarity between this house and their own cozy little homes ended there. Where theirs were freshly painted in sunny colors, the paint on this one had chipped away and discolored so much that the whole house looked a dirty gray. On the roof, only a few concave orange tiles remained intact. All along the front of the porch, there were spiraling columns — Nikki counted six, out loud — that looked as if they were barely still attached to the porch ceiling. It was clearly in what Jenny's dad would call "falling-down condition."

"Wow," Jenny breathed. "Oh, wow."

"It's beautiful," Nikki said, and it was, in a creepy way.

"Let's see if we can get in!"

"No."

"Why not?"

"We could fall through the floor."

"We won't go upstairs."

"There's probably glass, and snakes, and spiders."

"You are *such* a wimp. How can you not want to go inside? I want to!"

"Then just go ahead. I'll wait outside. Okay? You go ahead."

Jenny had a feeling that this time she couldn't talk her friend into it, and Nikki was being careful to stay out of her grasp. "Okay," she said in a brave, strong voice. "Watch me."

Nikki did. She watched Jenny stride up the wide front steps and cross the big porch toward where a front door used to be. Now there was only an open space. Inside, Nikki saw a huge winding stairway going to the second floor. When she looked up at the windows, she could see white fabric hanging down in shreds. She stared as Jenny stepped across the threshold and then disappeared from view. Then Nikki heard Jenny's voice call from inside, "Oh, Nikki, you have to see this! I bet a princess used to live here. It's so cool —"

Then Nikki could hear her, but couldn't understand the words.

And then she didn't hear Jenny saying anything.

Nikki waited. And waited. And her heart began to beat faster.

"Jenny?" she tried calling out, but her voice sounded weak.

She took one tiny step forward, and whispered, "Jenny?"

What if there was a monster man inside and he had snatched Jenny and killed her? What if there was a crocodile that came up into the house and got her? What should she do? Run away and get help? Oh, she wanted to run away! More than anything she wanted to. But Jenny was still inside, and what if she was hurt and needed —

And then Nikki heard a sound from inside of the house. A little sound, thin and wobbly. It took her a breathless moment to realize it was Jenny.

Jenny was screaming, inside the house.

Nikki began to cry for real, but also to

run toward the house. She didn't go in the terrible front door where her friend had vanished, but she ran around the side, toward where the sound of Jenny's voice was coming from. It was such a brave thing for her to do. If there were an award for children who do brave things for their friends in spite of the fact that they are scared to death, Nikki Modesto would surely win one. She spied a rickety lawn chair, and dragged it over to a window, scraping her shins, and sobbing.

She climbed up on it, hiccuping in terror.

Nikki put her trembling fingers on the dark, rotting wood of the windowsill.

She stared in, and she was so afraid of what she'd see.

But what she saw right away was that Jenny was okay, except she looked green as puke. But then Nikki saw there was somebody else there who wasn't fine. And there was a terrible smell. And there were flies. Nikki started to scream, too, and when Jenny saw her, she ran toward the window.

"It's a dead lady!" Jenny yelled in her face. "She's dead, she's dead!"

Nikki suddenly saw that she was going to have to take charge this once. "I want to go home!" she said with great and passionate

conviction, in a voice that brooked absolutely no argument. "Right now!"

The two little girls screamed all the way
back to the highway.

As they fled, the body — hiding its grisly
secrets — lay on the floor of the dining
room of the deserted mansion. She was
large-breasted, slim-legged, dark-haired.
Above her unseeing eyes, wooden beams
intersected a ceiling where a mural of
flowers and fronds was barely discernible
on the crumbling plaster. Once, parties
metaphorically raised these roof-beams; liquor flowed and waiters served dolphin on
silver trays to rich Floridians. But that was
decades gone, along with all but hints of
original elegance. Half of a black wrought-
iron drapery rod hung down from the one
remaining hook, caught on one of its
fleurs-de-lis. Outside that window, there
was a patio where weeds had broken all the
bricks. The centerpiece of the patio was a
dry fountain with a statue of a naked
cherub, now broken and shattered, in the
basin.

Forever beyond the reach of the dead
woman's outstretched and shattered arms,
elegant catamarans cruised the Intracoastal Waterway, where she would never

again go boating, trailing her manicured fingers in the water. Tourists strolled the beaches where she would never again raise her slim arms in lazy strokes through warm Atlantic waves. She had been pretty, but you couldn't tell that now. There were people who thought the world of her, who knew she would not have wanted children to find her like that, that she would have been horrified for them to see her. Worst of all, she was a minister's wife; to be found naked and exposed was a shame and a brutal embarrassment to her memory. But she had no say over any of that. Inside the hidden acre of property, her flesh and the house and the land were sliding back past civilization, back to dust and water and silence.

Susanna

2

"THE END," I type, and lean back in my chair, feeling breathless with relief.

What started with two girls stumbling across a body in a spooky mansion is finished. The guilty convicted, sentenced to die. The supposedly innocent set free. As of this moment, even my book about the crime is done. I've written all about it, beginning with the discovery of the body, and moving on through the investigation, the trial and startling mixed verdicts, and the incredible irony of it all. I hadn't intended to write another "Florida book" so soon after my last one, but what can you do when you're a true crime book writer and you live in a state that hands you sensational crime on a platter?

True crime in Florida resembles what fishermen up in the panhandle call a "jubilee." That's when sea creatures and fish of various kinds come swarming — for no reason anybody has ever figured out —

into the shallows and get stranded there. I've heard of jubilees so thick with fish you could walk across them.

It's kind of like that with Florida and criminals.

I could write nothing but Florida books for the rest of my life, and never run out of bizarre and original crime. You could almost accuse me of *liking* our felons. I wouldn't want to meet any of them in a dark alley, you understand, but I do appreciate how they help me earn my living. If I sound flippant about a serious subject, blame it on finishing my book. Other writers will understand. Now in the spirit of one of the many clichés of my trade, "it's left to the survivors to try to carry on as best they can." And all that's left for me to do is to print this out, pack it up, and call FedEx to pick up this manuscript.

Without giving myself too much time to think about it — sometimes it's hard to let go of a book — I start that process by switching on my laser printer. Then, with nobody there to see me in my office at home, I smile as I squint out my windows. Well, I'll be damned, will you look at that? It's a beautiful day in Florida! Is it March already? I do believe it is. Still winter up north. But here, the sun is shining like summer, boats are bobbing, and the Bahia Boulevard Bridge is sparkling as if it's made of tinsel instead of steel. How long has this been going on? Must be ninety degrees out there in that world beyond my air conditioning. Why, there's a whole universe out there, people are moving about their lives, going to jobs, making love, eating swearing laughing crying killing swimming running playing.

Who knew?

Not I; I've been shut up in this house for three weeks racing toward THE END. The research for this book started a year ago, the actual writing began six months after that, with the title, *Anything to Be Together*, and my pen name, Marie Lightfoot.

It is five hundred and fifty-six pages later.

Those pages are starting to roll out of my printer now.

Whenever I've been deep in the writer's trance and I come up for air again, it's as if all of my senses have been shut off and now they come flooding back in on me. Like now, as the sun coming through my wraparound windows hurts my eyes. I hear boats on the Intracoastal Waterway as if they had only this minute all started their motors. And what's that cherry-almond smell? Did I rub on lotion this morning? I don't recall. Suddenly, I'm hungry. Thirsty. Stiff. My left hip feels sore, as if I haven't moved in this chair for hours.

"Robot writer woman," I say, testing my voice.

There's a buzzing sensation behind my forehead, as if my frontal lobe is quivering from so much sustained concentration.

"Done at last, thank God, I'm done at last."

It's finished, this sixth of my true crime books. Will it be a bestseller, like all the rest? One hopes. One does, indeed, hope. Will my track record be enough to attract that many readers again, or will this crime do the trick all by its violent self? "Gruesome murder. Superb detection. Brilliant lawyers. Lives shattered," as the book jacket will probably say, "families torn asunder." The flap copy on true crime books tends to revel in clichés, and I should know, because I've written my share.

I think I'll just sit here and savor the moment.

I should call someone, and let them congratulate me, but I wonder if I have any friends left. Wait a minute, it's really March? Well, damn. March brings the dreaded, desired Spring Break. At this very minute high school seniors and college freshmen all over America are climbing the wave that will crest in our high tide, our tsunami of tourism. Well, shoot! I've surfaced just in time for the one period of the year when ten percent of the population leaves town, the retirees bitch about the traffic, everybody else works too hard, and it's impossible for anybody to go anywhere.

Not that I don't have anything to do at home.

So many phone calls left unanswered. So many letters unopened, bills unpaid, so much E-mail ignored. I wonder if I missed any appointments. Probably. I think I paid the mortgage for this month, but I'm not sure. Books are ravenous gods that eat the rest of life. All goes into their greedy maw, while the writer sacrifices her friends, her credit, her lover, her sanity.

"Congratulations," I tell myself.

"Thank you," I reply.

"Writers can get pretty strange by the end of a book," I observe.

"You're telling me?" I retort.

A lonely business, it is said of writing, but I don't feel alone. After all, I've just spent weeks with my "characters" — killer,

29

victim, police, survivors.

"Yeah, but they're only in your computer. You've hardly spoken to a *living* soul in weeks," I remind myself. "And look at you, look at your house. It's a mess. You're a mess. Maybe now you can become a human being again."

I have a writer friend, a novelist, whose husband once said to her, "No offense, but I can tell where you are in a book by your appearance." I laughed when I heard that, as did she; it's so painfully true. If I were to glance in a mirror right now I'd see a woman who hasn't changed her clothes in three days, whose hair is pulled back by a barrette but not combed, and who has barely been able to remember to slip on sandals to go to the grocery store for essentials.

For reassurance, I glance at a wall where I have framed mementos of my career. I want to know that it is possible for me to look better than this. In one of the frames there is a photograph of me that appeared in *Newsweek.* Now *that* woman, the one with a pen in her hand, *that* woman looks downright glamorous, with her combed, blond, streaked hair, and her flattering dress. We're in our thirties, she and I, but she could pass for younger. Me, I could pass for a bag lady. In my office, staring at the "other" me, I sigh. That's the author, the one who brushes her hair and goes out in public; this is the writer me. If my readers could see me now, they'd chip in to buy me a makeover.

I look around my office, as if seeing it for the first time since I launched this final push to the end of the book, and what I see through critical eyes is a disaster area. Books and papers piled everywhere. Old food crusting on plates. Coffee cups with milky sludge. And what's my brassiere doing over there, draped across that footstool? I must have taken it off on my way to the shower one night and never noticed it again until this moment.

And people ask me why I've never married?

There's usually a feeling of relief and satisfaction like no other I've ever known that comes with typing those two words in capital letters. THE END. At the beginning of a book, I think I'll never get there. There's too much to do, too much to write; there's too much research, too much information to synthesize. It's all too hard, too big, and even if I did it five — or even ten — times before, that doesn't guarantee I can ever do it again.

But now I've actually done it again, one more time.

I have only to gather up the pages. Post them to my editor in New York. Wait for her editorial comments. Make the revisions she requests, check the line-editing, then the galleys. And then I will forget this book and go on vacation before I start researching the next one.

I want it finished. I want to take a break. I want to start a new book.

There's only one small problem.

I shift uneasily in my swivel chair as the pile of pages grows.

The wee little problem, hardly even worth mentioning, is that I feel desperately unsure about this book.

"Who asked *you?*" I shoot back, resentfully.

"Maybe I'll want to see the movie?"

"Oh, that's very funny."

I'm hoping my editor, my wise, tough New York editor who knows more about my work and my audience than I do, will disagree with me. Maybe she'll call me and say, "Great work, Marie. This is your best book yet. I couldn't put it down. Loved every word of it. You've really outdone yourself with this one."

The way that conversation goes in my

imagination, you'd think I wrote fiction. It's wishful thinking. What I'm afraid she's going to say is, "Great beginning, Marie. Loved the first few chapters. But after that, there's something missing. I don't know what it is, but I feel as if you haven't quite gotten to the heart of this story. Do you think you can do that for us?"

To which my answer will be, "No."

"And your point is?" I ask myself, bitterly. "Is that a problem for you? I finished the damn book on time, what else do you want?"

Silence from inside me.

My stomach clenches and a sour taste rises.

My first giddy, trivializing relief at writing THE END is in direct proportion to the profound anxiety that lies beneath it.

Damn, where's denial when I really need it?

"You're scared," accuses the prosecutor in my soul.

"Am not," protests the defendant, but nobody on the jury in my psyche believes her. "What have I got to be scared of?"

Determinedly, I fill out a FedEx shipping form and call their 800 number for a home pickup. When I place the telephone receiver back in its cradle, my hand and wrist feel weak, and I know it's not carpal tunnel syndrome. It's worry, flooding into me, turning into fear before my very eyes, which I now hide for a moment behind my hands. There's a clutching feeling around my heart. I *hate* this. I know what it is. It's been waking me up at three in the morning for a few nights now. What we have here is a true crime writer who's afraid that she hasn't revealed the innermost truth. This should have been a sexy book, but it isn't. I've got no lustful facts, not even fantasy; all I've got between the first and last pages of this book is the hint of their murderous affair, but none of the actual details of it. He won't talk about it; she won't talk about it. Nobody saw them do it. I've got a preacher who took a lover. They killed his wife. Or, at least one of them did; a jury wasn't convinced they were both guilty. But still, shouldn't their illicit lust for each other fairly shout from my pages?

It doesn't; it doesn't even whisper seductively.

In my book, they and their affair are as cold as Florida air conditioning when they should come across as hot as August. This should be a tale of passion, of sweaty, slippery bodies; there should be a smell of sex, a taste of salty sweat, but there isn't. Oh, there's passion, all right, but it's the clean, neat fervor of a passion for truth and justice.

Before I slip the manuscript into a box, I pick up the next chapter to reread. It has a big problem — another one — that I can't fix. I always try to pick cases with great detective work and likable cops, and I thought I had one here. On the word of the state attorney for Howard County, I believed I had one. But I underestimated how much slack prosecutors give to cops. No matter how hard I try, I can't seem to turn the cop in this case into a hero. It's not fiction, so I'm stuck with him, and I don't like him very much.

I dread the reaction to him — and to the other cops — from my readers.

Wait'll they get a load of the contempt in the voices of the cops toward the poor dead woman in the mansion. I want my cops to *care,* dammit. And these don't seem to care about anything except getting even with a "perp" they personally can't stand. It's ironic justice they voice here, not a thirst for real justice for a murdered woman. Great, just perfect. A true crime book with no sex and an unappealing hero. What was I *thinking?*

Anything to Be Together
By Marie Lightfoot

CHAPTER 2

Even Detective Carl Chamblin winced at first sight of the decomposing body in the mansion, though he was a man who'd seen enough violent death in his long career to fill every morgue in Florida.

"Christ," he muttered under his breath, and then he mopped the sweat off the back of his neck with a handkerchief. It was too damned hot for homicide. Why couldn't he live in Minnesota where bodies froze and cops didn't sweat? In spite of the expletive, he didn't give the appearance of a man who'd flinch in the face of blood. At six-foot-five, Carl was 240 pounds of detective, with the big-jowled, scary face of a pit bull. At forty-six years of age, he was seven years away from the average life expectancy of the American cop. He thought about that more often lately, that risky gamble, the wager cops lay down on death or pension.

37

This victim, whoever she was, had lost her gamble early.

There was no purse, apparently, no identification.

Prostitute? Homeless? Addict? Those were some of his initial surmises about the identity of this dead woman who lay hunched on the filthy floor of an abandoned mansion, clothed only in her own blood and other bodily emissions. He eliminated those, however, when it dawned on him that her body was too lush, too smoothly well-fed to belong to a junkie or a whore. There was another possibility — a particular missing person — but he didn't seriously entertain that idea, not at this point, anyway. His mind simply rebelled at the notion that this corpse was in any way related to that case.

She looked as if she had curled up to try to protect herself from the blows that rained upon her here. "Here" was Bahia Beach, Florida, a seaside metropolis of approximately 100,000 people, sandwiched between Fort Lauderdale to the south and Pompano to the north, in Howard County. From January through March, tourists swelled the population of the city to many times that number. A few of those tourists never went home again, and some of their homicides fell to Carl Chamblin to identify and investigate. Was this woman a tourist who'd gone slumming in the wrong bar?

Had she been raped, too? Carl's guess was yes.

In the stifling heat of the ruined room, he watched the crime-scene photographer snap his pictures and film his videos. With those initial tasks finished, the techs could move in to start gathering evidence. One of them had the job of compiling all of the evidence that the others collected and of making sure it was bagged, boxed, or placed in preservative jars and then painstakingly labeled as to where it was found at the scene and who found it. At a crime scene such as this one, that could mean individually packaging hundreds of items ranging from the victim's clothing — if they found any — to sections of wood flooring or patches of peeling, blood-stained wallpaper.

For a few moments, Carl watched the techs as they placed dry items in plastic bags, and wet ones in paper bags, as per procedure, so that the wet things wouldn't rot. Hell, in this heat everything was wet, including his shirt where the sweat was running down, and inside his undershorts, and the soles of his feet. It was hard to think in this heat, but he tried to concentrate. It looked like the killer kept on slamming her with something after she fell. But with what? Where was the weapon? What would do this? He glanced up at a wrought-iron curtain rod hanging by a hole in its design. Something like that? That might do it, but he was guessing something thicker, something easier to grasp and swing than a thin, rusting rod. It wasn't going to take a medical examiner to tell Carl she'd been beaten to death. Pulped was more like it, he thought, sardonically. By the time her killer had gotten through with her, they could have run her through a mill and made paper out of her. He stared at her right wrist. It was flung, palm up, against the wooden slats of the scarred floor. Her left arm and hand were hidden under her body.

Despite the exotic setting and extreme violence, so far this was just another homicide to the veteran detective, merely the latest of hundreds he had investigated in his twenty-year career, most of that in homicide. Unlike Carl, however, one of the crime scene technicians in the room was anything but blasé, because it was the first crime scene she'd ever worked.

"Look what I found!" she exclaimed to

him, in a high, excited voice.

Carl glanced first at what lay in her plastic glove: a bloody ring. It was gold, with a large central diamond surrounded by smaller ones. Looked like a woman's engagement ring to Carl. Without touching it, he observed that it had notches in it, as if it was designed to fit into a matching wedding band. Only then did he look at the photo ID badge pinned to the tech's shirt: *Martina Levin*. He eyed her up and down. He'd never seen her before.

"You new?"

"Yes, sir."

She looked like an overgrown tomboy, he thought: short but sturdy in her navy-blue uniform, with a round face and short dark hair. Like Carl, she wore paper booties over her shoes; unlike him, she had dangling around her neck a type of gas mask meant to filter out smells. Carl hated the things and preferred mentholated jelly rubbed in his nostrils to cover the stench, although most cops claimed that worked about as well as coating your nose with water. He was surprised this girl was tough enough to remain in the room for so long without filtering the air.

She had to tilt her head to look up into his face.

"Find the other ring," he directed her.

"What other ring? I didn't see another one."

"Keep looking. If this is an engagement ring, there ought to be a wedding band. Have somebody turn her over and see if she's wearing it." After Martina Levin departed, he returned his attention to the corpse, but in his mind he was speculating about the ring she'd found. Why would there be a loose ring? It suggested to Carl the possibility of a lover's quarrel, and of somebody furiously throwing a ring at somebody else. Or, maybe this was a kidnap, rape, robbery, murder, and the perp had dropped some of his prizes.

"No, this was personal," he muttered to himself.

It wasn't just the appearance of the victim's body that spoke to Carl of an unusually vicious beating. There was blood everywhere, on the floor, the walls, even the ceiling. It was nearly impossible to avoid stepping in it, which surely meant that the killer had, too, leaving footprints behind him. He must have been a mess afterwards, covered in it. Some of the blood in the room had dried and gone black. Carl wouldn't have recognized it as blood if he hadn't seen blood like it before, so shiny it looked like glass. Some of it was so thick — and the temperature and humidity so high — that it was still damp. In those patches, it looked exactly like what it was, so that even a child could have identified the substance.

A child *had* seen it, Carl recalled. Two little girls.

He was glad he wasn't their father, trying to calm their nightmares tonight. His own three girls had heard it all, all the gory stories. Their mother had also been a cop once upon a time, which was how she and Carl had met. But Yvonne and Carl Chamblin had made sure their babies didn't *see* any of it. As far as the three grown Chamblin girls knew from their direct experience, life was suburban, safe and clean. It was too late to protect the little girls who'd found this mess.

The tech was back. "I wonder how she got here."

So did Carl. "You find the ring?"

"No. They don't want to turn her until they get the okay." She went back to her original line of inquiry. "I didn't see any car outside, did you?"

He shook his head, but then raised his glance to one of the glassless windows. Beyond a brick patio and a weedy backyard the length of a football field, there was water, the Intracoastal Waterway. He was facing east. Federal Highway was at his back, and past the Waterway, to the east, was beach and ocean.

The tech caught his glance. "Boat, maybe?"

Carl didn't see a dock down there, and didn't expect to find one. Boats would get bashed to splinters on this stretch of the Intracoastal. "She didn't get here by boat." Staring at the Intracoastal, it struck him that they shouldn't have been able to see all the way to the canal. The rest of the property was way overgrown. But somebody was keeping that back lot mowed and the driveway cleared, or else the police cars would never have been able to get up to the house. It was a jungle out there, he thought, half-humorously. It also suddenly struck him what a weird and perverted thing this was: he was standing here with a stranger young enough to be his daughter, both of them staring at the voluptuous naked body of a dead woman. What kind of way was this to make a living?

"How long's she been dead?" he muttered to himself.

"Not long," the tech said, thinking he was asking her. In Florida, bodies decomposed fast. She went off into a riff about

44

tissue morbidity and the life cycle of maggots, but Carl barely listened. He'd been gauging the length of time bodies had been dead for longer than this tech had been alive. He glanced at her name tag again: *Martina Levin.* He wondered why she was sticking so close to him when most young cops and techs were intimidated by him, his reputation, his length of service. Over the years, he had allowed a reputation for being gruff and taciturn to grow up around him because it served so well to keep pests, fools, and administrative assholes at a distance. Then it struck him that she was stalling. That's why she was hanging around him. She didn't want to get any closer to this job.

He didn't blame her, it was a particularly nasty one.

It was possible that the victim was killed somewhere else and then beaten post-mortem, but the excess of blood made him doubt it. It appeared she had died right there where she lay on the bare wood floor. He looked around. This was once a dining room. Two-story house. Open-air tower at the upper right front of it. He hadn't been up there yet, or anywhere else on the property except straight through from the gate to here.

The young tech misunderstood his interest.

"Cool old house, isn't it? Too bad it's so run-down, or maybe I'd buy it, fix it up."

"You'd buy it?" he asked, amused.

"Well, it's for sale," she said, defensively.

His head jerked around again and he stared at her so fiercely that she backed up a step. "It's what? For sale?"

"Yeah," she said, looking a little scared, but also confused, as if to say, "So what?"

"I didn't see a sign out front," he challenged her.

"It's in back," she told him, still defensive.

"Show me."

Nervously, with the big cop at her heels, the young tech led him through French doors onto the decrepit patio. And there, leaning up against the house was the FOR SALE sign. Carl took out a handkerchief, placed it over the edge of the sign so he could tilt it up to read it without getting prints on it.

FOR SALE, it read. A WING & A PRAYER REALTORS. SUSANNA WING.

"I'll be damned," he muttered, with a quickening of interest that he hadn't felt inside the house. This case had just gotten a whole hell of a lot more interesting.

46

Staring down at the sign, Carl smiled, but so coldly that the tech backed up another step away from the big detective.

"Is that important, or something?" she bravely asked.

"Hell, I know who she is," he said out loud.

"You do?" she exclaimed, impressed at this apparent evidence of super detective powers.

"Has to be her. Too much of a coincidence otherwise." This was no prostitute. No tourist, no homeless woman. There was a missing persons report on this beaten woman, but he hadn't connected the MPR with the nude, bloody body in the mansion. It just hadn't fit his mental image of — "A preacher's wife," he said out loud, his voice holding the satisfaction of a mystery solved.

"A *what?*" the tech asked in shocked, disbelieving tones.

Carl pointed at the FOR SALE sign: *A Wing & a Prayer.*

"But how do you know?"

"There's an MPR on her," Carl said.

"A missing person's report? Really?" The tech's eyes were wide. "Since when?"

"Last night."

"That's quick!"

"Yes," Carl agreed, and then added in a low, contemplative tone, "I expect she wasn't supposed to be found this soon." At the quizzical look on his companion's face, he explained, "Whoever killed her, he must have thought it would be a while before anybody found her body."

"Why didn't he just dump her in the canal?"

"Because bodies float."

"Oh, yeah," Martina said, flushing. "I knew that. Say, if she's a real estate agent, I'll bet one of her clients killed her, don't you? Maybe he lured her out here on the pretext of buying this property, and then he attacked her?"

"Could be," Carl murmured, but was distracted by the arrival of another homicide detective, Jill Norman, to whom he said, "Hey, Norm, looky here who our victim just may be."

The other detective stood only three inches shorter than Carl, but she was ten years younger, a short-haired blonde in a prim white blouse and dark trousers who could have passed for a preacher's wife herself. She focused on the real estate sign he was pointing at and a startled laugh burst out of her. "Oh, my God," she said, looking incredulous. "I don't believe it."

The two homicide detectives exchanged amused glances.

"Any other ID turn up?" he asked her.

"No. No purse, nothing with a name on it."

"Except this sign," he suggested, in a dry tone.

"And wouldn't it be something, if that's who this is."

"I believe there's a word for situations like this."

"Yeah?" Norm asked, in a tone that suggested she was awaiting a punch line. "What?"

"Poetic justice."

The woman detective laughed, and moved away again.

Martina Levin stared at them, shocked at their humor. She fumbled to cover the lower half of her face with her partial gas mask. "I'd better get back to work."

He heard how tight and offended her voice sounded.

"Let me explain something to you," he said in a tone that brooked no sentimentality on her part. "The victim's husband crusades against the death penalty. He's famous for it. The joke is, what's he going to do now? Protest the execution of his own wife's killer?"

"Oh, my God!" she responded. "Talk about your moral dilemmas."

Sweetheart, you don't know the half of it, Carl thought.

"Tell somebody else to look for the other ring," he said to her. "Let's find some shade. I'll tell you a story . . ."

Susanna

3

What am I going to do about Carl?

What he really said was: "Wing and a Prayer? Too fucking cute." And what he really said about the victim was: "Nice legs." He's a tough cop; there've been complaints, one shooting death of a suspected felon, a couple of hearings in front of the Florida Criminal Justice Standards & Training Commission, which licenses and disciplines cops. The Florida Department of Law Enforcement has a disciplinary file labeled "Chamblin, Carl E." But he has always walked away with nothing worse than a letter warning him to watch his step, as if he were merely a rambunctious kid in high school. Defense attorneys are suspicious of his means, of certain confessions he has obtained, but nobody's ever made any charges stick.

"I'm not popular with rapists and thieves, or with defense attorneys," he will tell you, with an aggressive jut to his jaw. "So sue me. They're the only ones who complain I'm too hard on suspects. You won't find any complaints in my files from the victims of crimes. They like me just fine."

So do prosecutors, who, to a man and woman, think he's a good cop and a clean one. It was, as I said before, the state attorney for Howard County who recommended Carl — and this case — to me. But if Carl's not brutal, at the very least he's ugly, he's brusque, he's lazy, and he's tired of being a cop; in other words, he's not exactly the heroic figure that readers like detectives to be. Have I softened his rough edges enough to make him acceptable to most of my readers?

Maybe, though I don't necessarily feel good about it.

I'm standing in front of my sliding glass doors, staring blindly out at the sunny day, feeling craven. It's not that Carl did a bad job on the case, or that he's dishonest; he's probably just an ordinary cop who's been on the job for too many years. Oh, well. If this book makes it to the movies, maybe an actor like Danny Glover can transform Carl into a gruff but lovable character. Carl's not black, like Glover, but he should be so lucky as to be played by an actor of that caliber.

At any rate, the manuscript — and Carl

in it — is gone now, flying to New York City. Hell, I *tried* to make him admirable — I threw in stuff about his family, didn't I? And I cleaned up his language. If readers think he comes off like an SOB in what I've written, they ought to see what I left out. For one thing, in real life his every other word is "fuck"; and for another, Carl doesn't loathe only that particular preacher. He hates them *all*, having been raised by a virulent example of them. To say it soured him on the clergy is an understatement. Nor have I mentioned the prior blots on his police record, the ones that have nothing to do with this case.

"So sue me," I challenge myself, sounding like Carl.

"Forget it," my kinder, gentler self replies. "Your book's in the mail. You should feel relieved. Try to relax, okay?"

"Easy for you to say."

I live close enough to the Bahia Boulevard Bridge that sometimes I walk across it, then stroll four more blocks to the beach. Maybe I should do that to celebrate now — warm my feet in the sand, splash them in the waves. And speaking of missing sex, I should call the man who may or may not still be my lover, invite him over for a glass of champagne and whatever ensues from that, if I can remember how.

But I don't move, I keep staring outside, avoiding real life.

"Shit," I mutter, getting that queasy feeling about my book again. "It's all wrong. My good guys look like bad guys and my bad guys don't feel bad enough. And there's too much innocence, not enough sin." My story should feel bloody and dark; instead, there's too much sweetness and light — the two little girls, to begin with. And then there's the victim — victims are always perfect, you know. And there's even Martina Levin, the naïve young crime-scene technician. Not to mention the fact that I could hardly get anybody to say anything bad about either of the defendants.

I don't know what to do about it; I can't change real people.

"I give up." My own life calls. Get on with it.

A few minutes later, I review my phone messages to see who I've ignored for the past three weeks. After I finish a book I usually have to spend a good week saying I'm sorry. Sure enough, I discover a batch of calls I don't want to return, and one that

I do. I know I should make the calls related to the book first.

"Do it," I command myself.

"You are such a bossy bitch." I pick up the phone and dial the first number on the list. "This is Marie Lightfoot," I tell the secretary who answers. "Is that you, Frances? Your boss has been —"

"Trying to reach you!" she exclaims. "Did you go out of the country, Marie? Hold on!"

Within seconds he's on the line: Antonio Delano, an assistant state attorney for Howard County — this county, my own. As the lead prosecutor at the Susanna Wing murder trial, Tony's one of the stars of the manuscript that I've just shipped off to New York. There'll be a black-and-white photo of him in my book, and readers will see a small, thirtyish, curly-haired, very Italian-looking man in a suit, staring intensely into the camera over a mess of papers on his desk. Not good-looking in the least, but compelling somehow, if you think intelligence and wit are attractive, which, as it happens, I do.

"Marie! So did you make me six-foot-four in your book?"

"Tony, I described you as a giant among men."

"Yeah, but that's just an intellectual giant."

"No, no. I left it to the readers to assess your height relative to the ground and your intelligence relative to the defense."

Over the phone, he snorts. "So since I got one conviction and lost the other, that means I come off as half-witted and midsized, is that what you're trying to tell me?"

I laugh. "I believe you called me first?"

"Repeatedly! Where the hell you been, girl?"

Tony's got a husky voice that I love to listen to in trials. It gives everything he says a slightly flirtatious edge, which is no handicap in a courtroom. I've told him that I think it makes him sound like law is only his day job, and singing blues in a smoky bar is his real profession, but he claims he can't carry a tune. As usual, he sounds both friendly and businesslike, an overworked lawyer with too many trials to conduct at one time. As far as the practice of law goes, Florida is no state for the lazy.

"I go into a cave when I'm finishing a book. T'sup?"

"It stinks, Marie."

I figure he's not talking about my work habits. I'm guessing he means the surprise outcome of the double trial he just prosecuted. A single jury convicted one defendant in the Susanna Wing murder trial — the preacher — but it set the courtroom and the media atwitter by acquitting the other one — his lover. It always infuriates prosecutors to lose at trial, but Tony was truly incensed in the hallways after this one. It appears he has not cooled off very much since then.

"Well, Tony, if they didn't both do it —"

"Are you saying you doubt it?"

"Who cares what I think, Tony? Or what you think, either, now." I won't insult him by soft-pedaling what I see as the truth. "In the end, you only had circumstantial evidence and hearsay on Artemis, and your codefendant refused to rat her out. The jury didn't buy it, and if I'd been on that jury I wouldn't have bought it, either."

He makes a disgusted sound on his end of the line.

"Well, would *you?*" I demand. "If you'd been on that jury, could you have sent somebody to prison for life, or recommended a death sentence, with only the evidence the jury heard?"

"There's more than one kind of court, Marie."

"You got me baffled here, Tony."

"There's the court of public opinion. Look at O. J. Simpson. He's got the mark of Cain on him and he always will, because no matter what that jury in his criminal trial thought, the media tried him and found him guilty as sin. We can do that in this case, too."

"Now wait a minute, Antonio."

"Marie, one of our defendants has got the mark of Cain now and the other one should, too. I couldn't get it done in court, and I regret that, but you can still do it. With your book! You can make sure the public understands that they're both equally guilty, even if the jury was too god-damned picky to —"

"And how am I supposed to do that if you couldn't, Tony? I don't have any information that you didn't present. I can't — won't — convict somebody in print if there isn't evidence in fact."

"Oh, come on, tell me the truth. Don't you think she did it?"

"Sure, yes. I think they're both guilty."

"Right. Well, there's things I could tell you, Marie."

That statement sits there all by itself for a long moment.

"Things I wasn't allowed to bring out at trial," he adds, seductively.

58

"Really?" I say, dryly, and then quote a country-western lyric, "Well, this is a fine time to tell me, Lucille. I'm only talking to you on the phone right now because my book is *done*."

"And so you don't care if it's wrong?"

That stings, so I bite back. "And maybe you're a sore loser, Tony."

"Touché. I'm asking you to come see me, Marie."

"Always a pleasure. But you lost, Tony. Why can't you give it up?"

"Oh, for chrissake, this isn't about me! It's about justice! It's about warning other people about a murderer who got out of jail free. It's about —" Suddenly he laughs, a short, sharp, cynical bark. "Public safety."

In the end, of course, I give him the appointment he wants.

We agree to meet in his office at the county courthouse tomorrow morning. In the casual tone of a mere afterthought, I inquire, "You going to ask Franklin to sit in?" I mean Franklin DeWeese, his boss, the state's attorney. There's a pause that I can't interpret before Tony says, "No, why should I? I hadn't considered it. Is there some reason you want him to be here?"

"No, no, I just wondered."

I hang up quickly. Before I can hang myself.

Then I return calls to the diehard supporters of the Reverend Bob Wing. They're as unhappy as Tony, and as unwilling to let this thing die, albeit for a different reason. They want publicity, too, but for their cause of saving their preacher from the death penalty. Don't these people understand that after a jury says guilty or not guilty it's supposed to be *over?* But that's disingenuous of me, isn't it? I have written about enough homicides to know that murder is a rock thrown into the pool of life. For some people, it disrupts the current forever, creating ripples that only seem to get bigger and wider as the years go by — as it probably did for the friends and family of a young woman in Lauderdale Pines whose murder was oddly and loosely connected to the death of Susanna Wing.

Anything to Be Together
By Marie Lightfoot

CHAPTER 3

It was only slightly cooler down by the water, where the detective and the crime-scene tech found places to sit on a seawall, under the shade of a live oak tree. A few feet away the Intracoastal Waterway pounded like surf on a rocky shoreline, from all of the boat traffic passing north and south. Yachts big enough to land their own helicopters, elegant sailboats, trawlers, fishing boats, and little runabouts all jockeyed for space on the famous stretch of man-made canal.

The story that Detective Chamblin told Martina Levin was a long one. It didn't seem to have anything to do with the murder they were investigating, but Martina Levin listened carefully anyway, feeling it was only respectful to do so, and besides, it sure beat going back into that bloody, stinking room that made her feel like retching.

With a sarcastic twist to his mouth, Carl

began his story, "Once upon a time, there was a nice girl named Allison Tobias, and she lived with her parents in Lauderdale Pines . . ."

"What's this got to do with Mrs. Wing?" Martina dared to ask him.

"Wait, you'll see," he told her. "Allison was a sweetheart —"

Everybody said so. If she had a fault, it was that she was a little too sweet, a bit too giving and generous, a shade too inclined to reach out a helping hand to anybody with a sad story, without first checking to make sure it was true.

In 1990, she was eighteen years old, just graduated from high school in Lauderdale Pines, Florida, and though a majority of her fellow seniors were going on to college, Allison hadn't taken any entrance exams or written any applications.

"I want to make some money first," she told her parents, Ben and Lucy, at the end of her junior year of high school. For a semester she'd put them off whenever they wanted to sit down and talk about college, and now they understood why. "I want to work for a while, so I can pay my own expenses and don't have to be a burden on you."

The elder Tobiases appreciated the sentiment, and it was true that they were not wealthy people. Financing their daughter's education, even just for the two years of an associate degree, would be a major strain on their single-income budget. Ben was a thirty-year man at a lumber yard; Lucy had devoted herself to taking care of him, their little house and their child. But they suspected that what this announcement of Allie's *really* meant was that their daughter wanted to be able to afford to rent her own apartment, so she didn't have to live at home with them anymore, which she would have had to do if she had enrolled, as they had expected her to do, in the nearest community college.

"I was hurt," her mother admitted.

But Ben Tobias remembered his own need to assert his independence when he was a teenage boy, and he reminded his wife that they had married when they were only one year older than Allison was then.

"She has never even dated," Lucy objected, thinking of the perils of too much independence too soon for a girl who was shy around boys at the best of times.

"Neither had you," her husband retorted.

His wife tried to smile at the good-humored jibe. "Yes, and that's just what I'm afraid of! She'll fall for the first man she meets out there, just like I did, and look where I ended up!" But then she softened it with a smile, to let Ben know that she wouldn't have had it any other way. For herself. But not for Allie. For her daughter, Lucy had other plans: college, slow maturation, a carefully thought-out career path, with marriage and children down the line at the appropriate juncture. But not now, and not anytime close to now.

"We can't tie her to the bedpost," Ben gently reminded her.

Still, Lucy Tobias wouldn't hear of it, at least not without laying down a few safeguards first. She finally capitulated enough to say that she and Ben would give Allie enough funds to set up modest housekeeping if — and only if — the girl could find an apartment within walking distance of their home. She would have to check in with her mom whenever she was out late at night, and once a day all of the rest of the time, and her father would need to install security locks and an alarm system in the new residence.

"She was only barely eighteen," Lucy says in defense of her concern, which in hindsight seems almost prescient rather than overprotective. "And a shy eighteen, at that. She had a couple of nice friends, but no circle that she hung around with, like some of those girls who get in trouble do. I wouldn't have that, no mall rats for my child. I always told her she had plenty to keep her busy, with schoolwork and piano practice, and a little soccer when she was younger, and helping me around the house. There was no need for her to be gallivanting around the town without her dad or me. Why, she'd never even taken a trip out of town without us, and here she wanted to go off and live by herself."

They didn't have any other children; they wanted to shelter their one.

Lucy Tobias secretly hoped that Allie wouldn't be able to find a place that met the criteria; theirs was a single-family residential neighborhood for the most part, with nearby rental space at a premium, it being so rare. But find it Allie did, though she had to keep checking the FOR RENT notices everyday for three months before she finally stepped into what seemed the perfect one, at 22 Hibiscus Avenue. It was a mere three blocks away, walkable even for Lucy. The only thing left from her mother's original conditions was for Ben to install enough security to fortify a Fort Knox, or a beloved daughter.

The Hibiscus address was a house, larger than its neighbors, with two upper floors that were always rented out, mostly to young, single working people and to students. Allison Tobias would have the sunny studio unit at the back of the second floor; directly across from her was a law student who was more often at the library than at home, and on the other side of the shared bathroom was a kitchenette/bedroom that was rented by a young tax accountant whose entire income was derived from freelance accounts, and who was also home a lot. The third floor was one large, self-contained apartment that was rented by a pair of self-described computer nerds who galloped up and down the stairs at the odd hours when they left for work and came home again. The owners of the house, a retired couple from Michigan, lived on the first floor and never kept a noisy tenant around long. They made an exception for the clatter of the "computer boys," up and down the stairs, because they had such an exemplary work ethic. Down in the basement apartment, where few people would have wanted to live, an elementary school custodian kept three rooms as neat and tidy as he maintained the halls and classrooms of the Briarwood Academy, a private school for privileged and scholarship children of the beachfront town of Lauderdale Pines.

Lucy Tobias had a brother who was a narcotics detective for the neighboring Bahia Beach Police Department, and she got him to look up the backgrounds of all of Allie's new neighbors on his police computer.

"Lucy, you know this is illegal," he told her.

"So is double-parking," his sister said tartly, "but I'll bet you do it now and then, and so do I. You can't tell me that you cops don't look up people you meet. If this were Marilyn" — his daughter, Allie's cousin — "you'd check them out."

He had to admit that was true.

"Clean," he reported back to her.

There wasn't a mark against the owners of the house or any of their tenants in any of the criminal records databases that Detective Lyle Karnacki — Uncle Lyle — checked for his sister.

That made her feel better, although she still would have much preferred for Allison to stay home. "Think how much money you could save that way," she argued with the girl. But her daughter, who had been so easy to get along with all of her life, seemed to have become uncharacteristically stubborn, and Lucy couldn't get her to change her mind about moving out. "You go over there and meet those people yourself," she instructed Ben. "There's nothing like looking people in the eye."

So Allison's dad made a point of introducing himself to everyone who lived there, and shaking their hands to get a sense of who his daughter was going to be near. They seemed like normal people to him, people with jobs who kept decent hours, except for the computer nerds, who claimed they didn't even know what their regular hours were supposed to be. They just worked as long as it took, one of them told him with a grin. Ben rather approved of that, because that's the way life was — you worked as long as it took at whatever it was you were committed to do.

"I didn't much care for the handshake of the fellow in the basement," Ben reported back to Lucy, out of their daughter's hearing. "You can judge people by that, you know, or at least I've always found you can. And that kid had one of those handshakes that makes you want to wipe off your hand afterwards. Kind of sweaty, you know? But I liked the way he offered to help me put the locks on Allie's door and on her windows."

The janitor was a young man — only twenty-one, he told Ben — but accomplished with the tools of his janitorial trade, it appeared. He wielded a screwdriver with confidence, handled a claw hammer as if he'd been born with one in his hand. No silver spoon for him, unlike the kids he cleaned up after at the Academy.

His name, he told Ben, was Steven Orbach.

But all the kids called him Stevie.

He was a burly guy, easily six feet tall and 200 pounds, with sandy-colored hair that he wore cropped in military fashion, and a square, open, if rather inexpressive, face. Ben Tobias almost asked him if he'd recently been in the service; he had that kind of shaved, muscular appearance to him.

"If your daughter ever needs any little repairs done," the husky young man said to the doting father, "just tell her to leave a note at the top of the basement stairs."

"I imagine I'll be taking care of things like that," Ben answered, rather stiffly, but he added, "Thanks just the same." Nor did he pass the offer on to Allie. Why encourage her to be dependent on other people, when she was going to have to start fending for herself? If she needed a drain unplugged, he'd clear it; if she had car trouble, he'd take care of it as he had always fixed the family cars.

Allie moved into her new little place the day after graduation.

Her mother took a white cake with lemon icing — Allison's favorite — over that night after dinner, and tried not to cry when she knocked on Allie's door and nobody was home. Lucy had insisted on making keys for herself and Ben so they could open the backdoor downstairs and Allie's door upstairs. "In case you're ever sick, honey," Lucy had explained in defense of the idea. "Or you go somewhere and we need to get in to water your plants."

But now, faced with the closed door on the second floor, Lucy couldn't quite bring herself to use that key, even though the delivery of a cake did seem to her like sort of an emergency. Somebody might knock it over, she reasoned, if she left it out in the hall. But Allie had made a point about saying, "Now, Mom, you can't just come in anytime you want to. You have to knock, just like you do on my door at home." That, itself, had been a battle royal several years earlier, with Mom arguing that it was her house and she had a perfect right to enter any room of it, and Daughter arguing it would be an invasion of her privacy. When Ben had weighed in on Allie's side, Lucy caved.

Lucy knew she'd better respect this door, too.

With a defeated sigh, she set the cake tin on the floor just to one side of the door and hoped none of those other people who lived there would step on it, or steal it.

"Don't cry," Ben told her when she got home. "She has to grow up."

But it was hard for Lucy to let go, and not to worry and feel rejected. Already she suspected that Allison was off doing things Lucy didn't know about, and probably with people that Ben and Lucy hadn't even met.

The two high school girls who were Allison Tobias's friends helped her celebrate her new freedom that first night at the Marina Bar & Grill, a popular hangout overlooking the Intracoastal Waterway. The girls were too young to drink legally, but they had fake IDs, like almost every other high school student they knew, and the Marina was too crowded to be particular.

If Ben and Lucy had known, they'd have had a fit.

"I love my parents," Allie declared, raising her first glass of draft beer and looking solemn. "God bless 'em." Then she broke out in a huge grin that was instantly mirrored in the faces of Emily Rubeck and Gretchen Hansford. "May they put my old room to good use!" The three gaily clicked their glasses together, and then chugged their beers. None of them normally drank that fast, or very much at all, but this was a special night of long-awaited independence for the most protected one of their trio. Emily and Gretchen were both headed for out-of-town universities, even though they didn't quite have the grade-point average of their smart and diligent friend Allison. What they did have were more permissive parents; Lucy and Ben were well known among their classmates for keeping their only child on the tightest of leashes.

"It'll always be 1950 for Lucy and Ben," Gretchen said, as she set her now-empty glass back down on the little paper coaster. Already her brain felt a little dizzy, but she was having fun; they all were, and they had agreed that they wouldn't drive on this festive night, they'd walk — or wobble — back to Allie's new place. If they didn't find a party first, or three cute guys to drive them. "Nineteen-fifties!" she repeated.

This observation struck the girls as hilarious.

But Gretchen and Emily knew that it made Allison feel guilty to make fun of her well-intentioned parents, so they didn't press the jokes too far. Besides, there was so much else to discuss over their second, and then their third, beers. What should Allie put up on her bedroom walls to decorate them? How much stuff could the other girls get into their dorm rooms without ticking off their roommates? And had Allie met any of the guys in the other apartments? Were they nice? Were they cute? Should the girls have a little party and invite Allie's neighbors?

"There's this really built guy who has an apartment down in the basement —"

"In the basement! Oh, yuck, I'd never live in a basement."

"And these computer guys who live upstairs, but I've never seen them, because they go to work, like, around two in the morning, and they don't get back until, like, one-thirty the next morning —"

"Never date a computer guy —"

"And the other two people on my floor are girls."

"Are they nice?"

"I guess. I don't really know."

"Yeah, 'cause you're too busy checking out the guys!"

Giggling turned to guffaws, until other patrons at the increasingly packed and noisy tavern turned to look at the three young women who were having such a terrific time together. "I hope you're not planning on driving," the waitress observed, on her fourth trip to their table. "'Cause if you are, I'm staying off the roads."

"Not us!" Gretchen told her, pretending to be serious for a second.

"Absolutely not," Allie echoed, with a straight face that she couldn't maintain. She laughed up at the waitress, who couldn't help but smile back at the girl with the face that looked so young, so innocent. The waitress, in her late twenties, remembered how it felt to be a graduate fresh from high school. She was tired on this night, as on most nights, and she thought to herself that these silly girls had no idea what life had in store for them.

"Gonna walk to Allie's place," asserted Emily.

Allison Tobias beamed with pride at those two words: "Allie's place." The waitress caught the look, and even intuited its import. She, too, had once known the excitement of moving out, getting a place of her own. Now it only seemed to represent more hard work, but once it had been exciting. She had a strange sense, one that she didn't recall ever having before, of wanting to warn the giggling girls somehow — but warn them of what, the waitress didn't know. Of life in general? Of enjoying this moment in particular, because it might never feel this good again? She didn't know, and the odd moment passed.

"Are you really sure you want another round?" she inquired.

Gretchen crossed her eyes at Allie. "Everybody's a mom."

"Yes, Mother," Allie said to the waitress, and then blushed a deep scarlet that made the waitress smile a little and shake her head at them. Encouraged, Allie added impishly, "We'll be good."

"I doubt *that* very much," the waitress teased as she left them.

The three friends drank, talked, and

laughed until one in the morning. No "cute guys" had approached them, but the more the girls had to drink the braver they got, until Gretchen worked up the nerve to do the approaching. By the time they weaved out the front door, they were accompanied by two men, strangers to each other, both a few years older than the girls who were flirting with them. One of the fellows seemed to have his eye on Gretchen, the other one was paying all of his attention to Emily.

Allison walked behind the quartet, trying to join in.

But that's hard to do when you're the odd man out, when everybody's got a partner but you. When it's supposed to be your special night, it really stings to be the one not chosen.

But Gretchen and Emily were good friends, loyal friends, and no fools, either. It was one thing to flirt outrageously with strangers in a bar, but it seemed to strike both of them at the same time that it was another thing entirely to leave that bar with men they didn't know. If it was possible to sober up fast, those two did. They managed to talk their way away from the two men, and once that was accomplished they each grabbed one of Allie's hands and started running away with her, down the sidewalk, giggling. It didn't take long for their friend to feel right in the thick of things again. But it's possible that she didn't quite sober up as quickly as they did, or perhaps the alcohol had hit her harder — she was thinner than both of them by a good ten pounds. Or maybe the feeling of being a wallflower stuck with her, even as the trio jogged together to her new apartment. Whatever the reason for it, when they reached 22 Hibiscus Avenue, Allie Tobias encouraged her friends to go on to their own homes.

"I'm going straight to sleep," she told them.

"I thought we were going to spend the night here," Emily protested, feeling a little hurt herself. She spied a folded piece of yellow paper taped to the door jamb. It was addressed to Allie, so Emily pulled it off and read it. "Oh, God, Allie, your mom's been here, and you're supposed to call her as soon as you get in."

Allie grabbed for the note and read it. "Uh-oh."

"Are you going to call her?" Emily asked.

"No way!" Allie said, looking aghast. "She'd know!"

"What are you going to tell her, if you don't call her?"

The three of them were used to this, to being "creative" in the pursuit of independence from their parents.

"I'll just say I didn't see the note." Allie gave the appearance of trying to wrack her tipsy brain to come up with a believable excuse to give her mother. "And I didn't call, because I was so tired from moving that I fell into bed early, and slept through all night, without even taking my clothes off."

"But what if she's called here? Wouldn't you have heard it?"

"No, if I was that tired, I might sleep through a hurricane."

Gretchen wasn't crazy about the idea of going to her own home at this hour with liquor on her breath. "My parents will know I've been drinking if I go home."

"You can come to my house," Emily offered.

Emily's parents were the soundest sleepers.

They both turned to look at Allie, still hoping she'd invite them in.

"I'm sorry," she said, and she looked so inebriated that Emily laughed and asked her, "Are you *sure* you can get upstairs?"

"I'm sure! It was great, guys. Thank you."

They watched her go inside and close the door. As they turned to run the two blocks to Emily's house, Gretchen said, "You think she's mad 'cause of those guys? Because they paid attention to you and me and not to her?"

Emily didn't know about that, but they both felt bad about the way the evening had turned out.

In the morning, Emily and Gretchen felt worse, with ferocious hangovers. They waited a long time to call Allie at her new telephone number, in order to give her plenty of time to sleep in. When they finally agreed they couldn't wait one minute more — at 11:30 a.m. — Gretchen dialed the new number.

She let it ring six times before hanging up.

"She's already gone out, I guess."

"Or she's in the shower."

"Or she's mad and she's not speaking to us."

"Allie wouldn't do that, would she?"

"I didn't even get her answering machine."

"That's weird. Why didn't it pick up?"

Gretchen shrugged. "I don't know, but I'm starved. Can we fix some breakfast? Do you think your mom would mind?" When Emily indicated that would be okay, her friend suggested, "Bring the phone, Em."

All through breakfast they called, and beyond that.

But they never did reach their friend.

In the little house on Thirty-seventh Street, where Allison's parents lived, Ben and Lucy weren't having any luck contacting their daughter, either. Over a period of ten hours, Lucy's feelings changed from hurt to annoyance, and then to fear, and finally to a sickening terror.

"Her very first whole day on her own and she doesn't call us," Lucy complained on the night when Allie was out celebrating with her friends. After leaving the cake, Lucy waited and waited to hear from the daughter who had *promised* to call her mother every day. "This is a poor way to start a new life, I must say."

"You want me to go over and check on her?" Ben asked.

"No, I'll call her myself."

"She won't like it."

"Well, she'd better get used to it, or remember to call me."

But when Lucy called, she didn't get any answer, because Allison, Emily and Gretchen were down at the Marina, giggling, drinking beer, and working up the nerve to flirt with guys.

Finally, around midnight, Lucy insisted that Ben drive her by the Hibiscus address, so they could see if there were any lights on in Allie's room. From the street down below, they saw that their daughter's apartment was dark. Lucy jumped out of the car and left a note in a prominent place on the backdoor where the tenants let themselves in: "For A. Tobias," it said on the front, because Lucy didn't want to give away any signal that a single woman lived there alone. Inside the little folded piece of paper was a note that said: "Call us when you get in, no matter how late it is! Love, Mom & Dad."

The telephone in their home never rang that night.

And although Lucy called the new number every hour on the hour all night long, no one ever picked it up. She didn't know what to think, or what to do. This couldn't be right; it wasn't like Allie to be so irresponsible as to fail to call home when she was supposed to. But what if this

81

was just a stupid way of trying to assert her independence; what if she was really there — or if she'd gone to stay at a friend's house'— and was just stubbornly refusing to give her mother what she wanted. Or what if she'd brought a boy back to her room —

It would be awful, to walk in there and discover that.

But wouldn't it be worse *not* to discover that?

How could she help her daughter, and be a good mother, if she didn't know everything that was going on in Allie's life? A young girl needed guidance in all things, because there were so many dangers, so many ways in which she could make mistakes, bad judgments, come to harm.

Lucy Tobias spent a miserable night.

The morning would only get worse for her and Ben, for Allie's two friends, and for everyone else who cared at all about a sensitive, unassuming eighteen-year-old girl with a bright and hopeful future in front of her.

It was one of those awful coincidences that make you wonder if there might truly be such a thing as a fate that cannot be denied: the day *after* Allison moved into her

82

new apartment, her police officer uncle in Bahia Beach felt something nudge his memory. It was a name, one of those that had been given him by his worrywart of a sister. Lucy was going to ruin that girl if she didn't cut the apron strings, Lyle Karnacki thought. They were apron strings made of iron; it would take a blow torch to cut them, he thought, and shook his head ruefully as he made the trek personally from his division to Juvenile.

When he got there, he inquired of a cop he knew, "The name Steven Orbach mean anything to you?"

The woman rolled her eyes, and said, "Stevie? Killed his mom when he was fourteen. Why?"

"Oh, fucking shit," Lyle breathed. "Tell me the whole thing."

"Well, that's it. Beat her, stabbed her, and choked her until she was dead. Stevie didn't get tried as an adult, unfortunately, so he — why?"

"His record's been sealed?"

"Probably. He was a juvie. What's he done now?"

"Nothing, I hope. My niece up in Lauderdale Pines has just moved into an apartment house and he's one of her neighbors. That could be him, couldn't it? I mean, this guy is twenty-one —"

"It's probably him. How many Steven Orbachs can there be? That's about his age, and that's where he moved to, last I heard. You might want to tell your niece to find herself another place to live."

"Fucking *shit!*" Lyle exclaimed, feeling as if he couldn't get to a telephone fast enough. "My sister's going to have a fit. Can I get an outside line off your phone?"

But it was already 9:00 a.m. when he called up to Lauderdale Pines.

"Lucy? It's Lyle —"

The medical examiner of Howard County later determined, at Lyle's grieving insistence, that he had been approximately six hours too late to save his niece. Ever after, his sister blamed him and he was never able to refute her accusations. He hadn't taken her request very seriously; he'd made a halfhearted check; and now no one could accuse him as harshly as he accused himself. But when the detectives launched their search for the killer, Lyle put everything he had into it, and nobody could ever say he didn't.

"Raped and murdered?" Martina Levin asked the veteran detective. Despite the shade from the tree above them, she felt as if she'd been left to bake too long in an oven. Even the hair on the top of her head felt hot when she reached up gingerly to touch it. The cop beside her had long since taken off his suit coat and laid it on the cement seawall. They'd both put on sunglasses, but she was still squinting behind the lenses of hers. "What happened to *him?*"

"To Stevie Orbach?"

Carl told her that in 1991 Orbach was convicted of the rape/murder of eighteen-year-old Allison Tobias in the early morning hours of May 27, 1990. Upon the unanimous recommendation of the jury and the fervent agreement of a district court judge, Orbach was sentenced to death, at a time when the electric chair was still the sole means in Florida of carrying out that punishment. When the state changed its laws he was presented with an alternative: death by lethal injection. To which he famously responded, "The hell with you. If I get off easy, that means you get off easy. You kill me, you bastards, for a crime I didn't do, then you can by God watch me fry."

"Jeez," Martina breathed, feeling fried herself.

"*That's* who our victim's husband is

fighting for," Carl told her with an angry jerk of his head toward where the body lay in the decaying mansion. "That's who the Reverend Bob Wing is trying to save from the electric chair. So do you get it now?"

The expression on her face told him she got it now.

"When's Orbach scheduled to die?" she asked him.

"Not soon enough."

When they walked back up to the house together, they discovered that the body had already been removed and that apparently the killer had covered his shoes in plastic to keep from leaving prints. That spelled premeditation to Carl. It suggested that a killer so careful would also cover his hands, taking pains to leave as clean a trail as possible. But one axiom of crime-scene investigation, as even young Martina Levin knew, was that every criminal leaves something of himself behind, even if it's only fibers or hair.

Carl learned they had not found a wedding ring to match the gold and diamond engagement ring and so it was assumed the killer had taken it. Later, when the cops found the victim's rings at home in her jewelry box, the notched ring was determined not to be hers. Neither would it be tied to the female defendant. Once the case was closed, the rings were forgotten. They were just one of the several unsolved puzzles that crop up in any homicide. "You don't have to find every little piece," cops will tell you, "if you can see the big picture without them."

Susanna

4

I wonder: Did I put in too much about the Tobias murder? I think I had good reason — it shows why the Bahia cops hate Bob Wing so much and it sets up the irony of the fact that he landed on death row right next to the very man he'd been lobbying to liberate. But I've got so much about it you'd almost think I should have written about that murder instead of Susanna's.

Well, too late now.

As if my telephone hasn't already tortured me enough with its demand for an audience with Tony Delano and its complaints from Bob Wing's supporters, it rings. Damn, and there's somebody I really do want to call. I feel weak-kneed just thinking about making that call, about seeing him again. Well, he'll just have to wait a little longer. For the first time in three weeks, I pick up a receiver, instead of letting the call shunt to the automatic answering mechanism.

"Marie?" A familiar bass voice inquires.

"Hi, George," I say, with some foreboding. It's George Pullen, up at the guardhouse at the front gate of the housing complex where I live in luxurious paranoia.

"You taking calls now?" he asks. "You surprised me, picking up like this. I expected to hear the recording. Well, say, you've got a couple of visitors who aren't on your list, and I'm calling to see should I send them on up to you?"

Just what I feared, visitors. There's no other reason he would be calling, except to announce the delivery of some package or other. Visitors. Damn. Just what I want in my disheveled condition — drop-ins.

"Who is it, George?"

When he tells me their names, I am slightly amazed at the coincidence of this event. "Send them up," I tell him, feeling resigned. "How's your asthma?"

"Not so good, thank you for asking. I'm trying not to use my inhaler so much, though. Afraid of the long-term effects."

"What are they?"

"Nobody knows." He chuckles. "That's what scares me."

"I see your point. There's nothing so dangerous as unintended consequences, is

90

there? In the short-term, though, a man's got to breathe."

"That he do. How 'bout you? Finish that book?"

I hate that question until a book is done. "I did, indeed, thank you. Not an hour ago. That's why the Federal Express truck was here."

"Congratulations! Did you put me in your book?"

"Not this time. I'm sorry, George. But listen, if you'd just kill a few people in an interesting way, I'd write a whole book about you. Can't you do that for me, huh?"

"I can think of a few people I wouldn't mind —"

I laugh. "Yeah, can't we all."

"You going on vacation now, you and that boyfriend of yours?"

"I'm just about to call him and find out."

"Take me with you?"

George is a fifty-six-year-old gay man with a longtime love. They're both former military men on good pensions, but they get bored; hence George's part-time job in our guardhouse, where he can read espionage novels to his heart's content.

"What would Bennie say if I did?"

"He'd be jealous. That boyfriend of yours is too pretty to be a lawyer."

I laugh, as will the "boyfriend" when I tell him this. "George, you've never told anybody but Bennie about my friend, have you?"

" 'Course not. Didn't you ask me not to? But listen, Marie, if you've got to conduct a relationship in secret, you might as well be gay."

I know he means well, but it annoys me to hear him say the truth. I can't even work up a laugh about it, and he meant it halfway joking, I know. Ignoring his last comment, I tell George to shoo my visitors up this way.

"Bye," he says, sounding contented.

I put my phone down, thinking: There's not enough time to clean up. The best I can do is unclasp the barrette and pull a brush through my hair.

That's the doorbell ringing, isn't it? I dimly recall that sound from the days when I wasn't writing night and day, from when I was a fairly normal human being. Now, let's see, what do people do when their doorbell rings? Oh, yes. They get up, they walk through their house to the door, and they peer through their peephole, because they are paranoid, in spite of living in a residential enclave with round-the-clock security. And they are sometimes completely bemused to find coincidence waiting for them on their doorstep. Hadn't I just been reading my own words about these people?

I recall how to open the door and do so, squinting into the noonday sun and the faces of the two people on my front stoop.

"Oh, Ms. Lightfoot, thank God you're here."

It's little Jenny Carmichael and her mother, whose name I can't immediately call to my mind. She's looking frazzled, as befits the mother of this child, and of four other little Carmichaels. Both of them are in sundresses and sandals with their gorgeous red hair held back by elastic bands. Jenny and her hair have both grown a lot since I last saw her. Jenny and her mom are carrying a large white canvas boat bag between them. Jenny's got one handle of it, her mother's got the other. Anne! That's her name, Anne Carmichael. She's a forty-one-year-old version of Jenny, and married to Herb Carmichael, who calls this child their "little handful." I wonder what he calls his wife.

"Anne?" I say, forcing pleased surprise into my voice. "Jenny."

The child glances quickly up at me, then down. This bold and forthright child looks scared. Of me? "I apologize for doing this," her mom says, frowning in the sunshine and talking so fast you'd think somebody was timing her, "but I've been trying for a week to get hold of you and I keep getting your message machine." She waits a beat, to give me time to make excuses for myself, but I just nod. "I didn't know if you were out of town or what, but we finally took a chance and came by to see if we might find you home."

"Why?" I asked her, trying not to sound rude.

"Jenny's got something to show you," Anne tells me, looking tense and sounding really angry at her daughter, whose averted eyes begin to leak tears that surprise and dismay me. "It's something that she didn't show you before, something she found in the old mansion, that she hid and never showed anybody. I think it's important, but I can't get anybody to listen to me!" Her eyes seem to be begging me to give them an audience, so how can I refuse her? But what really prompts me to admit them to my house, and what disturbs me as much as her daughter's tears, is the matching look of fear on Anne's face. While I hold the door open, she pulls her daughter past me as if somebody is chasing them.

Anything to Be Together
By Marie Lightfoot

CHAPTER 4

Early in the morning of the day Susanna Wing's body was found, a man called Bahia Beach 911 to report his wife was missing. His voice, which was being automatically recorded, sounded as if he was barely holding panic under control. He stated his name, Robert F. Wing, and then he gave his address, though that wasn't necessary since addresses automatically come up on the screen. Upon hearing why he was calling, the 911 operator told him he'd have to file a report with Missing Persons, and she gave him a number to call. In Bahia, as in most jurisdictions, an adult who is missing for fewer than seventy-two hours is not considered an emergency. Spouses who don't come home are given the benefit of the doubt, which means the cops assume they've left home for their own reasons.

In Missing Persons, a new transfer from vice spoke with the distraught husband.

Perhaps because she was new on the job she took his report more seriously than an older hand in the department might have at that point.

"What is your name, sir?"

"Bob — Robert F. Wing."

"And your wife's name, sir?"

"Her name is Susanna."

"Susanna Wing?"

"Yes, Susanna Louise Wing. I'm worried. She was supposed to —"

"How long has she been missing, sir?"

"A few hours. I was out of town this week, and she picked me up at the airport this morning . . . I mean yesterday morning . . . and brought me home, and then she left to go to work in her car. She was supposed to be home around five last night. We were going to a church dinner together — I'm a minister — but she never came home. You have to believe me when I say this is not like her. She would be here, or she would call. Susanna would never let me worry about her like this. Something has to have happened, or she'd have come home."

"You expected her around five, yesterday, and it's a little after midnight now, so you'd say she's been missing about . . . five, six, seven, eight, nine, ten, eleven . . . eight hours?"

"Yes, although if anything did happen, if her car ran off the road, or something like that, it could have happened a lot earlier, because she left the house at nine a.m." The caller had a beautiful baritone voice, resonant and compelling, even in the midst of strain. "She was supposed to be showing a house all day — she's a realtor — but I don't know if she even got there. My wife is self-employed, so there's no company I can call, and the house she was showing is empty, the owners have already moved out —"

"Where is that house? What's the address — do you know?"

"Four-twenty South Ocean. I've driven over there."

"Did it look as if your wife had been there?"

"I couldn't tell."

"What else have you done to try to find her?"

"I've called every friend that I could think of, and I've asked members of my church to drive around looking for her. I called 911, but they told me to call you —"

"Yes, that's right. You're doing the right things, sir."

"But we're not finding her! Please, can you help me?"

The gorgeous voice sounded anguished,

and so the police officer responded in a calming manner that was both businesslike and sympathetic.

"I'd like for you to describe her for me, sir, and I'll want a description of her car, and the license —"

"I can't find where all our pictures have gone!" He sounded frustrated, helpless, pleading. "I can't even find our wedding pictures. Susanna must have stored them away somewhere. She's a very organized person. That's one reason I know something's really wrong. I can ask my church members if they have any pictures of her —"

"Slow down, sir, let's take this one step at a time."

That first step was a physical description: five-foot-eight, 135 pounds — he guessed — Caucasian, thirty-two years old, very short dark brown hair, no distinguishing body marks except for a scar from a cesarian section.

"She's pretty," he told the officer. "And she's in good shape. She works out."

"You have children?" she asked, thinking of the cesarian scar, and of youngsters missing their mommy.

"No."

"Oh. Any other distinguishing marks?"

There was a brief pause, before he said

quickly, "I can't think of any."

"What about the car she was driving?"

"It's a 1998 Mercury Mystique. It's white."

"Do you know the license number?"

"It's a personalized one, WG-PRYR. That's the name of her realty company — A Wing and a Prayer. Because I'm a minister and she's a realtor." He cleared his throat, sounding a little embarrassed by it. "Will somebody come out to my house, or should I come down to you?"

"Not yet, sir. I have to tell you that most adults who seem to be missing have their own reasons for being gone. Statistically, your wife is likely to show up sometime soon, or maybe you'll realize there's a reason she left."

"No, not Susanna. Please, believe me."

"I'll send out the word to look for her license."

"Yes, thank you! But what else —"

"Nothing right now, sir."

"Nothing else? But —"

"She'll come home, sir."

"No, she'd be here if she could be. Please —"

But the young transfer from vice had done all she could do for the husband at that point. His description of his wife went into a current file, where it would wait until any further action might be required.

On second thought, and feeling bad about the minister, the officer attempted to get her boss to issue an all-points bulletin on the license plate. He laughed her out of his office. "Are you kidding? Can you imagine how embarrassing that would be for her, a minister's wife? We come rolling up to the motel where she's shacked up with a deacon, and then she sues us, or the deacon does."

"The husband says —"

"Yeah, they all do."

"He was really upset."

"They all are."

"Okay."

What could she do? Maybe his wife really was shacked up with a deacon.

No alert went out for the license plate.

At ten minutes to two a.m., the Bahia Beach police chief, Marty Rocowski, known as Rocco to everybody who didn't call him "Sir" was awakened by an urgent phone call. He reached for it too late to avoid waking his wife, who propped herself on an elbow and stared across the pillows at her thirty-seven-year-old husband who hardly ever got a whole night's sleep. Which meant that she didn't, either. The seven-year-olds that she taught in an inner-city school were going to get a sleepy teacher yet again this coming Monday morning. Seeing that she was listening anyway, Rocco put the call on speaker so his wife could hear, too.

"Rocco, this is Tammi Golding."

Police chief and wife exchanged surprised glances.

The caller was a prominent local attorney and regular golf partner of his wife's.

"Good morning, Tammi," Rocco said, with an emphasis on the word "morning." Knowing this couldn't possibly be a call bringing good news, he shot straight to the point. "What's wrong?"

Her familiar voice, grating and aggressive and stripped of all its usual characteristic humor, filled their bedroom. "I'm sorry to roust you out of sleep like this, but the wife of one of my clients has gone missing. My client, the husband, got detoured by 911. He got the runaround from Missing Persons — wait three days, that crap. But this is the real deal, Rocco. She's gone, and she's not a woman who would do this. I'm telling you that somebody's got to take this seriously. He does. I do. I want you to, and I want you to make somebody down at the department take it seriously, too. This is a minister's wife, for God's sake, Rocco. She hasn't run away from home. She's really missing, and she's been missing for hours, and the only possible explanation is that she's dead, or she's hurt, or she's been abducted. Or something else bad has happened to her. She's in trouble somewhere, we know it, and we can't find her, and we've called everybody, and we need help, and we need it right now. As you know, I am not given to hysteria, and I am on the verge of hysteria here."

"You sound personally involved," he observed, with a question in his tone.

"I care about these people," she shot back, sounding defensive.

"Who's your client?"

"Bob Wing. Sands Gospel Church."

"You don't mean that anti–death-penalty minister?"

"Yes, I do, Rocco, that's exactly who it is. Bob Wing. It's his wife, Susanna, that's missing."

The police chief, who was only human, after all, paused for a brief moment to appreciate the moment. Everybody knew that

Tammi Golding did the legal work for the Sands Gospel capital-punishment crusades. Locally, she and the Reverend Bob Wing were a pair of burrs under the seat of every cop, judge, and prosecutor who favored the death penalty. Rocco's own wife had been known to quote Tammi to him. He couldn't resist saying, "If his wife has been abducted, or killed, there is a certain irony in this situation, don't you think so, Tammi?"

"I don't give a damn about the irony," his wife's golfing partner nearly screamed at him. Across the bed, his wife made a grimacing, apologetic, expression at the noise. "I care about finding Bob's wife! Please, Rocco, throw your weight around, pull strings, do something, or what the hell good does it do me to have friends in high places?"

The police chief's wife smiled faintly at that.

"Have you got this on speakerphone, Rocco? Betty, are you listening to this? If you are, kick his ass out of bed. And don't count on me for golf today, not unless we find Susanna before our tee-off time. Betty?"

"I hear you, Tammi! I hope she's all right! Do I know her?"

103

"I doubt it, Betty," called the voice over the speakerphone.

"I've heard you talk about her though, right? Weren't you telling me some story about them —"

"Not me. Gotta go. We're organizing search parties."

The police chief, who didn't personally know the minister or his missing wife, couldn't help but feel amused as he called his own Missing Persons Department to get them moving on the report. Not that he wished anyone ill — of course he didn't — but as his old grandmother might have said, My goodness, how things that go around do eventually tend to come around. If this man's wife turned out to have been kidnaped or even killed by somebody who could get the death penalty for it, what would the good minister do then?

Picket his own wife's murderer's execution?

Marty Rocowski allowed himself a small smile as he placed his call.

The search to locate Susanna Louise Wing commenced officially five minutes later. Shortly after that the police chief was showered, shaved, and dressed, and heading down to his office at the Bahia

Beach Police Headquarters on Twenty-third Street, between Sunrise and Gulf avenues. Back home, Betty Rocowski rolled over and tried to go back to sleep. While she tossed and turned, Rocco drove A1A, enjoying the beach road in the darkness, rolling down his windows so he could hear the ocean, feel the breeze. Himself a firm believer in the death penalty, Chief Rocowski wanted to be sure this missing persons case was handled impeccably. He would make sure that nobody could accuse his police force of failing to do their duty for the wife of a man who was loathed by his officers.

Susanna

5

Confronted with two anxious visitors, I am not yet up to normal social response, much less solicitousness. "How'd you find me?" is the best I can do, after Jenny and Anne Carmichael scurry past me with their canvas boat bag. As stupid and trivial as the question sounds, their answer is important to me. I try hard to barricade myself from exactly this sort of thing, these uninvited visitors. Partly, that's to protect me when I'm writing; partly, it's to protect me, period, from some of my nutso book subjects. If I wanted to be found, I'd be in the phone book.

"You're on the tours." Anne looks back at me over her shoulder as I follow them into my living room. When she sees my puzzled look, she explains, "The tourist boats and buses? The ones that go past landmarks and homes of famous people? One time we took some relatives on one of those big boat tours, and they pointed out where your house is."

"They know where I live?" I am surprised, displeased.

"Because of your trees." Ah. Damn. I have six magnificent cypress trees in front of my house, three to each side of my front door. "You can see those trees from miles away, so it wasn't hard to find this place again. We think of you every time we take our own boat out and go past this neighborhood. Didn't you know you were on the tours?"

I shake my head. This would seriously annoy me if it weren't so amusing in an ironic way. Here I thought I was hidden under those trees, and now I find that they are fingers pointing right at me. *"And that's where the true crime writer Marie Lightfoot lives, folks. See those six cypress trees on that point of land over there?"*

"I hope they plug my books, at least," I say, with a wry smile.

Her frown relaxes a bit. "I don't remember."

"What's in the bag, Jenny?"

When the child glances back at me, I am again surprised to see what looks like trepidation in her blue eyes. And more evidence of impending tears. She doesn't speak, but turns around quickly and edges closer to her mother's legs, as a younger child might do. She is not such a little girl now, I note with a sudden pang. She looks a couple of inches taller, her hair is a little less red, a little more brown, and flatteringly long. The tomboy looks more feminine now, but I'll bet that Jenny can still scale fences with the best of them. Even with that fearful, sad tinge to her gaze, she has the same direct, alert expression that I remember from when I interviewed her.

We've come through the front hall, around a corner. When they step fully into my house, the view has the usual distracting impact on them that it has on everybody who sees it for the first time. I like to knock people out of their socks. "Wow!" Jenny says. She drops her handle of the bag and runs around her mother, toward the wraparound windows. "Cool house!"

"What a beautiful view," her mother echoes.

"Excuse the mess," I say, automatically, as I try to recall all I know about these two, which is significantly more than I've put in my book. That's always the way. I've heard that fiction writers do that, too — accumulate tons more material about their characters than they really need, all in the service of knowing them well so they can write with confidence about them. My brain is a file cabinet on every person in this case, and what's not in my brain is stored in my computer, along with hundreds of facts that I keep around the way some old ladies keep bits of string, because I never know when I might need them to fill a paragraph or enliven a metaphor. You probably didn't know, for instance, that Greater Bahia Beach boasts 550 tennis courts and eighteen major shipwrecks. We had almost 900,000 overseas visitors last year, and half that many from Canada alone. None of those tourists visited me. But now I have my own little statistic: two visitors in three weeks, and here they are now. I bring up the rear as they step around piles of reference books. I'm getting curious about the bag, and what's in it. "So what's in the bag, Jenny?" I ask again. Her skinny shoulders visibly stiffen and I get the impression she is not looking at me — or up at her mom — on purpose.

I turn to her mother. "Anne?"

But she frowns down at her daughter and says, "I want Jenny to tell you."

It suddenly seems merciful to change the subject. "How about some lemonade first? Anne, I've also got iced tea, or I could make some coffee." Why am I doing this? I ask myself, but too late. I seem to be encouraging them to stick around; maybe I'm a little lonelier for human company than I realized, especially since I still haven't been able to make the one call I want to make to the one person I want to see.

Jenny looks up at her mom as if expecting no for an answer.

"Can I have some lemonade, Mom, please?"

"I suppose so," Anne says, and then to me, "Iced tea for me?"

"I'll be right back with it." Then on an impulse, I invite Anne to come with me. Once we're in the kitchen, out of Jenny's hearing, I ask, "How's she doing, Anne?"

"Jenny's okay, I guess, except she can't play with Nikki anymore."

"What? But they're best friends. What happened?"

"It's *because* of what happened. Nikki's parents won't allow Jenny into their house anymore."

"Oh, I'm sorry. The girls must hate that."

"Jenny's miserable. I could just kill the Modestos. It's so unfair. Jenny gets blamed for everything."

I refrain from commenting that there is probably a good reason for that, given the nature of her willful, adventurous daughter. Nor do I point out that she herself appears to be blaming Jenny for something, too. I just cluck sympathetically.

"And —" Anne Carmichael starts to say something else but then stops, frowning.

"And?" I prod.

She shakes her head. "I want Jenny to tell."

Patience, I advise myself. Now that she's safe inside my house, Anne seems to be growing a little calmer, and I'm all for that.

"I wish they'd convicted that woman, too," Anne suddenly blurts out, and I turn to stare at her. She looks upset and angry. "Jenny has nightmares about her, and I worry about it all the time. What if that woman decides it's all Jenny and Nikki's fault? She's free now; she could do anything and nobody could stop her. What if she blames them? What if she thinks if the girls hadn't found the body, then nobody would have been arrested, and her lover wouldn't be in prison. What if she wants some revenge on the girls?"

She's talking about Artemis McGregor, of course, the "other woman," who was tried with Bob Wing but acquitted by the same jury that convicted him. I wish I could allay Anne's fears by telling her that

112

her worst nightmare is completely unfounded; unfortunately, I have known killers who did just the kind of thing she's scared about. They waited, they plotted, they took their revenge. Sometimes they got caught at it, sometimes there were only suspicions. Either way, the people they resented were just as dead. I can't bear to think of Nikki and Jenny and their families living under that kind of dread for years to come.

"I don't think that will happen, Anne," I say, cautiously.

She frowns. "You don't know the rest of it yet."

"What?"

"Let Jenny show you."

As Anne and I return to the living room with a tray of drinks, I wonder if my visitors realize that everything they are looking at is either man-made or put there by humans. That doesn't make it ugly; it is, in fact, beautiful. But while it looks like "nature," in fact every inch of it was plotted by architects and city planners, by botanists and that well-known landscape artist, the U.S. Army Corps of Engineers. I place a cool glass in Jenny's free hand, then pass the second glass to her mother. "You've heard of the Pleistocene, Jenny?"

She looks up at me and nods.

"During the Pleistocene era," I tell her, "Florida was mostly veldt, like they have in Africa. There were camels out there, and bison and tortoises as big as trucks, and llamas, and the ancestors of elephants. Isn't that amazing?"

"Elephants?" her mother asks.

"Mastodons," I tell her, lingering over the syllables with pleasure. Imagine that, mastodons in Florida. The proof, claim some naturalists, is visible whenever a new road goes through and ancient ivory is unearthed. I wonder if true crime writers will be dinosaurs one day, when satellites and video cameras record every inch of earth, and science can solve all crimes, so that nobody commits them anymore. Is it just me, the greedy writer, who recoils at that idea? "What's up, Jenny?" I finally ask, to get this over with. I like this child, and I like her mother, and I could talk about my state's natural history with them all day long, but right now I need a bath, not visitors. "What have you got to show me?"

They both turn around, and Anne gives her daughter a nudge. They set the canvas bag on my carpet, and the child bends over and digs something out of it. "I found this." She has something gripped in her right fist. "Here." She holds the fist out to me, and I raise my right hand and open my palm to her. She drops something small and light into it. When her own small hand moves away, I give a little gasp. She has given me a small, shiny gold ring. Like an archeologist holding a coprolite, I'm looking down at the treasure she has uncovered: a gold band with four diamonds. The diamonds are not so large that you could buy a home with the insurance proceeds from losing this, but they're definitely impressive enough to insure. The band has odd jogs in it, like a puzzle intended to fit another ring.

"The missing wedding ring!" I exclaim.

When I give Jenny an amazed stare, she says, "I found it in the haunted house where the dead lady was." Her blue eyes fill with tears, and she brings a fist up to rub the moisture away. Jenny suddenly looks very young and small and sorry. In a stiff voice, sounding as if she has been schooled, she says to me, "I apologize that I didn't tell you before, Ms. Lightfoot."

"Stole it!" corrects her mother, in a grim tone. "And didn't tell anybody, and probably never would have, except that I found it when I was cleaning out her closet. She says she was afraid she'd get arrested and go to jail for taking it." I don't smile at that, although I'm tempted. This is such a childish prank. And yet, there is something else at the back of Anne's eyes, a hint of an anxiety to match her daughter's. When I look at Jenny again, I see that tears are rolling down her cheeks, and I feel surprised and stricken for her. "Oh, Jenny!" I bend over, touch her hair.

"I'm sorry," she whispers, with an urgent look into my eyes.

They seem so disproportionately upset over this that I feel a need to calm Jenny down, set her mother at ease, put a little perspective on things. It doesn't seem to me like anything to get excited about. I can see why Jenny felt anxious, as any kid would whose mother had caught her stealing something, but I don't see why her mother needs to make such a federal case out of it. This is a childish misdemeanor if there ever was one. A little girl found a shiny bauble and wanted to keep it, that's all.

The ring sparkles in the sunlight as I hold it.

Anne Carmichael gives me a meaningful look and says, in a low voice that makes her daughter's eyes widen in fear, "What if it's *hers?* What if *she* wants it back?" And then she says, in a tense, angry voice, "Show Marie what else you found in the old house, Jenny."

Anything to Be Together
By Marie Lightfoot

CHAPTER 5

"Nobody equates religion with passion anymore," the Reverend Bob Wing was known to thunder from his pulpit now and then. "Not since the civil rights movement of the sixties. Nobody lays down their life anymore, nobody throws themselves with all of their heart onto the picket line of justice. But here at Sands Gospel, we still feel it." At that point, his fist would strike his black robe over his heart with a thud his microphone picked up. "Where there is racism, where there is injustice, where there is death that shouldn't be, we'll be there. We have a passion, all right, a passion for justice, for peace, for human rights."

The faces in the pews demonstrated his words, for they were young and old, black, brown, golden, and white and every shade in between. It billed itself as a liberal church — like the Unitarians — with no creed but with a wide-open welcome mat for Christians and Jews, Muslims, Buddhists, Hindus, Wiccans, atheists, agnostics, and anybody with a searching, doubting, crusading nature. It wasn't traditional or conventional, but then neither was he.

The tall, young preacher was mesmerizing and handsome. Forty-five years old, black-haired, with riveting blue eyes that held entire sanctuaries of people in their compass. There was about him the glamorous look of a western lawman — tall, straight-backed, and straightforward in his manner, he looked as if he'd be right at home in a long black coat with pistols at his side. His voice, that glorious baritone that reverberated in the hearts of his listeners, was part of his extraordinary appeal. Women adored him; men trusted him. Even his political enemies admitted he was as good as his word. Normally soft-spoken, he was known to be implacable as a bounty hunter when he got on the path of righteousness. He was scholarly too, with a doctorate in theology from Princeton and enough legal expertise to match most attorneys. If Bob Wing joined your cause, you cheered right up; if he opposed you, you girded your loins for battle.

His pet cause, the one that galvanized him, was capital punishment.

"Kill the death penalty," he liked to say, "and save this country's soul."

Argue with him and he leveled that blue stare at you and let loose with a devastating rebuttal to which few could respond. "Let me put this in terms even you can understand," he once famously sneered at a conservative opponent. "The way our criminal system is structured, if you favor the death penalty, you favor the occasional execution of wrongfully convicted defendants. It's as plain as that. The U.S. Supreme Court stated as much in *Herrera v. Collins*, where Justice Rehnquist wrote that, effectively, if the state has provided you with all of the due process you are entitled to under the Constitution and the laws of the jurisdiction in which you were convicted, and granted access to both substantive and habeas corpus appeals, and you nevertheless fail to overturn your sentence of death, the fact that you are innocent makes no difference. Got that? It makes no damned difference. The law doesn't care and you're a fool if you think it does. The system only guarantees the chance to prove your innocence, the court has written, because it is a subjective system with no absolute guarantees that every innocent person will be exonerated. The death penalty is absolute. Life in prison allows release. So, if you have the stomach for knowing that you, as a citizen of one of the states that are perpetually at risk of executing innocent or wrongfully convicted people, will be partially responsible for killing those people as a price for executing others, then fine."

Few stood up to that passionate onslaught.

"But some people deserve to die," his opponent objected.

"Like I said," snapped the preacher, "that's your choice, and you purchase your vengeance at a damned high price."

In the western suburbs of Bahia Beach, Sands Gospel members were awake and worrying in the hours before dawn. Their minister's wife had been missing for almost twenty-four hours now and they rushed to his side the way he rallied to the aid of so many other victims. Bob and Susanna lived in a suburb where clusters of homes dotted boulevards that are divided by grassy medians where waterfowl roost. Their development was called Bayfield, though there are no bays, and it's a good ten miles from the ocean. But each walled development has its own little lake, swimming pool, private gate, and homes association.

Church members arrived carrying comforting food they'd kindly brought to nourish their minister in his time of trouble. It was adults only, as this was deemed too upsetting for the children. This was the stuff of nightmares. Younger kids were left in the care of older brothers and sisters; baby-sitters and grandmothers hurried to help out, too.

At times, everybody seemed to talk at once in nervous bursts.

"Bob, I don't know what to say . . ."

"She's all right, Bob, I know it."

When they thought he couldn't overhear them, they whispered to each other, "Where do you think she could be?" And, "It isn't fair! Not after what happened to —"

"Shh," soft whispers warned.

By 8:00 a.m., the kitchen counters staggered under casseroles, canned goods, pies and cakes, coffee cakes and a meatloaf, loaves of bread, muffins, bagels, biscuits, several varieties of cream cheese, bags of potato chips, extra cans of coffee, and packs of sodas.

"Poor man, oh, that poor man. It's not

fair. First he loses one wife he loved, and now —"

"Don't say it. Don't even think it!"

Their minister had been married once before, to a lovely woman named Donna who had died only two years ago. When Bob had fallen in love with a new member, Susanna Davis, and then married her, his congregation rejoiced. It was heart-warming to see him rise out of sorrow and loneliness. But now . . . this.

"We'll find her," the president of the board said, forcefully. Stuart McGregor was a tall, lean man in his late thirties, with blond hair and an unlined face that could almost have passed for college-age. Though he hadn't been a member of the church very long, he'd taken to responsibility like a fish to water. He and the minister were good friends, as were their wives. His pretty blond wife, Artemis, nodded in agreement with her husband's sentiments as she walked around the living room carrying a coffee pot and providing refills for all the cups held out to her. "I don't care what it takes," Stuart assured people, "we'll find her."

"Of course we will," echoed one of the older women. She accepted a refill without looking directly at the comely woman who poured it for her. "And we'll take care of Bob till Susanna comes home."

Artemis McGregor — known as Artie — quietly continued her coffee duties, her big brown eyes filling up when the missing woman's name was mentioned. Petite, blond, and buxom as a high school cheerleader, Artie was normally the bubbly life of any party; but on this difficult morning she was uncharacteristically silent as she made her coffee rounds. She, too, was tired, and her hands trembled so much that a little hot liquid spilled on more than one recipient of her efforts.

Another member spoke up: "That's what this church is about, taking care of one another."

"But what if we *don't* find her?" somebody whispered, urgently.

"That's not possible," Tammi Golding said, firmly. "Between us and the police, we'll find her." She didn't look like a tough legal contender at the moment; she looked like a tired, worried friend of the family, dressed in white shorts, a T-shirt, and sandals, and wearing a frown that made her look older than her thirty-nine years. Like the church members in the house, Tammi hadn't slept since getting the emergency phone call from her client and friend.

"Tammi," someone asked her, "is the death-penalty committee still going to meet today?"

"No," she said quietly, with a glance toward the living room, where Bob Wing sat in his armchair. "Not with this going on."

"We haven't got much time. Every day —"

"Counts, I know. You don't have to tell *me*."

The other church members looked wilted; their shoulders sagged.

"We never had a chance," one of them murmured resentfully.

"Yes we did!" Tammi whispered back furiously, causing several other people to turn and look at them. "We still do! Don't anybody give up, you hear me? We won't give up. They'd just love for us to give up and let Stevie die. But I won't give them the pleasure. If we have to, we'll fight them until the second before they turn the current on him."

"Okay, Tammi," somebody agreed, wearily. "Okay."

When Artie McGregor moved past with the coffee a couple of the other women exchanged discreet glances — and then drew back from her as if to avoid getting burned.

"Do you think Bob wants coffee?" Artie suddenly blurted.

There was a moment of frozen silence when nobody responded to her question. Her husband, appearing oblivious to the silence of the others, smiled kindly at his pretty wife and said, "Why don't you ask him, honey?"

But Tammi Golding reached out for the coffee pot, took it out of Artie's hands, and said, firmly, "I'll do it." Left with empty hands and a look of surprise on her face, Artemis appeared close to bursting into tears. Seeing how emotional she felt, Stuart lovingly wrapped an arm around her. He gently led his wife out of the circle of church members, saying, "Come on, Artie, let's find something else to do. It'll be okay, honey, we'll find her and she'll be fine, I promise."

"I don't think so," Artie whispered, and somebody gasped to hear it.

"Sure she will!" Stuart reassured her.

"No," his wife said, tearfully, stubbornly, "she isn't."

Everybody heard her, and they heard her switch to the present tense. It was almost as if pretty little Artie McGregor, usually so cheerful and so effervescent, knew something dreadful that the rest of them didn't know yet. And they didn't want to know. The ones closest to the couple took a step backward, as if to remove themselves from the presence of a witch.

Their minister sat in an armchair by a telephone in the family room, looking exhausted and frightened. He hadn't slept all night, but then, neither had most of the rest of them. When he tried to pray, he never got past "Dear God . . ." uttered in tones of increasing despair and helplessness.

Eventually, seeing that their minister couldn't manage to pray without breaking down, Stuart McGregor got down on a knee, placed a hand on one of Bob's knees, and did the praying for him. While Stuart voiced their supplication to the Almighty, and others bowed their heads, Bob turned his face bleakly to stare out a window. Saturdays he coached a children's baseball team at this hour. Somebody was taking care of that for him this morning, he was told. His favorite baseball bat — an old-fashioned wooden bat, not a modern aluminum one — stood propped in its usual place, in an umbrella stand in the front hall.

Outside, cars, vans, and trucks lined the streets; it looked like Sunday morning at church, with everybody pouring in. When the Bayfield neighbors heard about it, they started dropping by, too, and when the word spread to other clergy in the city, many of them alerted their congregations to look for the missing woman and her car. Rarely had a search of this magnitude been launched for a single adult person.

It was about this time on Saturday morning that two little girls were propping their bicycles against a chain-link fence with signs that said KEEP OUT.

Susanna

6

"You won't *believe* what's in the bag."

The expression on Anne Carmichael's face and the tone of her words are dramatic enough to lead me to expect the Shroud of Turin, at least. I hang on to the diamond wedding ring as Jenny yanks other items from the canvas bag: a dark blue bath towel, an orange washcloth, one small and unopened green plastic bottle of water, three premoistened towelettes in foil wrappings, a package of condoms (which causes me to flick a glance up at her mother), and, at the bottom, a white sheet with elastic bands at the corners.

For the second time, they've managed to startle me.

This time, however, my heart starts pounding with self-serving hope.

"My God," I whisper. "The proof of their affair."

"Yes," Anne says, in a shaky voice. She grabs Jenny by the shoulders and pulls the girl back against her. "If the jury had known about this stuff . . ."

I finish the sentence for her: "They might have convicted her, too. Where were these, Jenny?"

"In the tower," she says in a small voice.

For a moment, I don't even remember that the mansion has one, and then I see it in my mind's eye, the "third story" on the right as you face the front porch. "Where in the tower, honey?"

"There's a cabinet," her mother says. "Set into the wall, as far as I can tell from the way Jenny describes it."

"I just wanted the bag," she says, defensively.

As I gaze at these banal objects lying on my living room floor, a personal memory pops unbidden into my head: once, I was interviewing the parents of a serial killer in southwest Florida, in the vicinity of the Big Cypress National Preserve. The three of us were sitting in their backyard looking out over their swamp, where an alligator lived. We were gazing into the thicket beyond when, suddenly, in the lazy heat, in the middle of one of my desultory questions — or one of their slow answers — we saw a flash of fauna between the flora. There. Not there. In and out. Gone. Now, the Florida panther is not extinct, but it's endangered and rare, only thirty to fifty of them remaining in the state. Claiming you've actually seen one is nearly akin to reporting a Big Foot sighting, so I'm not saying this was a panther, beyond all shadow of a doubt. But I'll say this much — perfectly aware that eyewitnesses are notoriously unreliable: it had a flat face like a cat, and a tail too long to be a bobcat's and too sinuous to be a dog's. I can't swear the tail was crooked on the end, the way a panther's ought to be, but I do know the creature was far too big to be a domestic cat, and there was nothing on the local news about anybody's pet mountain lion being on the loose. And it was the right color: not black, but tan. The parents of the serial killer saw it, too, for whatever that's worth as corroborating testimony, and they didn't make any claims about ever having seen anything like it before in their woods. It gave all three of us a shock, a shiver, seeing that creature flicker in and out of our view, and it left us staring at each other, and saying, "Was that what I think it was?"

I've got that panther feeling again, as though something improbable and dangerous has slipped in and out of my awareness.

"Does Nikki know about this?"

Jenny gives me a look, as if to say, "Well, duh," though her actual words are more polite than that. "Oh, yeah, Nikki helped me carry it to our bikes."

I had interviewed both of those little stinkers, and neither of them said one single word about —

"Why didn't you tell anybody?"

"Nobody asked us."

Her mother and I shake our heads at each other.

"She wanted to keep the ring," her mother says tartly.

"Mom! I was going to —"

"But you didn't. What should we do with these things, Ms. Lightfoot?"

"Marie, please."

What should they do with them? Now there's a question with an obvious answer, if I ever heard one. Take them to the police, that's what they should have done as soon as Anne found the bag at the back of Jenny's closet a week ago. They've waited a week, just to show *me?*

"Take it to the police, Anne."

"I tried," she says, looking aggrieved. "They didn't want it, and I didn't know who else to show, until I thought of you —"

"They didn't *want* it? Who told you that, Anne?"

"Detective Chamblin. He said it was too late to do any good."

"Did you offer it to the prosecutor?"

"Mr. Delano said the same thing. I even tried the defense attorneys. I just wanted *somebody* to take it away from us. But they didn't want it, either."

"Who didn't?"

"Ms. Golding."

I notice that Jenny is observing us closely, as if we are deciding her fate. No wonder she looks scared; the child's very bright; she understands that she may have hidden evidence. If this stuff could have been linked to Bob Wing and Artie McGregor, it might have put two of them on death row instead of just one. And if it couldn't have been linked to them, it might have provided fodder for the defense to suggest the presence in that house of somebody else who might have killed Susanna.

"They may not want it," Anne says, "but *somebody* sure does."

"What do you mean?"

Again she turns toward her daughter, but this time Anne doesn't sound angry at her little girl; she sounds gentle and anxious. "Tell Marie about the phone call, Jenny."

With wide eyes, the child says, "Somebody called our house and asked for me. And they told me I had to put the bag out on the front porch at night. They said I couldn't tell anybody about it. They said if I did my mom and dad would go to jail for . . ." She looks to her mom for help with the words.

"Withholding evidence," her mother says, and sets her mouth in a grim line.

"What?" I exclaim. "Was this before or after you talked to Carl and Tony?"

"After I saw them."

"This doesn't make sense."

"I know, but there's more. Jenny was so scared she didn't tell her father or me. She did what the person on the phone told her to do and put the bag on the porch one night. My husband heard a noise that night and woke up and went to look. When he turned on the porch light, somebody ran off our porch. They didn't get the bag, but it scared us all half to death. That's when Jenny finally told us the truth."

"Was it a man or a woman?" I ask them both.

But they shrug and shake their heads.

"I couldn't tell from their voice," Jenny says.

"My husband couldn't see who it was,

136

either." Anne Carmichael is literally wringing her hands. "I am really upset about this."

"I don't blame you. Who knew you had this bag at your house?"

"Just the people I told you."

"And who'd *they* tell?" I wonder out loud.

"I don't know, but I have a really big favor to ask you."

"You want me to keep the bag."

"Yes, how'd you know that?"

"You need to get it away from your family, but you also don't want to destroy it. But, Anne, the person who tried to take it is not going to know that it isn't there anymore."

"Oh, yes they are," she says with a grim smile. "There's a big sign on our front porch that says, 'Your Bag's Not Here. We Threw It Away.'"

I have to laugh at her wildly creative solution. "That's brilliant. When somebody comes in the dark, hit them back by daylight."

"Exactly. They're not going to hurt my children."

"No." I drop to my haunches to look that child directly in her eyes. "Is there anything else you have to tell us, Jenny?"

She shakes her head at me, but there's a look in her eyes that suggests she is surprised by my question and not very happy with it. Again, I get that spooky feeling of something elusive, something lurking in the shadows, like a panther. They're silent creatures, except during mating season, and then their screams can rip the sheaths right off your nerves.

I rise to my feet. "I'll keep the bag. Don't worry about it anymore."

When they leave, I have in my possession a gold and diamond wedding ring and the detritus, possibly, of an illicit affair. It's not much to add to my book, but at least the condoms and the sheet suggest that somebody had sex. What the ring means, I still don't know.

Anything to Be Together
By Marie Lightfoot

CHAPTER 6

Sands Gospel, the popular little nondenominational church, seemed to have everything going for it, except for one thing: money. It had an enviable location near the ocean and a vibrant congregation and a dynamic minister and the usual tax breaks. But it also had a lot of good works to support. The capital-punishment campaign alone ate money like waves licking at sand. The members were mostly middle and lower class economically, and they were folks who already gave a lot to charity before they even got around to writing a check to their church. Tourists didn't leave much in the collection plate, and the beach bums left less. But everybody left wear and tear, the wind and salt air most of all. The stucco on the outside was wearing out and the rugs on the inside were wearing thin.

A few members started praying for a benefactor.

They might better have heeded the wry old adage, "Be careful what you pray for, because you just might get it."

"I'll never forget the first time I saw Artemis," the church secretary avows. "Of course, she wasn't Artie McGregor yet, she was still Artemis Hornung. I'll swear, when she walked in, she was like a breath of fresh air, like a sea breeze. She was so nice, so friendly and polite, and she had the face of an angel. Just lovely. She introduced herself — and I thought, what a beautiful and unusual name, Artemis — and she said she was looking for a new church home. She said she hadn't actually set foot in a church for, gosh, twenty years."

What Mrs. Artemis Hornung didn't confide was that she was newly divorced from a man who was almost the exact opposite of her. Taylor Hornung was a "meat and potatoes" kind of guy who had married a woman who could whip up soufflés at the drop of a slotted spoon. Taylor's idea of a good time was a few beers and a football game; his wife liked museums, parties, and "good works."

It seemed almost inevitable when Artie and Taylor divorced.

"We were just too different," she told people.

"I couldn't keep up!" was his humorous version.

That was all right for a long time, though, because they were both busy with the operation of Hornung Dock & Pier, Inc. You know those wooden posts that pelicans sit on all over Florida? They're slatted and grooved and ringed with metal? Ever wonder who makes them, or where they come from? Hornung Dock & Pier, most of them. "There's a lot of water in Florida," Taylor Hornung liked to say, stating the obvious in his humorous way. "And one hell of a lot of sea-gulls. They all need perches, right? Wouldn't be right to keep them from landing somewhere. Even seagulls got to rest now and then, you know. Millions of seagulls and pelicans, thousands of boats, and lots and lots of piers and posts."

And, over the years, lots and lots of money.

After their marriage of twenty years they split their property without so much as a squabble because, "We started with nothing and earned it all together," as Taylor told his lawyer. "People say I'm generous to her, but they never stop to think that

141

she's had to be equally generous to me. I mean, it's her company, too."

"He's a sweet man," Artie was known to say.

"Too nice," said some of his friends who didn't view her contributions in quite the generous light that he did. "Like ten million dollars too nice."

Their business sold for twenty million dollars, with half for each of them, after taxes. Their union had not produced heirs. Taylor moved happily onto a sailboat and took off for the South Pacific, where he was reachable only by E-mail. Artemis moved into a smaller house and began to look for something besides business to fill her life and something beyond her wardrobe on which to lavish her money.

Later she would say, "I prayed for guidance."

Her penetrating glance fell upon Sands Gospel Church.

"She said she had heard good things about our pastor," Pat Danner, the church secretary, remembers about that first meeting with Artie.

A lot of people were hearing good things about Bob Wing.

SANDS GOSPEL PREACHER FILLS PEWS

one headline proclaimed on the religion page of the local Bahia Beach newspaper. And of course there was increasing publicity about his campaigns against the Florida death penalty. The word had gone out to tourists and residents alike that the sermons were lively at Sands Gospel, that the minister was young and charismatic, and that anybody could find a welcome there.

"Young" is a relative term, of course.

The Reverend Dr. Robert F. Wing was forty-three at the time of that article, forty-four at the moment when fate walked into his church in the guise of a "breath of fresh air" with the beautiful name of Artemis and the face of an angel. She was just turned forty herself. His first wife, Donna, had died of uterine cancer less than a year earlier; Artie, too, was just emerging from her divorce from Taylor Hornung. In fact, the church was full of suddenly singles. A "grief group" that Dr. Bob led twice a week was, sadly, packed with widows, widowers and divorced persons of all ages. Of all the places in which to look for happiness, surely a "grief group" was one of the least promising. And yet there seemed to be something magical about the "Recovering From Loss" group — its official name

— that Bob Wing started after Donna died. It seemed as if couples paired up left and right, as if he was as much match-maker as minister.

He, himself, had recently married a woman in the group. But his new wife was off on real estate calls the day that Artemis Hornung walked in, and so Susanna Wing wasn't there to greet their potential new member.

Only the church secretary and the minister met Artie that day.

She confessed to them that she felt a spiritual void in her life; he was a minister, trained to fill that emptiness with words of the spirit. Soon, the three of them were laughing and chatting away like old friends, as if Artie had found her natural church home, just as easily as that. When they found out that she was newly divorced, the church secretary kindly said, "You ought to attend Dr. Bob's group for people who've lost their spouses through death or divorce."

"I will," Artie told them, "and you ought to come to my next party."

And so it was set in motion by a good intention.

It all seemed so mutually congenial, such a fortuitous meeting of hearts and minds.

Bob Wing found it easy to say yes for his wife and himself, and Pat Danner accepted with pleasure on behalf of herself and her husband. It appeared that Artemis Hornung had found her church home and Sands Gospel — though they didn't know it yet — had found its benefactor, for Artie was not only newly divorced but richly so, with money to burn and a burning ambition to spend it.

The charming woman with the face of an angel said goodbye after a tour of the church. The secretary noticed that her handsome minister seemed to be staring at the front door after it closed behind their visitor.

"Nice woman," she said approvingly.

He turned, and she saw how he blushed. "Oh. Yes, she is."

Men, thought the secretary with fond amusement. Even ministers. Not a one of them could resist a pretty woman, especially one who admired their life's work. Well, who could resist that? And Mrs. Hornung had even managed to find something nice to say about the view of the parking lot! It was harmless, though. If ever there was a man you could trust to be true to his wife it was Bob Wing. He preached faithfulness, he lived it, and he even had the grace to blush just for looking at a pretty woman.

"Did you see the size of the diamond she had on?" Pat asked him.

He shook his head, no.

"Size of your head," the secretary marveled.

Dr. Wing grinned at her. "The size of my head *before* I preach, or afterwards?"

"Oh, before," his secretary teased him right back. "The way your head swells with all that praise, no diamond could be that big."

"That's what I thought you meant," he said with a deadpan expression.

"Maybe she'll repair our stucco," the secretary said, thoughtfully.

"Pat!" he remonstrated with her. "Let's don't spend the poor woman's money before she's even a member!"

"If she's got money, then she's not a poor woman," was her retort to that.

Knowing when he was beat, the reverend retreated to his office.

The church secretary never gave another thought to the way he'd stared after their visitor, except for one guilty, fleeting moment when the thought did cross her mind to wish this woman had arrived before Bob Wing had married Susanna. The secretary had seen the way Mrs. Hornung blushed when he spoke to her, and how she had noticed his wedding ring. Those two would have made a charismatic couple. The secretary quickly banished *that* wicked notion from her brain. There was nothing wrong with Susanna Wing that a little polish couldn't cure, and anyway, nobody was perfect. Dr. Bob had loved her enough to marry her, and the church secretary thought that should be enough recommendation for anybody.

One of the saddest things about Susanna Wing was that people seemed to want to like her better than they really did. She was a "looker," as men used to say, with a compelling face and a terrific figure, and when she smiled, they say it made you feel special. But she was also, as Pat Danner hinted, a little rough around the edges compared, say, to an easy, fresh-faced charmer like Artemis Hornung. If you had lined the two women up and said, "Pick the minister's wife," you'd probably never have pointed to Susanna. There were good reasons for that, though, and they were tragic ones. Susanna was an orphan, for one thing. Both of her parents were dead long before she was grown. She was raised in a series of foster and group homes where nobody kept her around for more than a few months at a time. With no other relatives who cared enough to keep track of her, when she died it was as if she had existed only in Bahia Beach, and only for the short time she'd been married to Bob Wing.

The church was packed at her funeral, but it was all church members and other friends of her minister-husband. Nobody came from out of town to mourn her, nobody at all. If there were people who would have wanted to come, if they had known, no one knew how to locate them. In keeping with the hard-luck story of her life, Susanna had grown up in Lancaster, California, where, when she was eighteen years old, a river had risen for the only time in recorded history and flooded the courthouse square, ruining every record stored in the basement of the courthouse, including the files of every juvenile for whom the court was acting as guardian. That meant the memory of the names of the people she lived with as a child died with her.

Susanna had once been married to money. She'd wed a computer start-up whiz, a Californian who had made and lost several fortunes before dying in a rock-climbing accident at the age of fifty.

"She didn't talk about Donnie at all," people at the church said. "It was too painful."

The obituary of Donald Scale in the *Sacramento Bee* portrayed a successful businessman who, like Susanna, had no other names of survivors to list in his death notice. Neighbors in the upscale neighborhood where the Scales lived in their Tudor-style home said the couple kept very much to themselves. Since the yards were large and surrounded by hedges, it was hard to get to know people unless you made a special effort or went to the annual block party. Donnie and Susanna weren't the sort to frequent such gatherings and nobody made the trek to their home to borrow a cup of sugar and start an acquaintance. By the time of Donnie's tragic death, all of his former companies had been liquidated — he had taken the cash, planning for an early retirement with Susanna — and the employees were scattered far and wide.

"She never talked about her past," people at the church said.

In many ways, Susanna was much better suited to her first husband, or so it seems now to those who learn the little bits about him that one can learn. He had no children, his parents were also deceased, he'd been an only child with no real talent for friendship, apparently, only for entrepreneurship. Nobody really knew why his widow moved to Bahia Beach, but they said that when she showed up for a meeting of the "grief group" at Sands Gospel, she seemed to be looking for love. They welcomed her, her new minister most warmly of all.

"Susanna was in his office a lot at first," Pat Danner says. "I heard crying in there." She admits that for a little while she feared that Susanna Scale was one of those women — there were a lot of them — who coveted the handsome preacher. "But Bob told me a little about Susanna's history and I realized she had a right to all the tears and attention she ever needed. After a while, I heard laughter more often than crying, and I felt glad for her, for both of them."

Maybe it was only natural that it turned into courtship.

"I'd say Susanna courted him!" Pat Danner laughs. "For a quiet lady, she could be quite determined, let me tell you. I mean, she *was* a realtor, so there had to be some backbone there, and some ambition, too. We saw that when she volunteered for the pledge drive. She didn't give up until she got what she wanted. I've seen Susanna turn on the tears for some skinflint member and string out a sob story about the church that you wouldn't believe, until she had him practically begging her to take his money. She was good, when she set her mind to it."

Coincidentally, a tall, good-looking man named Stuart McGregor also came into the "grief group" at about the same time that Susanna did. After her murder, Stuart spoke of how he had watched the melancholy widow turn into a merry wife. "I watched her and Bob meet, I saw them fall in love, I was there for the whole thing, and we all went to their wedding." And of course, shortly thereafter, the newlywed Wings would return the favor at Stuart's marriage to Artemis.

And no one guessed anything was awry with the Wings, until almost a year later, when Violet Lester, Annie Hamilton, and Margo Eby overheard something they were never meant to know.

The day the three women from the church overheard Susanna Wing in a tele-

151

phone argument with their minister, they were early to a pledge-drive committee meeting at the Wings' home. There'd been a confusion of times — the ladies thought the meeting was for 9:00 a.m. Susanna, as it turned out, had written it down for 9:30.

When Susanna didn't answer Violet's light knock, the three friends felt perfectly comfortable opening the door and walking on into the little foyer.

What they heard next paralyzed them with dismay:

"You've already got a wife, and I'm it, or did you forget that minor little detail?"

It was Susanna's voice, coming from the kitchen, ringing with anger.

"You leave me and I'll get up in the pulpit on Sunday and confess all of your sins! We'll see how she likes you then! You won't be leaving me when that happens, she'll be leaving you! Don't think you can leave me and stay with her, just because you love her . . ."

The word "love" was scathing, scalding to her.

"You love me, remember?"

Again, they heard "love" drawn up in a furious mockery.

"You couldn't live without me, you'd do anything for me, you'd love me forever — re-

member? And now you just switch all that to her? As if I never existed, as if we aren't even married?

"No! Don't say her name to me! Artemis! Artemis! Stupid name! Stupid woman. Stupid you! How could you let this happen? Love! You don't love her, you love her money. I believed in you, I trusted you, I loved you! How could *you?*"

The three visitors, mortified to have overheard Susanna screaming at Bob, and to have heard the awful content of those screams, tiptoed back out to the front stoop. White-faced and trembling, they just stared at one another. With unspoken accord, they waited quite a while before Violet dared to press her finger to the doorbell. When Susanna came to let them in, she greeted them with a brittle smile that looked just as ghastly as they felt.

The morning of the search for Susanna, the same three women friends from the church took charge of the gifts of food and drink. As they busied themselves in the kitchen, they cocked their ears to what was being said in the other rooms . . . and to what was not being said. Every now and then they looked up at one another, and then immediately dropped their eyes back to their work. Their minister was slumped in an armchair in the living room, waiting for the phone to ring, and none of the three women had been in to see him, to talk to him, or to try to comfort him.

"We could pray," one of them suggested to the others.

"To the same God that allowed this to happen?" retorted the second woman. "No thank you!"

"God didn't do this to Susanna," whispered the third.

There was a charged silence and their hands got still.

Finally, one of them made a mundane suggestion that broke the unbearable tension. "You'd better put that potato salad in the refrigerator until closer to lunch time, Annie."

Annie Hamilton quietly followed Violet Lester's suggestion.

"And the ham salad, Margo, over there —"

Margo Eby passed the ham salad to Annie Hamilton.

All three women looked tanned and Florida-healthy in their sandals, shorts, and T-shirts; but otherwise they could hardly have looked more different from one another. Annie Hamilton, the one closest to the refrigerator, was only thirty-eight, but her cropped, prematurely white hair gave her an older, sophisticated appearance that amused her friends, who knew how shy she was.

She carefully tucked cellophane wrap over the bowl of potato salad before closing the refrigerator door. Then she glanced at Violet Lester, who glanced at Margo Eby, who looked back at Annie Hamilton, completing the circle.

Violet, known affectionately among them as "the bossy one," heaved a sigh, and then started emptying yet another grocery sack of foodstuffs brought over by a church member. She was thirty-two, the mother of three, as plump as Annie was thin, with curly black hair and orange lipstick, and she was usually as cheerful as an elf. At this moment, however, she was trying not to burst into tears. She knew if she looked at her friends again she'd lose her composure.

"You don't think we ought to say anything?" asked Margo.

Annie and Violet stared at her, though Violet quickly looked away.

Margo, the thirty-four-year-old mother of a developmentally disabled child, looked at their expressions and said, "No?"

"No," Annie murmured.

Violet kept her head bowed and didn't say anything.

"But what if it would help find Susanna?"

Nobody said anything for a minute, and then Violet put her face in her hands and started to cry. Annie dropped everything and hurried to embrace her, and then Margo hurried over, too, and wrapped her arms around both of her friends. When somebody else started to come into the kitchen and saw them, he felt touched by the emotion being shown by Susanna's friends.

After a moment, Violet forced herself free of them. Then she turned and faced them, tears still streaming.

"I've already told about it," she said, with wide eyes.

"Oh, Violet, no!"

"I thought we agreed we wouldn't —"

But Violet glared at them and said angrily, "How can we not tell what we know? How can we? Our minister is having an affair with another woman, and we know it, and we know that Susanna was furious about it, and now she's missing. How can we keep that a secret? It might have something to do with her being missing."

"Oh, Violet," Annie whispered. "But that would mean —"

"I know what it would mean, Annie, and I can't help that!"

"You told!" Margo exclaimed, looking horrified. "You told?"

"We're not children," Violet hissed at her. "This is not some little bit of gossip we're not supposed to repeat. This could be a matter of Susanna's life or death. We had to tell, or one of us had to. So I did it. Early this morning. I called Tammi Golding, because she knows the chief of police, and I told her the whole thing."

"Did she tell the police chief?" Annie looked aghast.

Violet shrugged angrily. "I don't know what she did. I just know I had to tell somebody, so I told somebody I thought could make intelligent use of the information."

Margo said, thoughtfully, "You know, Susanna could have left him because of it, just left him, you know what I mean? Without telling anybody. This doesn't necessarily mean that anything bad has happened to her, you know?"

"That's right," Violet said, with an eager air. "She could have just left, and she did it like this to humiliate him, which God knows he richly deserves. I can't even stand to look at him in there, pretending to be so pious and so worried about her."

Annie walked to the door and opened it a crack.

She peeked out, and then looked back at her friends. "He does look worried. He looks like he lost his best friend."

"She was," Violet said, tartly. "He just didn't appreciate it."

Annie moved out of the way of the kitchen door just as it swung open.

A fourth woman stepped through the doorway into the kitchen.

"Hi," Artie McGregor said quietly, looking from face to face.

She was adorable-looking, a doll of a woman with short blond hair and big brown eyes. They had once been tremendously fond of her, but not anymore. She smiled tearfully at the three friends and asked, "Do you need any help in here?"

For a moment, there was no reply.

"No," Margo said carefully, when neither of her friends spoke up. "No thank you, Artie."

When they heard the kitchen door swing softly shut behind Artemis McGregor, shy Annie whispered, passionately, "Bitch!"

★ ★ ★

"Bob, the police are here! Look out the window."

At five o'clock on the Saturday afternoon that his wife was missing, the minister rose to his feet so fast he almost lost his balance, and had to catch himself with one hand on the arm of the chair. Church members gathered around him, and together they watched one . . . two . . . three . . . four police officers get out of two cars, slam their doors, gather together on the sidewalk, and talk for a moment. And then one of them — the youngest one — broke away from the other three and began to jog up the front walk.

He looked as if he couldn't wait to get there.

Bob Wing pushed his way through the crowd behind him and ran to open the door. He hurried past the umbrella stand that held his baseball bat. A feeling of relief and celebration began to sweep through the friends and neighbors who crowded in behind him. Why, anybody could tell just from looking at the cop's face that this was good news. The best news. They couldn't wait to hear it.

"Dr. Wing?"

"Yes! Have you found my wife?"

"Yes, sir, we have."

Cheering broke out behind Bob Wing's back.

Later, the police officer, who had been told to observe closely, would swear that the young, handsome minister looked stunned, as if he had just been given news that couldn't possibly be true. The other three police officers coming up behind him interpreted the preacher's reaction in exactly the same way. And, in fact, the Reverend Dr. Robert Wing said to the cop, in a shocked and hollow tone, "You found Susanna?"

"Yes, sir, we found her."

The minister's knees seemed to give way. He sagged where he stood, though a member of his congregation quickly moved to put an arm under his to support him.

"I don't believe it," Bob Wing said in an incredulous tone of voice.

It was a dirty trick the Bahia police pulled, and one for which they would be pilloried in the press, in pulpits, and the trial. They didn't care; as they would say later in their own defense, they had a brutal murder to solve and something important to prove. It wasn't as if they actually said that Susanna Wing was alive. They only said they had found her. He could have asked them if she was dead or alive, but he didn't. First he said, "You found Susanna?" And then he said, "I don't believe it." It made some people furious, what the police did, but the cops claimed that if they lied, it was only by way of omission. They defended their action by saying they wanted to gauge the reaction of her husband when he heard them say they'd found her. In hindsight, it would seem to be the reaction of someone who had not expected the body to be found, at least not so soon.

"She's dead," the minister stated flatly. "Isn't she?"

Behind him a woman gasped, and then cried, "No!"

"Yes, sir," the young cop said and then added after an almost imperceptible hesitation, "I'm sorry." Another pause, and then: "Would you please step out here alone, so that we can tell you about it, and ask you some questions?"

"Not alone," asserted Tammi Golding, stepping forward.

"Am I under arrest?" Bob Wing asked, in an unsteady voice.

"Arrest?" the young cop repeated, looking surprised. "Why would you think so?"

"She was murdered, wasn't she?"

"Bob!" Tammi said sharply. "With all due respect, shut up."

"Yes, she was," the cop confirmed, while his compatriots remained very still in the background, listening and watching. "But how did you know that?"

"Bob —" Tammi warned.

"I just knew it. It had to be something bad. I felt it in my heart."

"You think we want to arrest you for the crime, sir?"

The husband, who hadn't yet shed a tear over his wife's death, or even asked where she was killed or how, looked with knowing eyes at the police officer on his front stoop. "It's usually the husband, isn't that right?"

"Quite often," the cop confirmed in a soft voice.

"Not this time," snapped Tammi Golding, stepping forward from her role as concerned friend to her job as criminal defense attorney.

Susanna

7

The morning after finishing my book, I reluctantly roll out of the warm embrace of the naked brown arms of the state attorney for Howard County. It appears I do still have a lover. Apparently he is not high-maintenance. With a sigh for what I'm leaving behind in bed, I heave myself onto the floor. No rest for the weary writer. Or the horny one, for that matter, although that is considerably less of a problem now than it was at this same time yesterday.

I look back and smile at his sleeping face.

Franklin DeWeese sleeps with his mouth open.

It would be precious little on which to blackmail the man, but I haven't found many other faults, if you don't count the natural flaws of a born prosecutor. A bit aggressive, the way a Bengal tiger is a bit aggressive, but no more argumentative and bullheaded than a mama alligator with a nest to protect. A sweetie, really, if you don't mind brutal truth, or fighting him for every inch he gives you, if you don't mind being the perpetual defendant in the stand. Every now and then he gives me a break and lets up — like when he's just won a big case and doesn't have anything to prove for twenty-four hours or so. But, hey, it's good mental exercise; almost as good as the other kind I get from him. But, damn, I cannot stand here mooning like this. Got to keep all of the many appointments I have quixotically made for this day: with a homicide detective, an assistant state attorney — as if one prosecutor per day were not enough for any woman — and a reporter.

"What?" he says, opening an eye and smiling a little.

"Nothing. I was just enjoying the view."

The eye closes, the smile widens.

"Franklin, would you kill to have me?"

"Sorry, no," he says sleepily into his pillow. I return to sit on the edge of the bed, where I can stroke the silky mound of his right shoulder, on down to his bare back. "Mmm," he says.

"What do you think that would feel like?" I continue. "To want somebody so bad that you'd kill to have them?"

"Like sex, I suppose."

"You ever get a hint of that kind of sexual obsession off of Artemis McGregor or Bob Wing?"

He moves his head a little, indicating no.

"Me neither." I change my caress to a sharp swat on his butt. "I wouldn't kill to have you, either."

He laughs and darts out a hand to grab me, but I escape.

On my way back into the bedroom after my shower, the phone rings.

"Marie! I stayed home and read it all day yesterday."

My heart goes into overdrive. It's Charlotte Amstell, my editor. It's early; either she's calling me from her loft in Tribeca or she has subwayed to her office in Midtown Manhattan to break the news to me. Desperately nervous, as if I hadn't received phone calls like this on every prior book I've done, as if I were still the vulnerable beginner that all writers are in our hearts, as if I weren't as used to hearing good news as I am, I wait for her to say, "It stinks." Not that she would say it like that; Charlotte's much too kind for torture, but she's also much too good at her job to hesitate in going for the kill. If it's bad, Charlotte says so. She does it nicely, elegantly, but the knife still slices the verbiage clean off the page.

"Hi, Charlotte," I say, and go into a coughing jag.

The good news about being a bestselling author is that your stuff gets read immediately. It's very early by New York publishing standards; if she's at the office, that means she has come in early to talk to me without being interrupted by all the million and one things that keep editors from actually editing these days. When she says she had to stay home a day to read my manuscript, she means it; otherwise, she'd have to read mere snippets in between maddening meetings.

"Are you all right, Marie?"

Getting my voice under control, I ask, "So what do you think of it?"

"It's beautifully written."

Oh, shit. My heart goes from overdrive to park. My knees feel as if somebody removed my kneecaps during the night while I slept. The bad news about being a bestselling author is that you get the bad news faster. This is not what your editor is supposed to say after she reads your manuscript. She's supposed to say, "I couldn't put it down."

"I love the prologue with the two little girls," is what she actually says. "I don't see any changes there, it really pulled me into the story. And you've done your usual wonderful job researching the backgrounds of these people."

Oh, God, she's complimenting my research. This is worse than I feared. My research is something she ought to be able to take for granted, and the quality of my writing, too. Feeling hopeless, I wait for the ax.

"I just love it from start to finish."

I wait for her to say, "But . . ."

"Marie?"

"Yes?"

"Did you hear me?"

"You love it?"

"You sound so surprised." She laughs at me. "Don't I always? Are we having ourselves a little attack of neurotic writer, Marie?"

"Must be," I agree. "Did you find anything you didn't like, Charlotte? Any stuff for me to work on?"

"Don't you even want to know what I like about it?" She's highly amused at my perversity. "And you call yourself a writer? You don't want to hear all the praise first? But that's what they taught me in editor school. Praise first, criticize later. Do you want me to lose my editor credentials? I have to spend at least fifteen minutes gushing over you. Which I will do with utter sincerity, of course."

"Sincere gushing is my very favorite kind."

So I sit through a painful five — not fifteen — minutes of being appreciated for all my sterling writer qualities, none of which seems very much in evidence to me in the manuscript that she and Franklin have both read and which both now claim to like very much. As I listen to her talk about me, I make grateful noises, like a magpie doing a good imitation of somebody who believes what she's hearing. Finally, she gets past the gooey part to the problems. I knew it. I *knew* there were problems.

"I do have a couple of problems with it, Marie."

I brace myself. It's going to be major. But at least Charlotte's now going to tell me how to fix it. I gird myself for the sting of the wasp soaked in the honey.

"First of all, I wondered why you put in so much about the murder of that poor girl in Lauderdale Pines?"

"You mean Allison Tobias?"

"Yes. That's such a sad story, but I think you give it too much emphasis — in relation to your story as a whole, I mean — by going into such detail there in the beginning. Do we really need that much? Could you boil it down, do you think? Otherwise, I'm afraid your readers are going to think it's more important than it really is. To the story of Susanna and Bob Wing, I mean."

"Hm," I hedge. "I thought I needed it there."

"Really? Why do you have so much about her murder?"

"Well, uh, because her killer was the guy Bob Wing was trying to save from execution, and, uh, that's why the cops had to bend over backwards to be fair, because they couldn't stand him, and I thought that made it, uh, kind of interesting. And then there's the incredible irony of the fact that after the preacher is sentenced to death, he gets put into a cell right next to Stevie Orbach . . ."

"There's too much about her," my editor says, kindly, but briskly. "It diverts our attention from the main story."

"Okay. Let me think about it."

"Of course. And . . ." She pauses, while I'm still waiting for the worst of it. Rewrite the whole thing? Reorganize it all? Charlotte has uttered several words before I am aware that she's even talking. ". . . Marie?"

"Oh! I'm sorry, Charlotte. Would you repeat that?"

"I just said that I don't know Artemis very well, isn't that odd? Here, she's a major player in the case, and yet I don't have as clear a picture of her as I do of the other people."

"Hmm," I say, hardly surprised to hear this. What a coincidence — I don't know her very well, either. I'm taking notes, but still not listening very well.

"And that's it, Marie."

"What else did you notice?"

"I just said, that's it."

"That's all?"

"Marie!" She's laughing. "What's wrong with you?"

"Nothing," I hasten to assure her. "Hey, I'm a writer, and we're weird. You know that."

"You're telling me? Try shepherding a whole flock of them sometime. You are one of the few sane ones, so don't go getting all neurotic and writerly on me."

"Sane is my middle name."

"Really," she says, in a very New York way. "We left that off the cover."

"Maybe next time."

"Sure, right next to your photograph."

"Charlotte, thank you. Really. Thanks so much."

"No, thank you. You've guaranteed my salary for another year."

"Not that you want to put any pressure on me or anything."

"Heavens no. I merely expect you to write bestsellers every time. No problem for you, right?"

"Nope." No, writing bestsellers is no problem for me. Writing a good and true book, however, now that may be more difficult. As I hang up, I'm thinking: What if everybody else thinks this book is fine just the way it is, and I'm the only one who feels there's something missing? Can I let it go? If it appears to satisfy everybody else? I don't think so. "Letting go" is *not* my middle name.

In the bedroom, I find the state attorney still sleeping. It's 7:00 a.m. Late, for him. Mercilessly, I shake him awake. "You still here?" he mutters, turning over and smiling lazily up at me.

"Yeah, and I can tell you really miss me when I'm gone."

I can only see half of his handsome face, because he's got an arm thrown over it to protect his eyes from the sunlight, but I get a glimpse of a sly grin below his forearm. I ease myself down onto the edge of the bed, pulling my bathrobe around me, keeping just slightly out of the reach of his long arms.

"My editor just called, Franklin. She hates my book."

The grin vanishes and he sits up with satisfying alacrity. The covers fall away from his lovely brown body, and he says, with a vigorous indignation that does my heart good, "You're kidding. What do you mean, she hates it? How can she hate it? What's to hate, for Christ's sake? It's terrific. I liked it, what's the matter with *her*? What the fuck does she know? Damn, Marie. What will you do now?"

"Kill myself."

"After that."

I smile at him. "Just kidding."

"You're not going to kill yourself?"

"No, she loves it."

"She *loves* it?" He grabs for me, pulls me down on top of him and then starts tickling me. "You little liar!" Within seconds the tickling turns into something else, and soon I'm taking my punishment like a woman.

Anything to Be Together
By Marie Lightfoot

CHAPTER 7

It was not the police but a carload of Sands Gospel Church members who eventually found Susanna Wing's white Mercury Mystique with the WG-PRYR license plate. Although every instinct in them rebelled against the idea, when one of them suggested looking at the airport, they checked it out. Slowly, they cruised the lanes of all the lots, growing more and more sure this was a wild-goose chase, until they reached the farthest parking lot.

"Oh my God, there it is."

And there it was, nose in, license plate out toward them. The four church members in the car — one at each window, assigned to look out in that direction — didn't know whether to feel elated or dismayed. They didn't yet know about the trick the Bahia police had pulled on their minister, or even that Susanna was dead, so they finally decided that relief was the only truly spiritual response. "Hallelujah," murmured the driver, who was an agnostic. They all hoped that finding the car meant she was alive. But they also thought it might mean she had left her husband — and them — and had run away from home for reasons that were a mystery to them. If Susanna Wing had been unhappy living with Bob, they hadn't been aware of it, though there had been an undercurrent of nasty gossip recently, some unlikely story about Bob and that nice Artie McGregor. But they didn't believe that for a minute. No, if Susanna had felt restless or unappreciated as a minister's wife, they didn't know why.

"Thank heavens we found it," said one of the passengers.

After the initial excitement, a strange stillness descended inside the car, a feeling of a weight that instead of lifting had just grown heavier. Nevertheless, they tried their best to put a good face on things. "She's sure to be okay, don't you think so?" the left-backseat passenger asked the rest of them. "This has got to mean she took a flight somewhere, right? Here — somebody use my cell phone to call him." Nobody immediately took her up on that offer; finally, reluctantly, the passenger in the front seat reached over, grabbed the little black phone, and dialed in the number at the Wing home. It was hard to know how to present this information, and she decided to say it in a neutral, calm sort of way that wouldn't excite any false hopes, or betray any of her own misgivings about what this discovery might mean.

But her minister didn't answer the phone in his home.

Somebody else said, "Wing residence."

"We found her car!" The passenger couldn't help but burst out with the news. "That's got to mean she's alive!"

"No," said the voice on the other end, in a deadened tone. "She's not. They've found her body in one of the properties she had listed for sale. Somebody beat her to death . . ."

The woman holding the cell phone gasped in horror, but the church member who had answered the phone in the Wing home continued inexorably with what he had to say: "And the police seem to think Bob had something to do with it —" Again his listener gasped, while the other three in the car said, "What? What's happened?" and leaned toward her, touched her, tried to get her to tell them what she was hear-

175

ing on the phone. She pressed the receiver closer to her ear, batted them away, closed her eyes in dismay, as she heard the words, "— and they've taken him down to the police station for questioning. They haven't arrested him, at least not that we know. But you should have seen the terrible way they treated him when they came to tell us about Susanna. He was in shock, and they didn't even give him time to cry over Susanna. It makes me so angry! Is this what we pay our police to do?" His voice had risen in anger. "We're getting a legal defense team ready."

"Who's going to pay for it?" she asked, feeling frantic.

"There's still some money in the legal defense fund. If we have to take the attorneys off the capital-punishment appeals and put them onto this, that's what we'll do."

"Bob won't like that."

"We won't give him a choice in the matter."

It honestly didn't even occur to the church member holding the cell phone to wonder if her minister was guilty or innocent. Of course he was innocent! If there was ever a fact she could take for granted in this life, that was it. This was Robert

176

Wing they were talking about, her minister, one of the finest members of the clergy in the whole country, a man renowned for mercy and for charity, a famous opponent of the death penalty. This was Dr. Wing! Surely once the police realized the nature of the man, there wouldn't be any question of his involvement, and they'd release him immediately and look for the real —

She turned to face her three friends in the car.

"Susanna's been killed," she said, and began to cry even before she got out, "and the police suspect Bob."

In the right-hand seat in the back of the car, a member of the church turned his face and stared blindly out at the parked cars across from the Mystique. He had been a member of the ministerial search committee that wooed and won Robert and Donna Wing in 1996. One of the perks that had been thrown into the compensation package had been generous life-insurance policies on both of them. It wasn't cash, or a big house, but it was something nice the church could offer their clergy, especially to one like Bob whose crusades led to death threats now and then. When Bob Wing's first wife,

Donna, had succumbed to cancer two years later, the policy on her had paid out $100,000 to her grieving husband, who had turned around and started putting it to charitable uses rather than spending it on himself. Everybody in the church admired him for that, for not personally benefitting from Donna's death.

That money was almost gone, spent on Bob's crusade.

Now there would be a second payout, on his second wife.

The member in the backseat grew very quiet, even as his three friends were exclaiming and weeping over the terrible news. He felt sick, and couldn't bring himself to tell them what he knew. He sensed, with a terrible queasiness, that somebody was going to have to inform the police. Not that it meant anything, not at all! But it was the sort of thing the cops would want to know, wasn't it? For homicide investigations? It was just routine, anybody who watched television knew that, he tried to reassure himself.

It didn't make him feel any better.

The Major Crimes Case Squad met Saturday evening, eight hours after the body was found, four hours after the first interrogation of the victim's husband. At the request of the squad commander, Detective Carl Chamblin stood at the front of the conference room, summarizing the Susanna Wing homicide case for his fellow officers.

". . . one of the mothers called 911, who alerted us, and we were over there by twelve-thirty. The medical examiner puts the time of death at around noon Friday. Her husband looks good as a suspect. Reverend Wing attended a national church convention in Boston this week. We're checking that out. The victim picked him up at the Bahia airport yesterday morning from a flight that got in at around seven-thirty. Her car, the white Mercury. They drove home and had breakfast together. They also had intercourse. Before breakfast, he says. He says she left the house about nine-thirty to hold an open house at a property. He claims that's the last time he saw her alive.

"This is how I think it went down." As he talked, Carl wrote key words on a large white board at the front of the room. "Reverend Wing's wife drives him to the airport on Wednesday morning. He flies to Boston. Attends his meeting. She returns to the airport to pick him up yesterday.

They drive out to the mansion, not to their home. He forces her to have sex with him and then he kills her. He took care not to leave prints and he must have cleaned himself up before he left the crime scene. Maybe he took water along, and different clothes. At any rate, he dumps her clothes and his bloody ones. He returns the car to the airport, parks it in satellite parking at one-oh-five p.m., then he takes the satellite parking bus up to the terminal, where he gets a cab. He has the cab drop him off somewhere close enough that he can walk the rest of the way to his home.

"Her body could have rotted there before anybody found it. He could have been counting on that. It's a deserted house. No transient who finds a body is going to report it. The only other person who went in there regularly was a guy who was hired to mow the driveway and the paths. Tell them what he told you, Norm."

Detective Jill Norman stood up to report. "He said he mowed twice a month. Any day, except Fridays. He was told not to show up on Fridays because that's when Mrs. Wing showed the property to prospective buyers. So her husband would know they'd be alone."

"Wasn't the killer taking a chance that

the guy who mowed the grass would find the body?" one of the other cops inquired of her.

"No," she said. "Here's the kicker. He got fired last week. Says he got a postcard telling him not to show up anymore."

"Has he still got the card, Norm?"

"No. Tossed it."

She sat down again, leaving the floor to Carl.

"Who owns that place?" somebody else asked.

"A woman by the name of Artemis McGregor," Carl replied. "I'll come back to her." After pausing to gather his thoughts again, he summed up what they'd heard so far. "So the Reverend thought he could report her missing, eventually we'd find the car at the airport, and we'd all think she had run away from home."

"Whoa, Carl," somebody said. "You sound so sure. Why him?"

The squad commander interrupted to say, "We have reason to believe he was having an affair with another woman — Artemis McGregor, the one Carl just told you about. We have also been told — though we have yet to confirm any of these reports — that Susanna Wing has a big estate, a lot of money from a previous marriage. In addition, there was major life insurance on her."

↑ Somebody whistled, and an officer said, with dry humor, "Is that all? *Just* another woman, a rich wife, and life insurance? Damn, you mean we don't have video of him killing her? What kind of impossible case *is* this?"

There was laughter, because it all sounded so obvious.

"Can we go home now?" another joker asked.

"You think this was premeditated, Carl?" came a serious voice from the back.

"No," said the second joker, turning around in his chair to face the questioner. "That life insurance is just a coincidence!"

From the front of the room Carl said, "I think it sounds well thought out. Once we find the murder weapon, we'll be able to tell more about that. If it was something he picked up at the scene, he could argue it was a crime of passion, momentary insanity, if he can explain how he didn't leave tracks. Maybe his wife told him he had to leave his bimbo or she'd tell the church, I don't know. But if it was something he had to bring with him, something he'd stored in her car, say, then we've got premeditation."

"What was the murder weapon, Carl?"

"Heavy, wood, a baseball bat, like that."

"So, does the Reverend coach Little League?"

A murmur of grim amusement circled the room. No one had yet connected the crime to the innocent-looking baseball bat propped in the umbrella stand in the front hall in Bayfield Estates.

The squad commander interjected: "Check it out."

"She died somewhere she wasn't supposed to be that day," the case squad commander said when she took over the conference from Carl. "At least not according to her own husband. He said she told him she had an open house at 420 South Ocean. But there is no evidence to suggest she ever showed up there on Friday. We have a lot of work to do, ladies and gentlemen, a lot of things to check out, and just because the Reverend looks like a good suspect for us, that doesn't mean he's the one. Keep your eyes open. Do your jobs. Let's not convict an innocent man, all right? Just because he's a preacher, that don't make him a bad guy."

Laughter eased around the room again.

"Commander?" an officer called out. "Isn't this the anti–death-penalty preacher?

The one who's always picketing outside the courthouse?"

"And outside of the penitentiary," somebody else said, sounding bitter. "He's the moron thinks Stevie Orbach ought to get a new trial."

There was a rumble of anger at that idea.

"Yeah, same guy," the commander agreed. "Now, I personally don't have any problem with that, because as you all know I do have some problem with capital punishment. Call me crazy, but I don't think it's a perfect system. I know that some of you feel the only good murderer is a dead murderer."

An approving chuckle or two could be heard in the room.

"But I have this nutty idea that we ought to be sure they're actually guilty before we fry them. Afterwards is a little late to say we're sorry. So what I'm saying is, this isn't about politics, girls and boys. This is about the brutal murder of a woman. And maybe her husband did it. And maybe it's true that most husbands are the guilty parties. But we don't know if that's true in this case. Let's not jump to conclusions here, just because some of you think it might be fun to watch him picket his own execution."

There was outright laughter at that jibe, which would become an ongoing irreverent joke in South Florida.

"Be cops," she warned them, in the serious but good-natured way that made most of them respect her. "Don't be judges."

"Excuse me, Commander?"

"Yes, Norm?"

"Has the Reverend got an alibi, Carl?"

He stood up again to answer her. "Depends if it checks out, Norm. He says he was visiting nursing homes with a member of the church." Carl allowed himself a very small smile. "Guess who?"

"Don't tell me! Mrs. McGregor?"

"Bingo. The Reverend says that Artemis McGregor picked him up at his house at ten a.m. and they drove around for the next couple of hours. Then he says she dropped him back off at his house, and he worked there all afternoon. Never made it to his church on Friday. Seems that's normal for him, that he likes to stay home and work on his sermon for the following Sunday."

"What does the McGregor woman say?"

"Nobody's talked to her yet."

"But there'd be witnesses at the nursing home?"

With a deadpan expression, Carl said,

"Well, now, that's an interesting point you raise there, Norm. It seems that the Reverend and Mrs. McGregor never actually went into a nursing home, they just drove by. It appears they got to talking and never actually got a lick of work done in two hours' time."

There was an exchange of glances among the officers.

"So, Carl," one of them said, "you think she's the woman?"

But he merely shrugged, and smiled again. "Maybe she had a problem and just needed two hours of personal counseling from her pastor."

A cop suddenly voiced a thought out loud: "Carl, did you see any indication there could have been more than one killer?"

His smile vanished. "She was beat to a bloody pulp. The medical examiner says every bone in her body was broken. One person could do that. But two people could do it faster."

It wasn't true that every bone in the body was broken.

"Bones are made of calcium phosphate and collagen," explained Adam Strough, the chief medical examiner for Howard

186

County. Dr. Strough is known in law enforcement and media circles as a bit of a character and a born professor. He was more than happy to provide the gory details to anyone who wished more than a mere superficial understanding of what happened to the victim's body. "Seashells are made of calcium. I think of bones as being as fragile as seashell, but strong like them, too. It just kills me to see somebody break bones on purpose; I want to protest that God and a pregnant lady worked hard on this skeleton, so have some respect."

To reporters who craved excruciating detail, he added:

"There are two hundred and six bones in the human body, and one more in those of us who have a wormian bone in our skull. Now, not everybody has one; it's a small, irregular bone, a little island unconnected to any other bone. But barring a birth anomaly, we all have twenty-four ribs, twelve vertebrae in our necks, seven bones in each ankle, and eight in these marvelous wrists that can swing a tennis racket or play a Mozart sonata.

"Almost all of those were broken in the victim's body.

"The distal phalanx was broken in her right thumb and in her left. The calcaneus bone of her heels was fractured, as was the mandible, both femurs, the coccyx."

He provided a list of the Latin names of all the bones broken.

"Our skeletons have three primary functions, apart from storing organic salts and forming blood cells," the medical examiner lectured, when given the opportunity. "Those functions are: protection of our soft inner organs, support, and motion. All three failed her. No one could have stood up under those blows. The violence that rained down on her produced breaks that ranged in severity from cracks to fractures to splintery smashes, to say nothing of the destruction of the organs within."

Susanna Wing had a wormian bone, and it was broken, too.

"I wondered how much she felt," the medical examiner mused away from the microphones. That was what people always wondered — especially the victim's survivors — about horrific deaths. Did she suffer? How much? Or was she mercifully dead before the worst of it? "It's hard to know precisely which blow killed her," Dr. Strough theorized, "and in what order they were struck, because there were so many of them. If he hit her skull first, it could have incapacitated her immediately and she truly wouldn't have felt anything after that. But if he hit her lower first, then she felt quite a lot of it before she died."

He was positive about one thing: it was the beating and nothing else that killed her. The actual murder "weapon" was most likely a sliver of her own breastbone that punctured her heart.

It was possible she had been raped.

"She was either raped," the medical examiner announced, "or she engaged in rough sex just prior to being killed. There are abrasions, bruises, she bled. One way or another, it was violent. Brutal." To the cops, he added, dramatically, "This guy's a real bastard. I want you to remove him from the streets of the city where my wife goes to work and my daughters play!" Some of the cops would have smiled at that, except that they felt the same way. They might not have put it so theatrically, but they shared his sentiments all the same.

The medical examiner saw the cesarian scar that her husband had told the police about, but he also found a tiny scar in the crease below each of her heavy breasts, where silicon gel sacs had been inserted. Those, apparently, were the other "distinguishing marks" that her minister husband had hesitated to mention to the officer in Missing Persons. It didn't make him look any better in the eyes of the cops. But didn't a woman, even a preacher's wife, have a right to feel attractive?

After Dr. Strough's lecture on abraded genitals and fractured bones, Detective Chamblin thought about hate, rage, jealousy, fury, psychosis, temporary insanity, steroid rage. All the old familiar "reasons" why one human being might pulverize another. For some reason, jealousy stuck in his mind. Carl admits to having a bit of a jealous streak himself. "Who doesn't?" he asks, rhetorically. Of course, he hopes there are no circumstances in which he might feel driven to behave like an idiot. Still, there was something, some chord that was struck in him as he examined the appearance of the body in the autopsy room, that made him think: This is what I might do if I were crazy and jealous and cold-blooded as a shark. People think it's hot-blooded people who commit violent crimes — like that's some kind of compliment to them, like they're to be admired for being passionate, or something — but that's bullshit. It takes a cold-blooded son of a bitch to kill somebody, even when they do it in a so-called moment of passion. All they're really thinking about is themselves. What's more cold-blooded than that?

He said about as much to Dr. Strough, who replied, "Do you know, Detective, that the Latin root of the word 'joint' is *'art'?* When I look at that poor woman, I see the destruction of a work of art. I'll tell you something. There's only one thing wrong with the death penalty. And that is . . . that we ought to be allowed to take a baseball bat to the person who did this." The medical examiner's respect for nature's genius did not extend to those who cruelly undid its handiwork. "And I would like to bat first in the lineup."

"Funny you should mention the death penalty," Carl told him, and went on to explain who their main suspect was. "And funny you should mention baseball bats."

By that time, they'd made the bloody connection.

Within forty-eight hours the Bahia Beach police had built a devastating case against the crusading preacher: Bob Wing had no confirmable alibi for the time of the death of his wife; he had in his house a baseball bat with traces of her blood and tissue and bone caught in the cracks of the old wood, although he denied knowledge of how it got in that condition. His fingerprints were all over the handle of the bat, which was not surprising, and he also had, provably, the two oldest motives of all — money and sex. If "coveting" is close to jealousy, then Carl wasn't far wrong in his original guess. As for "cold-blooded," crimes didn't get much more cold-blooded than this one. The preacher's alleged paramour, Artemis McGregor, wife of the church board president, Stuart McGregor, was arrested and charged as a codefendant a short time later.

In South Florida, where the Reverend Bob Wing was well known, the response to the crime, the charges, and the eventual verdicts was sensational. Statewide, it made a splash. Nationally, coverage was limited to tabloids, and included the cheeky headline KILLER PREACHER LOVED HIS NEIGHBOR A LITTLE TOO MUCH.

Bob Wing went to jail, refusing bond. Artemis McGregor was arraigned, then freed on a steep bond paid by her husband, Stuart. Tammi Golding took over the defense of both of them. Their plea? Not guilty. They opted for a joint trial, though their legal team advised passionately against it, hoping to pit one defendant against the other in front of different juries, if all else failed. But the defendants

192

wouldn't be used like that, they informed their lawyers.

"We're innocent," Artemis said, "we didn't do anything wrong."

"I know that," Tammi Golding assured her, "but we don't have to establish that. All a jury needs to acquit is reasonable doubt. That's all we have to do, just build a case for reasonable doubt."

At the same time, over in the state attorney's office, Antonio Delano declared to his staff: "We've got them. I know it."

Susanna

8

"For a true crime writer, you're a hell of a liar."

Having administered his delicious sentence for my crime, Franklin releases me. We sprawl on the bed — me in my bunched-up bathrobe, and he completely naked — and grin at each other.

"So this is great news about your manuscript, Marie."

"Right," I say, and roll over, suddenly feeling dulled again.

"I was right about it," he says, smugly, behind me. "It's terrific."

"You liked it because I told you that if you didn't I'd never sleep with you again."

"Yeah, that's it, you've found me out."

I roll back over so I can see him. Even without touching him, I can still feel the luscious touch of his skin on mine, the smell of him, the feel of the curves and angles of his body under my hands, the curl of his fingers in mine, the feel of the top of his feet under the bottoms of mine, the taste of his tongue. Inside me, I can feel where he was and it makes me want him again. What would I do for sex, I wonder? How far would I go for love?

"Will I see you when I visit Tony today?"

"I don't know, sweetie, it depends how busy I am."

Suddenly he is staring at me, and looking prosecutorial. "I'm not sure I like the whole idea of this appointment with Tony. What kind of bug has he got up his ass? He just can't shut up about that damned case. But it is over. We won —"

"And you lost."

He makes a face. "Oh, thank you. So good of you to remind me. Be sure to make a bigger point of that in your book, will you?"

"Count on it."

"And my man Tony's got other cases to work on now."

Even though this is the first time I've spent with him in three weeks, even though we don't have much time to talk this morning, even though I'm really happy to be with him, there's something that's got to be said between us. It's the reason I have diverted any talk of a shared vacation; there won't be one if this isn't solved. I didn't want to say it last night and spoil our delicious reunion. But now I take a breath, and force the words out: "Franklin, it feels awkward to sit there pretending that you and I barely know each other." The Howard County State Attorney and I have been "involved," as they say, for some time now, and we've kept it a secret from the start, for reasons that seemed like good ideas back then. They don't seem as good to me now. "What if your staff already knows about us? What if they're pointing and giggling behind your back, and all the time you think they're looking at you in awe because you're such a great boss."

"Would they still be giggling then?"

"Yes," I say, deadpan. "In nervous awe."

"This didn't bother you when you were interviewing cops and lawyers for this book of yours."

"Yes, it did, Franklin."

"But I like our little secret, Marie." The sly smile returns and he waggles his eyebrows at me. "I thought you still enjoyed it, no?"

"No."

Franklin almost manages to hide his surprise at my tone. The owner of the face that gives nothing away to juries — unless he plans it — cannot quite hide from me that I am taking him by surprise.

"No? You're the one who said secrecy is sexy."

"You must have me confused with another girlfriend."

"Yeah, that must be it. But admit it, it's more fun this way, Marie."

"Okay, I'll admit it turned me on for a long time. But it doesn't now, Franklin. We're grown-ups, we ought to be able to do things that grown-ups do, like go to movies and restaurants, and not just hide out in my bedroom."

"Your bedroom is my favorite place."

"What's the real reason, Franklin?"

He lowers his lids and gives me a penetrating look from under them. I watch him decide whether or not to level with me, and while he's taking his time doing that, I am deciding that quite a lot rides on the honesty of his answer.

"Are you trying to pick a fight?" he asks, a question that I take for avoidance. "Are you mad about something else and you're taking it out on me?"

"Yes. No. What's the real reason, Franklin?"

"The real reason, Marie, is that I'm still not ready to tell my kids about you."

That hurts, and I can tell that he sees that it does.

He didn't even say "about us." He said "about you."

He could add "I'm sorry," but he doesn't.

There was a time when we first fell into this affair that we told ourselves that secrecy would protect us when it ended; nobody would know, so nobody would gossip, or take sides. We must not have expected it to last very long. But here we are, much later, and what started out thrilling has become kind of sad and exhausting to me.

"I'm not talking about meeting them," I say, with a bite to my words. "I'm talking about going to a movie. You and me. In public. Do you have to tell your kids about that?"

"No, but if somebody saw us out together . . ."

"They're going to call your six-year-old and tell her?"

He makes an exasperated face, which probably mirrors my own. I hate feeling put on the defensive about something that seems so simple to me. Why is he making this so difficult?

"The divorce is still too fresh, Marie. For one thing, they might think it had something to do with you."

"But it didn't, and you can tell them I came later."

"Right, a whole month later, but they're three and six, and math isn't their strong point, nor is it their mother's."

"You're afraid of what Truly will say? Gee" — I can't help but fall back on sarcasm — "I could have sworn you divorced her."

"She can poison the kids against me, Marie."

"No wonder you divorced her, a woman like that."

"If you had kids, you'd understand better."

"That's such a cop-out. I really hate that particular argument."

"Too bad. Kids need time to adjust, and seeing Daddy with a new woman is more than I want them to have to adjust to right now, while they're still getting used to living alone with Mommy. Hell, they only see me on weekends, Marie, and that's not enough time to prepare the ground for meeting you, at least not this soon."

"Soon? Franklin you've been divorced almost a year!"

I feel mortified to think I've been putting up with this for so long. But it didn't start to bother me until the initial romance wore off and the feelings of a real-life relationship started to settle in. The problem was, they couldn't settle in, because of our game of seek-each-other-and-hide-from-everybody-else.

"It's so unfair when you pit your kids' feelings against mine, and I know that probably makes me sound like a selfish jerk, but there you have it. Maybe you're right, Franklin. Maybe if I had kids, I would be more understanding. And maybe not, because maybe this isn't about them, but about whether or not I can continue to tolerate this behavior of ours. And you know what? I can't. It's too damn much work to maintain and it feels a little silly to me now."

Suddenly, he's flinging himself out of bed.

"Let's talk about this later, Marie."

I hate that officious tone he gets.

"I know what it is," I say, trying to joke, "you're just embarrassed to be seen with a white woman."

He feigns dismay and shock. "You're *white?*"

"Only on my mother's and my father's side."

"That settles it, I'm never taking you

home to meet the kids."

He's joking, too, but I'm thinking: *That's probably true, you probably never will. There goes Cancun, or Paris, or Katmandu.*

On the way through my living room to the garage, we pass the canvas boat bag and Franklin asks me what I'm going to do with it.

"You sure you don't want it, either?" I inquire.

He shakes his head. "Can't try her twice for the same crime."

"Well, I think I'll hold on to it, see if anybody calls *me*."

He has already told me there's nothing his office or the cops can do about the person who called Jenny and then tried to grab the bag off their front porch. Even if they traced a phone call, no crime was committed. As I scoop up the handles to carry the bag with me, he warns, "Don't be taking any chances, all right? Just because I can't charge anybody with a crime doesn't mean they aren't dangerous."

"Who do you think wants this stuff?"

He shrugs as we enter my garage, his mind already on his work. All up and down the line, the official attitude toward the Susanna Wing homicide case seems to be:

solved, finished, over, don't bother me about it anymore.

"How long do you think your kids will need, Franklin?"

Taken by surprise, he stops in front of his SUV and looks back at me. "There's no set timetable for these things, Marie."

There's that officiousness again. I grit my teeth, then say, "All right. Then all I can say is that I know what I need. This has become too much like dating a married man. If you're not willing to be seen in public with me by the end of this month, I'm out of here, Franklin. I mean no disrespect to you and your kids, but I have to think of my self-respect, too."

"You're making way too much of this."

"No, you are."

"Okay, I hear you," he says, unexpectedly.

"One month. All right?"

He says nothing, but he looks frustrated, angry.

Finally, I get a grudging "All right."

"As plea bargains go, that was not a very satisfactory answer from the state attorney's office."

"It's the best I can do at the moment."

"That's good enough for me."

But when he walks back over to kiss me

goodbye, I can see it in his eyes, the fear of telling his children, his trepidation about his ex-wife's reaction.

I hope it's a good month, if it's going to be our last.

In my car, I test my emotions to see what hurts. Maybe I'm lucky; maybe I haven't actually fallen in love with the man yet and I can still get out of this without getting badly burned. If that's the case, I intend to treat this month as if we're the last two people on earth, and this is our last time together. He wants sexy, I'll give him sexy. He wants secret, I'll give him secret. I'll give the man something to miss, by God. By the time I've pulled out of my driveway I've almost managed to talk myself into feeling good about the prospect of losing my lover.

I'm still following his car down the road when my cell phone rings.

"That's great about your book," he says. "I'm not surprised, and I'm glad she likes it so much."

"She thinks I need to work on Artemis some more, though. When you read it, did you feel as if you got to know her very well?"

"Why would I want to? You did her fine, Marie."

He really is a very nice man sometimes.

"Thank you," I say, and manage not to cry over the phone. What's a mere book — or a lost romance — in the larger scheme of things? Everybody else seems to like my book. So what if I'm unhappy with it? I'm just the writer, so who cares what I think? And, anyway, I like some of it just fine.

And he loved me just enough, until now.

On my way out, I pause by the gate to have a conversation with Bennie, who's on duty this morning. With his help, I'm going to set a trap today, and maybe we'll see who gets caught in it.

After all, Franklin DeWeese isn't my only secret.

Susanna

9

Another thing that nobody but Franklin knows about me is that I've never actually met Artemis McGregor, the infamous Artie, the notorious "other woman." Not that I haven't tried, repeatedly, and by every hook and crook I know. Mail and E-mail, intermediaries, lawyers, fax, and phone, I've tried them all, even showing up on her doorstep, just to get the door closed in my face, even loitering in an inconspicuous car across the street from her house — like a cheap private eye — in the vain hope that I might follow her out and waylay her in the grocery store.

Apparently, her husband, Stuart, does all the shopping.

She has consistently refused to have anything to do with me or any other member of "the media." Mr. McGregor has been only slightly less shy. He and I had one strange, stilted dialogue in a hallway at the courthouse — I hesitate to call it an interview, still less a conversation. It consisted of me asking questions about her and him answering politely to each one of them, "I really can't speak for her. I'm afraid you'd have to check with Artie about that."

As if anybody could, I pointed out to him, to no avail.

He is unfailingly courteous; she is unremittingly silent.

Most of what I think I know — and have written — about Bob Wing's codefendant has come to me secondhand, or from the courtroom. Ask me what other people say about her and I can fill you in. Ask me about her credit rating, her history of real estate transactions, her arrest record (nothing before this), even her genealogy, and I'm a veritable databank. I've even had E-mail conversations with her ex-husband on his sailboat in the South Pacific. He seems a nice guy, loyally, even indignantly, supportive of her, and you'd think it spoke well of a woman when her ex-husband had nothing but nice things to say about her, wouldn't you?

All of that is in the book, but it's camouflage for my dirty little secret, which is that I don't really know the woman at all. I've never run into this problem before; eventually everybody talks to me. Oh, I've known murderers who were gun-shy, so to speak, but I can almost always count on their egos to pull their trigger eventually, although what comes shooting out may not be anything you'd want to know. And some survivors — or surviving victims — find it difficult to let it all out, for a while. But most people want — need — to talk to somebody. I'm accustomed to being that person. But not this time, not with this woman.

Her codefendant, Bob Wing, has talked to me several times.

But I know *her* voice only from hearing it in court, recognize her face only from there, too, and from photos her mother showed me. I know her personality not at all, really, because the reports vary so dramatically depending upon who is explaining her to me, her friends or foes.

Saint or sinner —

That's all I've ever heard about her. I've relied far too much on other people's opinions of her. It makes me feel uneasily like an historian, because when it comes to Artie McGregor I have relied entirely on secondary sources for my information. Would secondhand reports give an accurate picture of me, or of anyone? Personally, I don't think so. I need to see faces, body language, responses; I want to hear tones of voice and the exact words that people use.

But now maybe I have some bait to lure her.

I use my car phone to try her number one more time, and get their message machine. Of course. "Mrs. McGregor, this is Marie Lightfoot," I tell the machine. In a carefully neutral tone, I continue: "I have a canvas boat bag that belongs to you. This afternoon, I'm going to take it back where it was found, snap some pictures of it for my book, and then I'm going to leave it there. Nobody else has any use for it. So if you want it back, that's where it will be."

There. Now let *her* wonder about *me*, for a change.

I pull into a "visitor" parking space at the rear of the Bahia Beach Police Department. As I walk up to the metal detector at the back door, I am still thinking about the mysterious, elusive Artemis McGregor. Surely it was for women like her that the phrase "appearances can be deceiving" was coined.

"Is this the missing wedding ring?" I ask Carl Chamblin. "Does this match the engagement ring that you guys found at the scene?"

We're in the Homicide Investigative Division of the Bahia Beach Police Headquarters on Twenty-third; I'm at the side of his desk, in a chair so uncomfortable that I would confess to a crime just to get out of it; Carl's leaning back precariously in his own black plastic chair that looks two sizes too small for him. Under the glass top of his desk there are photographs of his family: himself, his wife, two daughters, sons-in-law, four grandchildren, all of them smiling. *They* appear to love him, regardless of what I or my readers may think of him.

"How'd you get that?" he wants to know.

"The Carmichaels gave it to me."

"Why the fuck'd they do that?"

"Because you told them you didn't want it, Carl, and because I'll collect anything to do with this case. You scared them away."

His fierce face cracks a grin and he laughs. "It's what I do best, Marie. I like to scare the good citizens so they won't report crimes and force me to do some actual fucking work around here." He puts out his hand for the ring.

I hand it to him. "So, is it?"

"Probably." He perches the ring atop his right index finger, unable even to slide it past the first joint of his finger. "Whoever

211

wore it, she was a skinny thing," he observes.

"Whatever happened to that other ring?"

"It's in the evidence room, unless somebody's stolen it." He's not kidding. A diamond ring would be a temptation to a dishonest cop with a little credit-card debt. Almost playfully, he says, "What do you think I should do with them?"

It takes me a second to realize he is taking possession of it.

"I could pawn them, maybe," he continues, looking at me to see if I'm falling for this. "What do you think this one's worth, Marie, a few thousand? I wouldn't get that much, if I pawned it."

"And you'd have to split it with me."

"Your word against mine."

"You better be nice to me, Carl. My book's not out yet."

"Oh, right, I'm gonna be famous. Felons all over South Florida are gonna want my autograph. I guess I'd better behave myself till your literary masterpiece is in print. I hope you told them how handsome I am?"

"There's a photograph of you in the book."

"Damn." He looks suddenly disgusted, but not, it turns out, about his appearance. "Do you know we have twenty-seven effing pawnshops in this city alone, Marie? And a hundred and twenty-nine in just this one county? And that I checked every damn one of them, on my own, without a computer, when I was looking for a lead on that engagement ring?"

"I know you did, Carl. I pray for a big budget increase for the police department, every night."

"Right. You could give us your royalties on this book."

"Yeah, that's gonna happen." He laughs, and so do I. There's no central computer in Howard County for comparing pawn slips with stolen or lost property reports. That means that cops have to do it manually, and sometimes that means cross-checking literally thousands a day. It's a source of unending and well-justified complaints, but so far no money has been allotted to lighten the load on them. "So what *are* you going to do with it?"

"Check back with me on this, Marie."

"Meaning, you don't know?"

"No, I just thought you'd want to make sure I really did tag it for evidence, instead of pawning it like I said I would."

I give him a wry look. "If you're not an honest cop, Carl, I'm going to look pretty stupid for turning you into a hero."

He looks smug, catches the eye of a cop across the room, and grins at her, before looking back at me. "Is that what you did? Aw. Why didn't the little girl give us this ring a long time ago?"

"It's pretty, and she wanted to keep it."

"Also, she didn't want to get caught stealing."

"Also that. You're not going to get her in trouble, are you?"

It's his turn to give me a look. "Yeah, I make it a practice to arrest ten-year-old suburban white girls and charge them with grand larceny." Suddenly, his expression changes. "Which, now that I think about it, this may be."

"If it's worth that much."

"Why are you interested in these rings, Marie?"

"I am interested in everything about this case."

"I thought you already finished your book about me."

"About you?" I can't help smiling. Cops are pretty damned amusing, sometimes. Funny, caustic, quick-witted as hell. My own riposte is less than original. "You wish."

"I've told all my relatives."

"Of course. I make sure I only write

about cops with big families. More book sales for me that way."

"We're a library family, sorry to tell you."

"Is that right. Well, maybe I'll have to rewrite my manuscript, and get more about Norm in there, a little less about you." Sergeant Jill Norman was his partner on some of the investigation, but she didn't play enough of a role to be as big a star in my book.

"My family just got bigger. You gonna give me a free copy?"

"Several, a box load if you want that many."

"What if I don't like what you wrote about me?"

"So sue me."

He laughs, unaware that I mean it. I try like hell to portray the real people in my books accurately, and with some compassion for the fact that after I make use of them they still have to live in the world. But there's no guarantee that I will write about them as they want the world to see them. They have no idea the risk they take with their reputations when they put their words in my hands. I smile back at the detective, but I feel queasy, because I know that Carl Chamblin is not a man who will take it kindly if I don't completely share his own high opinion of himself.

"If I don't like it," he suddenly says, "you better not fucking park on my streets." At his own supposed joke, Carl Chamblin laughs loud enough to attract the attention of other cops in the room. When I glance around at them, however, it seems to me they are looking at me, and not at him. I spot two of them — two women — talking behind their hands, and when they see I am looking at them, they smile at me in a kind of embarrassed way, and quickly turn away from each other. Hmm. Call me paranoid, but it seems to me there is something in their expressions —

"Carl, you ever hear any rumors about my private life?"

He looks surprised, then foxy. "What should I hear? You got a little secret you don't want us crack detectives to find out about, Marie?"

I feign innocence, and stand up.

"You know," he says, looking up at me from where he's leaning back in his chair, "now I won't rest until I find out what it is."

I nod in the direction of the two women cops. "Ask them. Maybe they know. And

when you find out, tell me, okay? I'm sure it will be as great a surprise to me as it is to you."

Carl laughs, and makes a move, as if to escort me to the door.

"So you don't think the rings are connected at all?"

"Oh, let it go," he advises me, and props his butt on his desk. "It's over. We got a conviction, you got a book. The fuck else do you want?"

"Just these loose ends."

"Fuck 'em. They're not important. Somebody stole some rings and that house was where they hid them, and if you go looking for who those people are they may not be real happy if you find them."

It sounds as if he is warning me away from my own curiosity.

"Don't you want to investigate it, Carl? If they're stolen?"

"The sign on the door says homicide, not theft."

I notice something and ask, "Speaking of signs, what's that, Carl?"

He turns to see what I mean: a big white cardboard sign with a fat black "8" on it. "The number of days left till the execution of Stevie Orbach," he tells me. "That's our countdown calendar."

"You do that for all your killers?"

"No, just Stevie. Somebody rapes and murders the niece of one of our guys, we're going to pay special attention."

"Will you do that when it's time for Bob Wing?"

"No." Carl shrugs. "He's nothing to us."

"One more question."

He fakes a put-upon sigh.

"It's about Artemis McGregor. Do you think she's dangerous?"

He gives me an amused, cynical look. "No, I think she's scared."

"Scared?"

"Sure. I think she got caught up in something she never intended to happen and she feels lucky to have got off so easy."

"Doesn't it piss you off that she was acquitted?"

"Nah. We got the bad guy. Her life is ruined, she'll never pick up the pieces from this. She was just a pawn. If they'd gotten away with it, she'd probably have been next on his list."

"You think he'd have killed her, too?"

"Sure, first they killed his wife, then they would have killed her husband, and then Wing would have killed her. She's got money, right?"

"So," I say, a shade ironically, "you're

saying that in a way you may have saved her life."

"Listen, we don't need to execute her. She'll fall for another one just like him. Women like that, they do themselves in, every time."

The assistant state attorney, Tony Delano, tried to make the case in court that Artie McGregor was a canny, manipulative femme fatale who bashed her rival to death with a baseball bat. And now here's Carl Chamblin saying she's nothing more than a fool and a helpless tool for a good-looking man.

"What about the stuff in the boat bag, Carl, the condoms and stuff?"

"What about them?"

"Seems like evidence of their affair. I'm going to put a photo of it in my book. I'm taking a photographer out to the mansion with me today to pose the bag in the cabinet where Jenny found it."

"You got permission to go in there?"

"I've notified the owner."

Carl's good-bye smile is cruel. "If you ask her nice, maybe she'll recreate the murder for you. Get pictures. Ask her to sign one for me."

In the lobby, I stop to use a pay phone to drop my third piece of bait. When defense attorney Tammi Golding comes on the line, I say, "Tammi, it's Marie Lightfoot, and I won't take but a minute. You know that canvas boat bag that Jenny Carmichael found? Well, they gave it to me. I'm going to take it out to the old mansion this afternoon and get some photos of it up in the tower where Jenny found it. Is there any chance your client would come out to have her picture taken, too?"

Tammi expresses the opinion that I must be nuts.

I laugh, and say, "I have learned that it never hurts to ask. Will you at least run the idea past her this morning?" I get the reluctant agreement I'm seeking and hang up, thinking: Almost hooked now. I figure it has to be Artemis who tried to get her hands on the bag, and Tammi's my best bet for being the one who told her about it, however innocently. But I need to contact everyone the Carmichaels told, just in case Artemis fails to listen to her messages and there is another route by which the news gets passed along. That's why my next stop is the assistant state attorney's office, and my excuse is that he's the one who asked to see me.

I don't make it out of the back door of the police station, however, before I'm waylaid by the chief of police himself.

"Marie?" I turn to find Marty Rocowski bearing down on me, looking dapper in a light summer suit with a matching shirt and tie, so that he's dressed all in cream. After a few polite preliminaries, he gets to the point, with a self-effacing grin. "How you doing on that book of yours?"

"Mailed it to my editor yesterday, Marty."

I can't bring myself to call him Rocco.

"Hey, congratulations. Would you let somebody read it now?"

"I don't usually do that." That's a partial truth; frequently, I allow some people to read short excerpts, to check for accuracy. But I don't want a chief of police getting his hands on my manuscript, because he'd naturally be inclined to try to censure anything he didn't like that I had written about his officers. "Why, Marty?"

"I'm only asking for my wife." His grin grows wider and more charming. "Betty is one of your biggest fans. She can't wait to get her hands on this one, and her birthday's coming up. I'd score bigtime if I could take a copy of it home to her before any of her friends could read it."

"I'll give you a signed copy when it comes out."

He hides his disappointment fairly well, but it leaves us in an awkward moment of silence, which he fills by asking, "Now that you're finished with it, will you take a vacation?"

"Hope to, although I still have some work to do on it."

"You ought to go," he urges, enthusiastic as any travel agent.

"How about you?" I ask, to get his attention off me. "Can you and Betty escape any of Spring Break?"

"For a few days. We're going to Ft. Meyers to play golf right after the execution."

"Excuse me?"

"Stevie Orbach. I'm taking a group of officers up to watch, friends of Lyle Karnacki's. Then I can go play golf."

"Is that usual, for groups of you to watch executions?"

"I consider it part of the job."

I'm truly curious now. "Why, Marty?"

He looks at me thoughtfully, then says, "My philosophy is that we ought to see the consequences of the laws we enforce. If we arrest people and testify against them, then we ought to take it all the way to the end and see them executed, if that's the case. Families aren't the only ones who need closure. Cops do, too."

"You mind if I use that quote in my book?"

He smiles down at me. "Not at all. If you change your mind about the manuscript, call me, all right?"

"Sure," I say, while thinking that as much as I want to keep on the good side of my hometown police department, that particular favor is not gonna happen. As I return to my car, I have a moment of realizing how lucky I am to have the easy access I do. Computers have made life hard for regular crime reporters on newspaper beats. There are new security systems to keep you out of anywhere the cops don't want you to go, and there's the new fashion of "escorts" who keep you from wandering off into interesting corners, and new gag rules on cops, prohibiting them from talking freely to reporters. Not only that, but there's no paper trail to follow anymore. If you're a journalist with a police beat, you want to be able to search inventory lists, for instance, that show everything the cops seized with a warrant. But those physical files are gone, replaced by impenetrable computers. To get inside information now, you may have to file for it under the Freedom of Information Act, and you'll be lucky if the city attorney okays it. At that point of maddening frustration, some reporters write the only story left to them — about how the cops won't cooperate with the press. You can just imagine how popular that makes the reporter and how congenial that makes the cops. As I sail past the metal detector, I know these same doors would lock me out if I were any writer but me doing any other kind of crime writing. But since I am only writing about good cops doing good jobs in cases that are already solved, they let me pass "go."

I pause to look back at the incongruously pink building.

What if I had to write something really bad about them? Would they let me back in again? My portrayal of Carl Chamblin and the other detectives is pretty blunt in the new book; I hope there's enough oil left on the hinges of their good will to keep the door swinging open for me.

This is Franklin's domain: the state attorney's office.

The moment he spies me, Tony Delano launches right in. "I'll tell you why *he* got convicted and *she* didn't."

I nod, even as I'm clearing off a chair on which to sit.

Tony is short, stocky, intense as his Sicilian forebears are reputed to be. The fingers on which he ticks off his points are stubby as sausages, but better groomed. "We got *him* on five points: the baseball bat, the semen, the uncorroborated alibi, and enough motive to choke a rhinoceros. After the testimony about the life-insurance payout, he was a cooked goose."

I nod again. Tony's right: he had a strong enough mix of direct physical evidence and circumstantial evidence to convince any jury. The murder weapon was proven to be the baseball bat. The bat belonged to the preacher and it was found in his front hallway with her blood and tissue embedded in its cracks. The semen wouldn't have been convincing — they were married — except that the medical examiner thought she may have had forced sex before she died. The alibi was a farce. It amounted to, "I was with her," the "her" being his codefendant, whose alibi was, "I was with him."

Satisfied that I'm agreeing with him, Tony plunges on. "Now I'll tell you why we didn't convict her."

"All right."

"We didn't establish any physical evidence to tie her to the scene."

I wait for him to go on, but he just sits there looking at me until, finally, he says, "That's it."

"I don't agree, Tony. I mean, I agree it was bad that you only had circumstantial evidence on her, but I think you still might have convinced the jury. That's the impression I got from a couple of jurors."

He winces like a man who doesn't want to hear bad reviews of his own performance in the courtroom. "Okay." He sighs. "Hit me."

"You lost her at three points in the trial, Tony. The first was when Tammi demolished those three witnesses of yours, the church women who said they knew about the affair. Tammi made them look like jealous gossips. The second was Artie herself, who sat there looking like the first angel at the right hand of God. Nobody could convict that woman of anything, Tony. She looks too damned sweet and innocent. They were never going to believe that she stood in that house and watched him force sex on his wife and they sure weren't going to believe she picked up a weapon of her own — which you never produced — to help kill Susanna. You're lucky they didn't convict *you* for saying all of those nasty things about her. And the clincher was when Tammi put on that nurse from the retirement home who told about how all the old folks adore Artie."

"Barf."

"You might have tried that." I give him a sympathetic smile. "That might have convinced the judge, but I don't think Franklin DeWeese himself could have brought in a conviction on Artemis McGregor. And where *is* your boss this morning?"

"He might drop by."

"So what's the information you have for me that you couldn't bring out at trial?"

"Those church women." Tony's looking serious now. "The ones that Tammi turned into petty, gossipy bitches?"

"Yes?"

"Marie, they're not."

"*That's* your new information?"

"Listen, okay? Think about the implications of what I'm saying, what they said, the telephone conversation they overheard. They really did hear it, I'm totally convinced of that, and I'm not exactly naïve, Marie. Maybe this sounds stupid to you, for me to say this, but they are not goody-goody hypocritical white-glove church ladies. They're kind, intelligent women, and their only sin was accidentally overhearing

a damning telephone conversation between a husband and a wife, and then
making the awful connection between it
and her death, and then having the guts to
go up against their beloved minister and
the whole congregation who idolize him
and say so. Marie, those women have been
pariahs ever since it became known that
they took their evidence to the cops. You
saw how Tammi treated them in court,
like they were dead fish and she was dangling them by their tailfins. They were cru-
cified on the witness stand, and I feel
damned bad that I couldn't protect them
once Tammi got rolling."

He pauses, takes a breath, which he
blows out like he's winded.

"But this isn't even about how lousy this
is for them and their families, Marie. This
is about what it means if they really did
hear what they said they heard. Now, you
tell me — what would that mean?"

"That Bob and Artie really were having
an affair."

"Yes. What else?"

"That she's probably guilty."

"Yes, at the very least of being a co-
conspirator or an accessory. And, there-
fore, a guilty woman —"

"Got off. To which I still say: Sorry,

Tony, you lose. You're the lawyer, you tell me — isn't that how our judicial system works?"

"Or doesn't," he says, looking glum.

"Right. Or doesn't."

"So that alone," he says with a challenging air, "doesn't inspire you to correct in print the egregious wrong that has been done to those nice women, those good citizens? You don't even want to raise the possibility in your book that they did overhear what they said they did? And at least let your readers draw their own conclusions. Or, are you going to be satisfied with portraying them in the way the defense manipulated them to appear?"

I give him a look as if to say, "Well, when you put it that way . . ."

"What if I told you where you could get your hands on new evidence?"

I smile at him a bit smugly. "If you mean the canvas bag, I've already got it."

His eyes widen. "You do? How the hell — ?"

"They brought it to me when you didn't want it. Why didn't you?"

"Too late. Besides, the chain of evidence is fatally compromised by now. But you'll mention it in your book, right?"

"I'll do better than that, Tony. I'll even

put in a picture of it."

He smiles happily at me. "All *right*."

"In fact, when I leave here, I'm taking the bag out to the mansion to have some pictures taken of it right where Jenny found it."

"I knew you cared about the right things." Tony picks up a ballpoint pen and clicks it a couple of times. "Would you go to a movie with me sometime?"

I blink in surprise. Where'd *this* come from? The universe seems to have heard about my desire to go to a movie with a grown man, but it has gotten the fulfillment of it a little confused. Usually, I can see these things coming, but Tony has blindsided me here. I'm suspicious. Is this a test? To see if I'll confirm some gossip?

"Why do you want to take me out, Tony?"

It's his turn to blink, then to smile. "That's a new one. I've heard 'No' in all its permutations, but I don't believe I've ever had a woman actually question my motives." He makes a show of thinking it over. "I want to take you out because you're shorter than I am."

"I'm not, actually."

"Close enough."

"I suppose I've been asked out for worse

reasons. I can't, Tony." I decide to tell part of the truth and see if he reacts to it. "I'm busy getting my heart broken by another man. Believe me, going out with you would be a lot more fun, but what can I do? I have an opportunity to be really miserable, and I'm determined to take it, by God."

He's shaking his head in amused sympathy.

I can see nothing in his face that shouldn't be there.

"Tell me who he is, Marie. I'll have him arrested for something. What charge would you like? Felonious mischief? Leaving the scene of a romance?"

That makes me laugh, though I still wonder what he knows.

"We could probably keep him in jail until he comes to his senses."

"Thanks, but he's already arrested, Tony."

Tony doesn't miss much, including my little pun. "Arrested development? I hear it's epidemic among American men. Not me, Marie. I may not look it, but I promise you I'm a grown-up. My heart is mature." He places his right hand over his chest dramatically, making me smile again. Suddenly he takes his pen and scribbles on a slip of paper, which he then hands to me. "Here. If you ever need cheering up, use this coupon that's good for one night out with a man who guarantees that he will appreciate you."

"What a deal." I take it, smiling, and make a show of putting it in a safe place in my purse. "Thank you. You are an honorable but devious man, Tony."

"Kinder words could never be said to a lawyer. Who's going to play me in the movie?"

"Who do you want?"

"Well, I'm pretty much the spitting image of Russell Crowe."

I throw him a kiss as I leave. "I'll see what I can do, Russ."

The gate to the property that Artemis still owns is padlocked. The NO TRESPASSING signs are more numerous than ever. If Tammi does call her and tell her what I'm doing, and she objects to my being here, there's no way to tell me now. And if locks, signs, and a fence couldn't keep out two ten-year-olds, it certainly can't keep out Bennie, George, and me. One of them is playing professional photographer, the other is playing photographer's assistant, and I'm carrying the bag.

Like the girls, we have to leave our vehicles outside and then clamber over, equipment and all. Together we walk up the overgrown driveway, playing our roles, talking of the weather, the trees, our fears of crawly things. Then, cautiously, we climb to the tower, stand in the windows and admire the views, then set up our pictures, which I may in fact use, and take them. George, our "photographer," gets carried away and starts snapping pictures right and left, trying for "artistic" shots, until Bennie and I pull him away.

The bag stays behind in the cabinet in the tower.

No way was I coming in here alone, not even in daylight. And when we come back tonight, from a hidden side path, without any baggage, my ex-military bodyguards will flank me all the way.

But first I have an appointment I have to keep at home.

Bennie drives me back so that he can relieve his substitute at our own gate. George, meanwhile, glides into the shadows, to watch the property until we join him later.

I doubt the fish will jump until dark, if she rises to the bait at all.

Susanna

10

"You must hear about hundreds of murder cases every year," the young reporter exclaims. Her startling light-blue eyes are open wide and staring at me as if she thinks I'm the ninth wonder of the world; she's way more impressed with me than is good for my ego. Her name is Deborah Dancer, and she's a feature writer for our local daily newspaper, the Bahia Beach *Sun-Journal*. She's here to interview me and to apply for a job as my part-time research assistant. God knows, I need somebody around every now and then; I'm spending far too much time talking to myself. Deb, as she tells me she likes to be called, is several inches taller than I am, skinny as a lamppost, with an energy so intense she looks as if somebody threw a switch and lighted her from the inside out. Her shoulder-length hair looks electrified, too; she's got it dyed a pale blond that doesn't flatter her complexion. Young is how she looks; untested; eager as a lamb and twice as bouncy. She's wearing clunky high-heeled shoes and a red-and-white striped sundress. It appears she is too young to have developed any taste; is she old enough to have any sense?

She's perched on the edge of a cushioned porch chair at my patio table overlooking the Intracoastal Waterway. I've just served us iced tea and sandwiches, and now I'm sitting back across from her in a matching chair, brushing crumbs of whole wheat bread from my lap onto the ground for the palmetto bugs to clean up. (There's a flip side to Florida, and it's disgusting, huge, and brown, and it flies.) There is something so fresh and ingenuous about her that I feel like Lillian Hellman, by comparison; any second now I'm going to whip out a cigarette and gripe about Dashiel Hammett.

"With so many cases," she continues enthusiastically, her ballpoint pen poised over a notebook, "how do you ever choose which ones to write about, Ms. Lightfoot?" She's only six months out of journalism school, I have learned, but I have noted a more mature desire in her face as she looks around my property, a look of, "Some day, this will be me." I doubt that; so far, she hasn't asked me anything interesting. I know what I would ask me, and it isn't these predictable, safe questions about my work. I'd ask, "Why don't you ever talk about your personal life, Ms. Lightfoot? Is that your real name? I've heard it isn't, I've heard you changed it, is that true? Why can't I find out anything about your family in any of the interviews you've given, or any place on the Internet? Is there something you don't want the world to know? Are you hiding your own secrets, while you investigate everybody else's?"

I smile, quite happy to avoid that line of interrogation, and I try to give her what she thinks she wants. To be fair, I've got to admit those aren't the questions most people would ask on an employment interview. But then, this isn't just any job. I need somebody sharp enough to catch my mistakes, and bold enough to point them out to me.

"When I pick a murder case, I look for certain qualities," I tell her, choosing that last word with care. The bald truth is that I have certain cold-blooded criteria, but phrasing it that way wouldn't look tactful in print in her newspaper. "I want a killer who is unique in some way. I want a sympathetic victim, heroic police work, and an unusual or glamorous setting, like here, where it's beautiful and glittery."

She is scribbling, so I slow down.

"I look for murder cases that have at least one shocking twist to them, although I'd prefer two or three."

I pause, to let her ask the question.

"What kind of twist?"

"Oh, like a prison escape." You'd think we were trading recipes, so congenial is our conversation. "Or a surprise witness who alters the outcome of the trial, or a hidden motive that makes everybody gasp when they hear it."

She visibly shivers. "Like Raymond Raintree."

"Exactly." She is referring to a killer in my book *The Little Mermaid*. "Or a bizarre method of murder that the killer uses, or the way he ensnares his victims. Sometimes it's amazing coincidences that make it interesting."

"Or," she interjects, "the shock of finding out the killer is a well-known minister."

"Yes. Let's talk about that, shall we?"

As preparation for this dual-purpose interview, I messengered over to her home the first third of *Anything to Be Together* with a request that she read it with a critical eye. This is the real test, to see if she has the guts to confront me about my own work. I also want to gauge her instinct for "story." If she doesn't have a feeling for that, she won't be a good researcher; without it, she'll bring me irrelevant facts instead of meaty, pertinent ones.

"Oh, yes! I could barely put it down to come over here. But you don't want praise, right?"

"Right."

She swallows, visibly working up her nerve. "Well, then, I have one criticism, and a question."

"Good. Shoot."

"I think you hurry too fast over what happened to that girl in Lauderdale Pines."

"Allison Tobias? Really? That's funny, my editor says I devoted too *many* pages to her."

"Oops. Sorry."

"No, no. You think I need more?"

"Yeah," she says apologetically. I wait to see if she'll hold her ground against the opinion of a New York editor. "This may sound awful, but I felt like what's missing is what really happened to her."

"Raped and murdered," I remind her, dryly.

"Well, yeah," she retorts with a sarcasm that amuses and pleases me. "But you just *tell* us that and skip over the gory details. How'd he actually get *to* her to do it? And where did he do it? Down in the basement where he lived, or up in her apartment? Did he kill her the same way he killed his mother, or —"

"I see what you mean."

"You're not mad I told you?"

"Of course not. But do you want to know the embarrassing truth? I don't remember all the gory details. That case is peripheral to my story, and I really only used it to establish the irony of how Stevie and Bob ended up in adjoining cells on death row."

"That was amazing!"

"Oh, and I was also trying to make the Bahia cops look good, because they had to work hard to overcome their anger and bias." I think for moment. "But I must have some of that stuff in my files somewhere, and if I don't, that would be a great place for you to start your research."

Her face lights up. "Are you hiring me?"

"Only if you call me Marie."

Her grin is happy and huge. "I'll try."

I start to get up, but she says, "That was my criticism, about not having enough about Allison's murder. I've got a question, too."

I ease back down in the chair.

"Whatever happened to the note?" she asks me.

"What note?" It's so many weeks since I wrote that Tobias chapter, I can barely remember the names of her parents, much less the details of the story.

"The note her mother left on the door."

"What about it?"

Deb's face flushes, but she perseveres. "It's just that you never mention it again and I think it would be a poignant detail if they had found it beside her telephone, or something. Like she was going to call home, but never got the chance."

I have to think about it to recapture it: *When Allison didn't call home as she was supposed to, Mr. Tobias drove his wife over there and she left a note on the door for their daughter. Then, when Allie and her friends showed up, one of the girls tore down the note and handed it to her.*

"I don't know what happened to it, Deb. I don't recall seeing it on the inventory list from either Stevie's apartment or Allison's, and I doubt it was evidence in the trial. But you're right, it could make a nice little touch if we could find out." I don't know that it really would, but it might, and I want to encourage this initiative she's showing.

"I'll research it for you," she offers eagerly.

I give her a grin and a hand to shake. "You just do that, Deb."

Before she leaves, I load her down with a copy of the rest of my manuscript, with instructions to be tough on it as she reads it, and also my file on the Tobias homicide. "If I have anything about the note, it will be in here."

Deborah hugs the pile of paper to her thin chest and vows, "I'll guard this with my life."

"Please don't," I joke. "No research is worth dying for."

Finally, at the door, she makes a comment about Steven Orbach's execution coming up in eight days. "Can you imagine, knowing that, counting down the days?" She shivers in the waning sunlight. "It almost makes me feel sorry for him. Almost." As I watch her wobble away on her ugly shoes, I am struck by the fact that I have hired a very intelligent, sensitive, and nice young woman.

But now it's time to go fishing.

"Reminds me too much of Vietnam," Bennie breathes into my left ear, from behind me. "Let me go in front of you,

Marie." He's got a very small flashlight, which he has dimmed down to a minimum and even that low light he's shielding with his hand, so that only a bit of path is illuminated in front of him. It's indistinguishable from the moonlight filtering through the tree branches above us. He looks back and I see his teeth flash white in a grin. "You scared of snakes?"

I shake my head, proving a person doesn't have to speak to lie. These guys — George Pullen and Bennie Gonzales — are delighted with this private commission, this break from guarding pampered homeowners, this chance to use old skills to make a little cash on the side. We haven't heard from George since we left him here, which means that nothing has happened; the bag's still in the tower, nobody has come to snatch it. Nothing may happen at all, though we're all prepared to spend a night waiting to see if it does. To the guys, this is a game. To me, it's a long shot. If it pays off, I'll have a hell of an epilogue for my book.

"What'll you do if she shows up?" Bennie asked me this afternoon.

"Nothing," I confessed. "I'm not a cop, and you guys aren't detectives. I just want to watch. And, George, if I'm not there and you're the only one who sees her, don't stop her. I don't even want her to know that we've seen her. If we see her take the bag, I'll know she's guilty. Nobody really knows that for sure, Bennie. That's all I want, I just want to know."

Now he and I are sneaking up to the shadowed edge of the seawall where the real detective once sat with the crime technician to tell her the story of Allison Tobias. George said to meet him here at the time we said we'd be back.

But George isn't here now.

I check my watch, and Bennie checks his, too. We're right on time.

After one minute turns into five and nothing moves except leaves and small unseen creatures in the foliage, Bennie leans over to me and whispers, "I'm going to look for him. Don't go away."

I don't even say, "Be careful," because what is there to be careful of? It's merely dark. It only looks spooky here, but it isn't, really. And George is off in the woods taking a leak, no doubt. I wait, feeling like Nikki waiting for Jenny to emerge, only not so scared. After a little while, though, like her, I want to call out to my friends to locate them in the shadows. I want to shout, "Bennie? George?" But I don't, and the longer I don't — the longer I stand there by myself — the more spooked I get, until I'm actually scared. Where *are* they?

Then, like Nikki, I finally hear a cry.

It's a heartbroken cry that is shattering to hear. I plunge out of the shadows, racing to find the source of it. I would do anything to stop the sorrow and pain in that terrible cry. I stumble around the nearest corner of the mansion, frantically following the sound until it winds down and all I am left with is a trail of imagined echoes that pulls me onto the ruined patio. There by the fountain, on the far side of the broken statue, Bennie is holding George in his arms and rocking him. George Pullen is dead, the canvas bag is gone, and I am responsible for this foolish, senseless, terrible loss.

Susanna

11

The weekend is a bad dream capped by the fact that when I sleep I have nightmares visited by killers I have known. These nightmares are like fever-dreams in which bodies entwine, strange mixes of people from my books come and go, floating in and out, wielding knives and gun, saying insinuating, cruel things to me and to each other. None of it makes any sense, and that can surely be said for real life as well, in which the waking hours are a hell of tears, explanations, police reports, and loneliness. Franklin wants to help, wants to be with me, but he has the kids and I understand that he can't leave them. I don't want him to. I want to wallow in sadness and guilt. There's nothing I can do for Bennie. He has flown to Tampa to stay with his grown children until our medical examiner releases George's body for the funeral and burial. The autopsy will reveal the obvious, that while he was bending down to do something simple like tie his shoe, he was struck from the rear by a piece of the broken statuary from the fountain on the patio.

I'm not convinced she meant to kill him, though I doubt she cares.

When I'm awake, and alone, I can't get scenes from my own book about them out of my head. It's as if my mind has tossed all of it up in the air in the hope that when the words fall back down again they will make sense. But nothing about these people makes sense, and if I'm honest, I'll admit it never has.

It doesn't make sense that they could fight so hard against the death penalty, and yet be killers, themselves. Unusually vicious ones, at that. It seems so incredibly perverted. Once, when I interviewed Bob Wing in the prison where Florida stores all of its death-row inmates, I asked him why he'd picked Steven Orbach for his latest crusade. This was after his own guilty verdict and sentencing.

"Why Orbach, of all people, Dr. Wing?"

The preacher gave me a long, steady look, as if to gauge my capacity for tolerating whatever it was he was going to say. It was so weird to realize that the very man of whom we were speaking was just down a long hallway and through a couple of bolted doors. When Bob Wing returned to his own cell, after talking to me, he would pass Stevie Orbach's cell. Like Wing, Orbach would have on the blue pants that all inmates wear and the orange T-shirt that denotes death row.

"I'm going to have to quote Scripture at you," Wing said, with a disarming smile, as if warning me of something I might not enjoy. Up close, even in his penitentiary garb, the man had a lot of charm; everything I'd heard in that regard and about his physical appearance was true. In fact, he was nearly irresistible. When he smiled, it was damned hard not to smile back instinctively. When he leaned in any direction, I felt my body respond by following in his direction; when he leaned toward me, I felt the closeness like a pull between magnets. Amazing. And he did, indeed, have a rugged handsomeness, a compelling voice, and, to top it all off, a surprisingly self-deprecating sense of humor. "Can you stand it?"

"I'll try to bear up," I assured him, with a smile.

"Well, don't say I didn't warn you." He blew out a breath. "I get my marching orders from First Corinthians, twelve and thirteen." Wing raised his eyebrows, as if to ask me if I knew it.

I smiled slightly, and shook my head to tell him no.

"Well, that's where Paul says we are all imbued with the same Spirit, whether we're Jew or Gentile, slave or freeman. Then he compares the Church to a human body, saying every cell has an important part to play in the whole, and the whole must take care of its parts."

As before, he checked to see if I was following this.

"I'm still with you."

"Great," he said, with a nice smile. "Now here's the part that electrifies me —" He stopped, realized what he had just said, and actually began to laugh. "Oh, Lord, I'm sorry, what an awful pun." But he kept laughing, as if he couldn't help it. He was like somebody who hadn't laughed for a long, long time and once they finally got started, they just can't stop. As for me, I was so startled — and his macabre amusement was so infectious — that I ended up laughing with him, and feeling damned strange doing it.

"It's the strain," he managed to say, but still couldn't stop chuckling. "Not sleeping." He went off into another gale of laughter until he was weeping with it, wiping his eyes, and groaning that his stomach hurt from laughing. I'd never before had the experience of sharing a good laugh with a murderer.

Finally, in the silence of simmered-down hysteria, I suggested, "Beats crying?"

He heaved a big, spent sigh. "Not necessarily."

I decided he should know; I'd take his word on that.

"Where was I," he asked, "before I commenced to make a complete fool of myself?"

I checked my notes. "You were somewhere in the New Testament. First Corinthians, I believe. Chapters twelve and thirteen."

"Oh, right. Thanks. Okay, so the part that . . . gets . . . to me is where Paul says the following." He then proceeded to quote slowly from memory: ". . . *Our indecorous parts get a special care and attention which does not need to be paid to our more decorous parts. Yes, God has tempered the body together, with a special dignity for the inferior parts, so that there may be no disunion in the body, but that the various members should have a common concern for one another. Thus, if one member suffers, all the members share its suffering; if one member is honored, all the members share its honor.*"

After that mouthful, he looked at me rather like Franklin sometimes does, appraisingly. I felt like a Bible student expected to provide instant exegesis. Never one to be afraid to ask a stupid question, I said, "And that says to you . . . what, exactly?" He laughed a little at my candor, and then leaned toward me and began to talk in an intimate, passionate manner, as if it was vitally important for him to make me understand. "It says to me that when Allison Tobias suffered, we all suffered. Not in a physical way, as she did, but as a society, it hurt us, it pulled us down. And it says to me that the more we love our fellow members of society — our Allisons, for instance — the more painful it is for the rest of us when any one of us gets hurt. But it also says to me that if Steven gets put to death, we will all pull the switch. Now I realize that's just fine with a lot of people, but it's not fine with me. And the reason it's not fine with me is that Corinthians says that God wants us to pay the most attention to the least among us. Ms. Lightfoot, who do you consider to be the least among us?"

"Children?" was my reflex answer.

"Maybe," he agreed, "but maybe it's not the children, at least not in this society anymore. Maybe it's the men right here in this building and in others like it."

"Criminals, you mean?"

"Yes. Our worst are the 'least' among us."

"Murderers."

"Rapists. Child molesters."

"And why, exactly, do you think God wants us to pay more attention to them?"

"Because they need it the most," he exclaimed, as if that was the most obvious fact in the world. "Those of us who are already blessed don't need any extra attention. It's the ones who are cursed who need it. Just think about it: Isn't that true even at the most basic level of raising children? If you're a parent, who needs your undivided attention the most? Your problem child, of course. Even if the other kids don't like it. Tough, they've already got the blessing of your love. God expects us to be generous and kind toward those who are not generous and kind. They can't get their acts together without our help and His; they're not capable of that yet. But we are. And it's not like there's nothing in it for us, Ms. Lightfoot. When someone rises out of evil into goodness, then the rest of us are elevated, too."

"So you think that your calling is to serve the worst among us."

"Yes, those whom society perceives to be the worst."

"Like Stevie?"

He sighed again. "Yes, although I don't know if he is one of those, really. I don't know if he's guilty or not, though I tend to think not. The police were awfully quick to pin it on him. But his guilt or innocence is not the point, for me, although it is for members of my church who are convinced that he is not guilty. They don't want to let a boy they think is innocent be put to death. I don't want to let down God, who has instructed us to serve the least among us."

"Some people would say you are one of them now."

He withdrew from me in that instant. The spell was broken. It happened so quickly I felt as if a cord that tied us together tautly was cut, flinging me backward. I nearly, physically, recoiled. I hadn't meant to be cruel or to offend him by saying what I did; if anything, I'd meant it sympathetically. But he withdrew into himself as effectively as if he had reentered a cell and locked it. The interview was over in that moment, though I asked him one more question: "How do you feel about Artemis getting off?"

"Innocent people should get off," he said, coolly.

"You feel good about it then?"

"Good? That she was accused of something terrible that she didn't do? Good, that she was humiliated and that her life may have been ruined? Good, that a faithful wife was made to look like a whore? Do I feel good about that? No, I don't feel good about that, Ms. Lightfoot. Artie is one of the best of us. Every day she practiced what I preach. I wish she had never heard of me or my church, that's how I feel about Artie McGregor."

"Are you in love with her?"

He stood up so suddenly it frightened me. But all he did was push back his chair, walk over to the door and bang on it with his cuffed hands, to indicate that he wanted to be taken back to his cell.

My heart was beating hard in my chest when he left.

It appeared I had transgressed against him. When I recovered my balance, I took a sanguine attitude, because of my experience with other people on death row. Murderers have notoriously thin skins. And not a single one of them I'd ever met would have sat still for being termed "the least." Afterward, I looked up those verses in the New Testament and read them in full, making sure to read the same version that Wing had told me he was quoting. I discovered that he had left out a lovely and more familiar part: *"I may speak with the tongues of men and of angels, but if I have no love, I am a noisy gong . . ."*

It was chapter twelve that he had quoted to me. This other part was in chapter thirteen, but he had named that, too, as being — what had he called it? — his "marching orders."

This, too, was familiar, though I'd never heard it said so plainly as this: *"Love is very patient, very kind. Love knows no jealousy; love makes no parade, gives itself no airs, is never rude, never selfish, never irritated, never resentful; love is never glad when others go wrong, love is gladdened by goodness, always slow to expose, always eager to believe the best, always hopeful, always patient . . ."*

It did not describe any murderer I'd ever known. But then, Bob Wing didn't look or sound like any killer I'd ever met, either. When the jury found him guilty, I admired them for being able to look beyond his appearance and charisma to the evidence against him. It couldn't have been easy. Even I, when he shut me down in that interview with him, felt for an instant as if the sun had gone out. It was very easy for me to understand how a lonely widow like Susanna Scale had fallen head over heels for her handsome minister.

That part, at least, made perfect sense.

In talking to his lawyers, Bob Wing related how he went home and told his wife all about the nice woman who'd walked into the church that day.

"What did you tell Susanna?" Tammi Golding asked him.

"I said that a really nice woman came into our church today and that she had invited us to a party at her house."

"What did Susanna say?"

"I think she may have said she didn't have a thing to wear."

The lawyer chided him, "This is no joke, Bob."

"But it was all so normal, Tammi. Susanna was curious, she wanted to know was the new woman married, was she attractive, did she have any money —"

"Bob, why would your wife ask you things like that unless she felt threatened by women in the church? Was Susanna jealous of you?"

"No, Tammi! Susanna wasn't jealous, she was a matchmaker! You *know* that! Didn't she ever try to fix you up with anybody?"

"No," the never-married attorney said, wryly.

"Well, I'm surprised. She was always on the lookout to fix up the single people in our church."

"So who'd she have in mind for Artie?"

"Oh, Stuart McGregor, right from the start."

"So that was Susanna's doing, getting them together?"

"Yes. She called Artie and asked if we could bring along a single friend of ours to the party. That's where Stuart and Artie met. Susanna knew Stuart was lonely since his wife's death. And we knew that Stuart had inherited from his wife, and Susanna wanted to be sure that no woman was after him just for his money. So that's why she wanted to know if Artie had any money of her own, that's all."

"And you told Susanna that Artemis was wealthy?"

"I told her how Pat had pointed out to me that Artie was wearing a diamond as big as my head."

So first came the party, for Artemis and Stuart. They got much better acquainted after that at Bob's "grief group." Susanna continued to attend, although she was married now. She went for the company, Bob Wing averred, and to help him. As it had for Bob and her — and with nudging from Susanna the matchmaker — attraction blossomed between Stuart and Artemis, quickly flowering into engagement and marriage.

The two couples became friends in the process.

Once, when Artemis got cold feet, after being persistently wooed by Stuart, Susanna counseled her to grab this opportunity for happiness, because who knew if she would ever get the chance again?

"What do you think of Artemis?" Tammi asked Bob Wing, bluntly, practicing for the trial.

"She's a wonderful woman," he said, with feeling.

"You like her?"

"Yes, very much."

"Have the two of you ever been lovers?"

"No, Tammi."

"Have you ever engaged in sexual contact of any sort with her?"

"I have not."

"Has she with you?"

"Absolutely not. Not ever."

"Were you ever unfaithful to your wife?"

"No, never."

"You and Artie were just friends, is that right?"

"Yes, we're friends."

Later, in the trial, Tammi Golding turned to the jury as if to say, "You see? This is a *minister*, for heaven's sake, a minister who has sworn to tell the truth. Who could possibly doubt him?" But as Tammi turned her back to refer to her notes, she hoped the jury had not noted Bob Wing's unfortunate omission of one word in his answer.

"You were just friends, is that right?" had been her question.

"Yes, we're friends," came the answer.

But without that "just," there remained a big gap of possibilities.

There was also a gap in the questioning, or at least one juror later said she thought she'd noticed one. After asking Bob Wing if he "liked" Artemis Hornung McGregor, his lawyer skipped right on to a question concerning fidelity. The juror thought, at the time, that the natural next question should have been, instead, "Do you *love* her?" But Tammi Golding didn't ask him that.

Which left at least one juror wondering why not.

Was the lawyer afraid of the answer he might give?

There were other problematic answers and at least one non-answer.

"What did you and Mrs. McGregor do for the two hours you were together in her car?" Bob Wing was asked first by the detectives, then by his own lawyers, and finally by the state attorney in the trial. He wouldn't tell the cops, but he opened up a little bit to Tammi Golding.

"We drove around Bahia, up and down the beach."

"Did you stop anywhere, Bob?"

"We had car trouble. On the highway."

In fact, the nursing homes they were supposed to visit that day did report that Dr. Wing had called to say they'd had car trouble. But when questioned about it, he couldn't remember exactly where it had happened and there was no independent corroboration for the story. Tammi knew right away that she didn't want to dwell on it in court, as it would surely sound suspicious to jurors.

"Did you spend the time talking?"

"Yes, that's all we did."

"What did you find to talk about for two whole hours?"

"I'd rather not say."

"Bob," his attorney told him, "you *have* to say. If you won't tell me, I won't put you on the stand, because the prosecutor is going to ask you that, and if you don't answer, the judge is going to command you to answer, and then you'll either have to, or you'll be held in contempt. Look, if you talked romantically, or even if you stopped somewhere and had sex with her, that's a hell of a lot better than leaving the jury to think that the two of you spent the time murdering your wife. So what did you talk about, Bob?"

With a show of great reluctance, Bob Wing finally said, "Our marriages."

"Oh, great," Tammi thought, but she only said, "What did you say about them?"

"Tammi, I really don't want to say this. It's a breech of confidentiality. Artie told me things that she trusted me not to tell anybody else."

"And she wouldn't want you to tell if your life depended on it?"

"You'll have to ask her."

"I will, Bob. What did you say to her about *your* marriage?"

Later, Tammi Golding would remember

262

how haunted his face looked when he answered her. "I told her it was failing. I should never have married Susanna, Tammi, and that's what I told Artie. Maybe I shouldn't have done that, but . . ."

"But you did, and what else did you say?"

"Nothing."

"You didn't tell her why it was a mistake? Why it was failing?"

"No, that would have been a betrayal of Susanna."

"Well, Susanna's dead. So tell me, even if you didn't tell Artie. Why was your marriage failing?"

"It was my fault. I didn't love her. I never did."

"Why did you marry her, Bob?"

His face twisted in what looked like grief and guilt. "I think I let her talk me into it, Tammi. She seemed to love me and she was so kind and good to me, I thought that I could learn to love her, too. Good intentions . . ."

His lawyer said, "I can't put you on the stand, Bob. No way I'm going to let you get up there and say these things so that Tony Delano can twist any which way he wants."

"Don't you have to let me testify if I insist?"

"Yes, but please, please don't insist."

But he did, in the end. Bob Wing insisted that he just had to look the jury members in the eye and tell them he was innocent of adultery and of the murder of his wife. Most people thought it was the suicidal arrogance of a man who could not even imagine that people wouldn't believe anything he said. The jury returned the favor by looking at Bob when the judge read their guilty verdict to him.

Unlike her fellow defendant, Artie McGregor took her lawyer's advice. She did not take the stand in her own behalf. So Tony Delano never got his chance to ask her the same questions. But then, she hadn't answered any of them for Tammi Golding, either, not even in the privacy of the law office, where nobody else would ever know.

"Artie, what did you and Bob talk about that day in the car?"

"I don't remember, Tammi."

"Did you talk about your own marriage?"

"It would be natural to mention Stuart."

"What did you say about him?"

"I don't recall."

"Did Bob discuss his marriage, or Susanna?"

"If he did, it wouldn't be right for me to say."

"Artie! Your life's at stake here. What did you talk about?"

"I don't remember."

"It must have been important for the two of you to skip those nursing homes. I can't even imagine you doing that, Artie. You're usually so dependable when it comes to things like that, so what in the world were you doing with Bob, or talking about with him, that would keep you away from the old folks?"

"I felt bad about that," was Artie's quiet reply.

She never even mentioned car trouble.

At the defense table, Bob Wing and Artemis McGregor sat separated by two attorneys; they rarely looked at one another, and when they did, they looked away so quickly that some observers thought they seemed embarrassed, and other observers thought they were trying not to show what they felt for one another. Mostly Artie sat with her head down, looking angelic, scared, and sad; Bob Wing held his head up, but he frequently flushed or paled, depending on the testimony against them. It was noted by many that he seemed most agonized by any testimony that reflected badly on the woman seated down the table from him, the woman for whom he claimed he did not kill his wife.

When she was acquitted, he wept and looked deeply relieved.

Artemis broke down in tears at that moment, too, a moment that followed his own guilty verdict, which he had absorbed with little change of expression. It was only for her verdict that he wept. And then, for the first time in the trial, she moved past the lawyers, toward him, and put out her right hand to touch his left arm. People standing nearby say that she looked up into his eyes, with her own eyes brimming, and whispered, "I'm sorry, I'm so sorry . . ."

No matter what his claims or her silence, at that pregnant moment Bob Wing and Artemis McGregor looked like two people in love.

Detective Jill Norman — "Norm" — thinks that Stuart McGregor was wrong to think he had watched Bob and Susanna fall in love in the grief group.

"*They* didn't fall in love," Detective Norman scoffs. "*She* did. He fell in love with her inheritance. It was just what he needed for himself, since he was busy turning himself into a saint by giving away almost all of the insurance money from Donna's death. Here came this pretty, lonely, kind of unpolished woman — just ripe for picking — and not only did she come with an inheritance of her own, but if he got married again the church would take out one of those enormous policies on her like they did on Donna. It was a double play for him."

As Antonio Delano, the assistant state attorney would tell the jury with chilling effect in his closing argument, "That grief group was a perfect setup for manipulating and seducing vulnerable women, and the defendant knew it. If Bob Wing had been a spider and those lonely women had been flies, that group could not have been a more deadly trap. Sooner or later, one of them was bound to fall into it. All he had to do was string it and wait. Hold meetings regularly. Get the word out to the community. Attract new widows and divorcees, who are surely among the world's most vulnerable and needy people."

Antonio spread his arms wide toward the jury.

On paper, his closing argument sounds melodramatic, but in the courtroom that day it was so compelling you could hardly breathe for the tension upon hearing it.

"And what did those women find at Sands Gospel Church?" Tony demanded. "Solace in their time of trouble? Oh, yes." This was said with indignant sarcasm. "Did they find an understanding minister to counsel them? Oh, yes. Indeed, they did. Did they find in him a shoulder to cry on, an ear in which to pour their troubles, a font of advice for all the lonely aspects of their lives? Oh, yes. That's what Susanna found when she walked innocently into the trap known as the grief group. With all her sorrow, with all her money, Susanna walked into the trap, and it closed over her."

Then with even greater conviction, the prosecutor turned his final argument toward the other defendant sitting at the table, separated from her alleged lover by their own lawyers. "But even spiders have mortal enemies. Male spiders are smaller, weaker than their mates, and if their mate is a Black Widow, the male himself gets caught in the trap. In this spider's web, ladies and gentlemen of the jury, we had two deadly predators. A perfect match. Perhaps he would not have carried out his awful scheme if Artemis McGregor had not come along to encourage and assist him in it, almost as if they were joined in an evil perversion of wedding vows. 'Till death do us part.' Only it was Susanna's death they sought, so that they would not have to part. We do not know which of them struck the first blow. Or the second, or the twentieth. We do not know which of them first voiced the dreadful idea: 'Let's kill her.' We only know they did it," he intoned, employing one of his boss's favorite lines to use in closing arguments in homicide cases. "We know they are guilty of her murder. Their motive was sex and money, the oldest and most convincing motives of all. Their means was a baseball bat, cruel and effective. And their opportunity was a Friday in August when they were together and Susanna was once again alone and defenseless.

"Please, do not leave her alone now, ladies and gentlemen of the jury. For once in her life, let there be people who care about her. You. And me. There was no one to care about Susanna after her parents died, no one to love her in all those foster homes, or when her first husband passed away. Please, do not leave her alone again.

"Be her friend, by being her advocate along with me.

"Stand up with me and say no! This sad life must not end without some vindication. There must be some justice for this lonely woman who had no one to protect her. Now she has me, which may not be much. But she also has the law, and you, and you have the power — the only power — to stand up for her now. I ask you, on behalf of Susanna, to find them both guilty of her brutal, lonely, terrible death."

It was theater at its best, sincerely meant and delivered, and riveting, if only half successful.

I can't get the damn book out of my head.

Though it beats obsessing about George Pullen's death.

When Antonio Delano calls to say he heard what happened, I recall an earlier comment of his. "Why can't you give it up?" I'd asked him. "This isn't about me!" he'd exclaimed. If all else failed, if he couldn't convince me otherwise that Artie was a killer, he had sarcastically advised me to think about "public safety."

"I should have listened to you, Tony," I tell him over the phone. "If she's the one who killed George, I'll never forgive myself for taking her so lightly. What are the chances of convicting her on this one?"

"About as good as the last time, Marie.

A search warrant hasn't turned up the bag at her house or in their cars. If we can't put her at the scene with some kind of physical evidence, we're going to lose this one, too."

I say nothing, feeling awful.

"Marie, if it's any comfort, you're hardly the only one to underestimate Artemis McGregor. A whole jury did, remember? I'll bet Bob Wing did, too."

"How can somebody look so sweet and do so many good works, yet be so evil? She didn't fool you, Tony. I should have paid attention."

"So should your two friends," he says, gently. "For god's sake, they owned a security company, Marie. They're ex-military. If they couldn't anticipate hazardous duty, how could you?"

But as I hang up from his call, I know that guarding our cul-de-sac hardly prepared George and Bennie for what I led them into. It's many years since Vietnam. They were too old for this job, their skills were too rusty for what I asked of them, even if none of us guessed I was asking it.

Suddenly I feel another emotion arising out of the morass of regret and self-pity I've been struggling in. It's rage. I *hate* her. Hate it that she can kill people with impunity. And I hate the idea that my book is going to let her off, just as the jury did, and only because nobody can seem to prove anything against her. I *hate* it. This is personal now.

When I think about a certain moment in the trial, a moment that turned the verdict in her favor, my skin crawls.

Tammi had put a character witness for Artie on the stand, a nurse from one of the retirement homes that Artie and Bob visited regularly. This young woman from the EverCare Center cried on the stand when she told about one demented old man.

"He doesn't have anybody. No family. No sons or daughters. And he's so sweet. Mrs. McGregor is the only person on earth who ever came to see him. Her and Dr. Wing. But she'd hold his old hands and talk to him as if he could understand her, and he'd just smile and smile. He misses her visits so much! Even though he doesn't know exactly who he's missing, he knows that somebody he loves is gone. I wish she could come back and see him again."

That did it. One juror said afterward, "My mom is in a nursing home for Alzheimer's patients and it takes everything out of me to go see her, and she's my own mother. Anybody who would go visit senile people she doesn't even know has got to be a saint. Nobody like that could ever kill another person."

It makes me feel sick to think about it.

And there's not a damned thing I can do about it.

But Sunday night I wake from a nightmare of being chased and feel in my gut an even more sickening thought: What if we've all been wrong? What if they've never been guilty, they've always been innocent? That's what they've claimed, without any quarter, both of them. What if an innocent man is sitting on death row and an innocent woman is holed up in her house, afraid to go out, pilloried by former friends and by people like me?

Sitting up in bed, I realize the key to that interpretation lies in the very words of my own book that have been haunting me since Friday, when George was killed. Suddenly the admirable qualities of Artemis McGregor and Bob Wing pop into high relief, forcing me to look at them without prejudice: her selfless good works, the high recommendation from that unusual source — her ex-husband — and the way she looks, and conducts herself, like a sweet, kind, modest person. Then there's her reputed lover. But there's no proof of that beyond the infamous phone call and — possibly — the contents of a canvas bag that has never even been established as belonging to either of them. Contrast that, I instruct myself, with what is *missing* from the testimony against either of them: no other allegations of impropriety, no other women coming forward to accuse the handsome minister of sexual advances, not even a hint of infidelity by either one of them. If he's the sexual scoundrel he's made out to be, wouldn't there have been some other hint of it? Think of his dedication to the lives of other people, his crusade to extend the lives of other people, not to end them.

Once I have admitted these thoughts into my consciousness, I am forced to consider the fact that somebody else *could* have placed that bloody bat in Bob Wing's house. Many, many people had access to that foyer. In addition, why would a man so careful about footprints, a man who hid his own and Susanna's bloody clothing so well that it was never found, why would that man leave his handprints all over the murder weapon?

Tammi Golding made some of these points in her closing statement, but the jury — and I and most observers — didn't buy it. Maybe if she'd been able to offer up another suspect — anybody at all — she might have been able to create an aura of reasonable doubt, but she didn't. The jury was left with the murder weapon, the semen, and, worst of all, the lousy alibi, all pointing, reasonably, toward the Reverend.

I can see my way around those pieces of evidence.

But what I can't get around is the overheard conversation. *You've already got a wife and I'm it.* If Tony's right and those three women told the truth, then Bob Wing was having an affair with Artemis and I believe they killed Susanna. Which means I still believe that Artemis struck George Pullen over the head and killed him, intentionally or not.

When I fall asleep again, the nightmares do not return, at least temporarily. By entertaining a fair doubt of my own prejudices, I have granted myself some peace of mind at last. As a result, I wake up feeling more rested, but also filled with even greater resolve to bring some kind of justice to the memories of Susanna and George. I rise from bed, thinking, "There must be *something* else left to investigate, some little thing we've all overlooked until now. There must be." I can think of only two anomalies that have haunted me throughout my involvement in this case and in the lives of these people: one is sex, the other is rings and panthers. And while panthers are elusive creatures, I decide to go hunting for them first, because it feels as if the sex — the passion — is hidden even more deeply in the foliage, if it's there at all.

Susanna

12

On Monday, before I can leave on my hunting expedition, my new research assistant calls to report on what she had been doing for me. It feels like a total non sequitur to hear her talk about the Tobias chapter when I'm focused so intensely on more important things.

"I can't find out anything about the note," Deb Dancer tells me. "There's nothing about it in your file and I checked with a couple of the sheriff's deputies who were there at the time, and they don't remember. You've got a copy of the inventory lists, and it's not on them. I went ahead and called Lyle Karnacki — remember him? Lucy's brother? Allison's uncle who's a Bahia cop? And he said he made them go over the place with a fine-tooth comb, but he doesn't recall ever seeing it. So is it okay with you if I contact Mr. and Mrs. Tobias and ask them if they know?"

This seems so trivial compared to the weight on my heart from George's death. I can barely concentrate on what she's asking, much less give a damn, but I play along because it's not her fault that I'm such an emotional wreck this morning. "Why would they know?"

"They probably don't," she admits. "But I also want to know what happened to that cake tin — remember that? — and I want a description of it for your book."

"I like your attention to the telling detail, Ms. Dancer. Be tactful, all right?"

"Tact is my middle name," she says, sounding strangely like me.

We're just about to hang up when it occurs to me to say, "I ought to warn you that you may not like Allison's parents. I don't know if it comes across in what I wrote about them, but she's an incredible control freak and he's like her slave who'll say anything to keep the peace with her."

"Yeah, I sensed that, plus I read your background notes on them."

"Okay, well, good luck. Let me know how it goes."

"Ms. — Marie?"

"Yes?"

"Are you all right? I'm sorry, but you sound kind of down."

"I am a bit, but you've cheered me up, Deborah." And it's true that her energy has reinfused me with some of my own. "Call any time, okay?"

"Okay," she agrees, sounding pleased and happy.

She didn't mention George Pullen's murder and I don't want to talk about it, so I didn't say anything, either. If she hasn't heard about it at the newspaper where she works, then maybe I'll get lucky. So far, it's been a brief news item, only one of several violent crimes that happened in Bahia on Friday, and not even the "worst" of them. There was a multiple homicide that distracted everybody. So unless some reporter learns that it was connected to the Wing homicide and that a celebrity author was involved, I may escape without the publicity. It's going to be hard enough to report it — confess to it — in my own book. I felt painfully foolish explaining to the Bahia cops why we were there in the first place, although Bennie told me not to feel that way. "Look," he said, even in the midst of his own grief, "we were trying to do what these cops never managed to do — prove once and for all that she's a killer. As far as I'm concerned, George died in the line of duty, trying to do a righteous and necessary thing. Don't apologize for this, Marie, because if you do I'll consider that an insult to his memory."

I pray he's right and not just trying to make himself feel better, too.

But now it's time to corner little Jenny Carmichael and find out if there's anything else she's hiding from the grown-ups. When she and her mother brought their surprises to me, that mischievous slip of a girl made a slip of the tongue and I think I'd better check it out. Besides, they deserve to be told what happened to the bag. If nothing else, it should reassure Anne that she was absolutely right to be afraid of it for her family's sake; although she may also judge that it was a mistake to turn it over to me.

To distract myself from the annoying traffic of Spring Break, I play old interview tapes from my research on Allison Tobias. If I can't do anything profound for Bennie, maybe I can do something small for Deborah by listening for hints about the details that interest her, the note and the cake that Lucy left. A less sympathetic mother I have never met, and Ben Tobias wasn't much better. In my book I tried to put them in the best light I could, because they've suffered enough without my adding gratuitous insults to their grievous injury.

I particularly remember how the landlord hated them.

When I interviewed the old man, he had become a renter himself. After the murder, he told me, the Tobiases sued him and his wife for failing to provide security adequate to protect their tenants. A jury awarded the parents a large verdict that forced the landlords to sell the Hibiscus Avenue house and their other properties and would have confiscated most of what they both earned for the rest of their lives. Rather than allow that, the couple — already in their sixties — retired and lived on their Social Security payments. The old man's wife died three years later, he told me, from "heart."

"There's nothing special to remember about the night she was killed," the old man tells me on the tape of that interview. "No screaming, no unusual commotion, nothing like that. The computer boys came home together real late like they always did. The other girls, they were always so quiet we hardly could hear them on the stairs. Oh, we heard Allison come in, all right. She was drunk, you know, and even quiet drunks are loud. We heard her laugh in the back hall and we figured that must have been when she met up with Stevie. I guess we were both asleep when she went upstairs, 'cause neither the wife nor me heard any of that. We felt just terrible that we helped that boy. Thought we was doing a good deed for a young man needed a fresh start. You don't never want to do a good deed," he tells me, bitterly. "It'll come back on you real bad like it did on us."

After that, I managed to locate one of Allie's friends who had gone drinking with her that night — Emily Rubeck Richards — later a teacher, married, with two kids.

"There isn't a day I don't think about it," she says in that interview. It seemed to me that she still had the earnest appearance of the "good girl" she was in high school. A nervous temperament had turned her into a nonstop talker and she told me more than I needed, or could use, in the book. "Did you know Allie's dad made us leave the funeral? We went in the church with our parents, and Mrs. Tobias saw us and made him come over and tell us we weren't welcome. He said it would upset Mrs. Tobias too much for us to be there, since it was all our fault for taking

Allison out and getting her drunk. It was terrible when he did that in front of everybody at the funeral. I think it was the worst moment of my life, except for when I heard Allie was dead. Gretch never has got over it, I don't think. It's kind of ruined her, but I never believed that, that it was all our fault. My parents felt real bad about Allie, but they were furious at Mr. and Mrs. Tobias for doing that to us. Gretch and I never forced Allie to go or to drink, and it wasn't us who wanted her to be all by herself. She wanted that. What were we supposed to do, force her to let us stay there? We were just kids ourselves, doing what teenagers do. It's *not* our fault, it's that horrible Stevie Orbach's fault. But Mrs. Tobias was always a bitch, so I wasn't all that surprised when she treated us so rotten. Do you know, she used to ground Allie for *weeks* if she got in five minutes late? Weeks! She'd stand at the door and grab Allie and yell, 'Get in here!' She was a trip. We hardly ever went over there. He was nice enough, but kind of a wimp. Whatever Mrs. Tobias said, that was the law. After Allie died, I felt bad for Mr. and Mrs. Tobias — like you would for anybody — but that didn't give them the right to act so mean to Gretchen and me and to hurt our parents' feelings like that."

Emily and the old landlord helped me locate three of the tenants, so now I listen to their interviews, too, fast-forwarding over the extraneous parts. Finally, I go through the painful interview with the parents, but there's nothing on the tape for Deb, just a reiteration of how Lucy set the cake in its tin outside her daughter's door and how, later that night, she taped a note to the door of the house.

This seems like a ridiculously small bit of business to be paying Deborah to research, but I can feel myself getting caught up in it, too. I'm catching from her the bug of obsession that compels a writer to worry some little detail to death. Sometimes entire books can turn on just such a detail that opens the door to greater revelations. Not this time, though. These are just small, human touches to round off a chapter and lend it that verisimilitude that makes readers trust me. It won't hurt, however, to go to the trouble to get it right.

Susanna

13

The seven Carmichaels live in a sweet stucco house that would be roomy for three people but is noisy and crowded with all of them there at one time, which they are when I arrive. Anne's clever warning sign is still propped up on the front porch so it can be seen easily from the street. Herb's mowing the lawn, with two little boys trailing behind him, dragging lawn bags in his wake. Inside, I find three more red-haired children — with uncountable numbers of their buddies — and Anne, unloading more bags of groceries than I thought any person could buy at one time.

"Welcome to Bedlam," she calls to me, from the kitchen to the front door.

I open the screen and go on in.

"What's everybody doing home on a Monday, Anne?"

"Spring break."

That's right. I forget that our own children get a spring break, too; it just *seems*

285

like it's only everybody else's kids who do. Herb's a teacher, so that explains his presence, too. When I start to tell her about the canvas bag — and George — she makes the children leave, and calls their father in to hear it.

"You can take the sign down now," I tell them, at the end.

"My God," Herb says, looking somberly at his wife. "It could have been one of us."

"It could have been you, Herb," she says. "If you'd tried to stop her."

Like me, they're assuming it was Artemis McGregor.

"Mind if I talk to Jenny?" I ask them.

"Tell her what happened," Herb says, looking grim. "Maybe this will scare a little sense and honesty into that girl."

"No!" his wife objects. "She'll blame herself, Herb. Jenny will think that if she hadn't taken the bag and kept it a secret, that poor man might not have been killed. That's a terrible thing for a child to think."

"But it's true."

"She's just a child! Jenny didn't hurt anybody, Herb. That awful woman did, she's the one to blame. Not our Jenny."

Herb may have a point in theory, but his wife's got the right idea, in my opinion.

And there's no way I'm going to lay that burden of guilt on a ten-year-old. They can tell her what they agree to tell her, but I'm staying out of it.

I have a hard time getting Jenny off to myself, because wherever Jenny goes, a horde of other children follow. I don't want to arouse her parent's suspicions and get Jenny into even more trouble with the question I have to ask her. The only way I finally manage it is to exclaim, "Jenny! What have you got in your hair?" Then I grab her by an arm and pull her into the bathroom and lock the door behind us.

"What's in my hair?" she cries, racing to look in the mirror.

I confess there's nothing and sit down on the edge of the tub to talk to her.

"Jenny, when you were at my house, you said something funny."

"What?"

"You meant to say 'ring,' but you said 'rings.' "

She pulls her long red hair down over her face and picks through it as if looking for cooties there. It's a very effective maneuver, since now I can't see her face.

"Jenny?" I reach over and brush her hair back. "Rings?"

"I don't know why I said that, I really don't."

"But you remember saying it, do you? That's interesting. Why would you even remember that unless there was something to it? Look, I'm not mad at you, Jenny, honest, I'm not. And I won't try to get you in trouble, okay? It's just that I really need to know why you said 'rings.' It seemed like a funny kind of mistake."

She scratches her head with both hands in a show of frantic thought.

"Are we locked in here forever unless I tell you?"

That sounds to me like something somebody would say when they're dying to confide or confess something and they're looking for any good excuse to do so.

"Yes," I say, solemnly. "Forever. We'll die in here. We'll have water, so we'll last for a while. But no food. And you're going to get really tired of sleeping in the sink, because I'm taking the bathtub."

She giggles.

"Jenny, please tell me."

I can see that this is a struggle for her. She agonizes over it for a few moments and then she says, "I can't. I promised. I have to talk to Nikki first."

Great. Now how am I going to arrange that? Nikki's mom wants nothing to do with this little terror.

"Okay," I say with more confidence than I feel. "Let's go over there."

"Really?" Her eyes widen, and she looks half scared, half thrilled. "Right now? I get to go see Nikki?"

"If your mom says we can."

"Are you going to tell her why?"

"No, that's our secret, yours and mine."

"What are you going to tell her?"

I have no idea, but I unlock the bathroom door anyway.

Three children are waiting outside. "What'd you have in your hair, Jen?"

We make our escape with a truth, since I wouldn't want to be setting too horrible an example for the kid. "I need to see Nikki today," I tell Anne Carmichael. "And I'd like to take Jenny in the car with me to see if they'll let the girls see each other. Maybe if I'm there, her parents will loosen up a little bit."

Anne seems glad of the idea, but she's afraid of Jenny getting hurt.

"I won't, Mom, I promise."

Anne gives me a stern look as though to say, "*You* promise."

It turns out to be easier than I have any right to deserve.

The Modestos aren't meanies, after all; at least, they're not mean enough to make Jenny sit out in the car and not come into their house. Mrs. Modesto even gives her a little hug, and says, "You look so grown-up!" I think I detect a note of hope in her voice. I tell her that I'm collecting a little more information for my book, which is true, and I promise not to upset the girls by making them relive the worst moments of that horrifying day.

"May I talk to them by themselves?" I ask her.

"Let's go to my room!" Nikki offers.

The girls are shy around each other for about ten seconds. Then intense giggling, hugging, and chattering breaks out. They happily lead me to Nikki's cubbyhole of a bedroom while they catch up on each other's toys, friends, lives. I feel happy just being around these two cutie-pies. Best friends reunited, it's great. Maybe if I had kids I wouldn't have done this, wouldn't have sabotaged Nikki's parents like this. But my excuse is that I don't know any better, so I get to play God for a day.

Jenny introduces the topic of our visit by

busily whispering in Nikki's ear. "Psst, psst, psst," is all I hear as they madly whisper back and forth. Nikki, it seems, needs a bit of persuading.

"Okay," she says, at last, looking at me. "But you got to promise not to tell, Ms. Lightfoot, you've really really got to promise, and you've got to really mean it, because I'd be in really really big trouble if my mom finds out."

"Me, too," Jenny asserts.

There's sure a lot of promising going on today.

"Cross my heart," I tell them, and demonstrate it.

"It's in my backpack," Nikki says, wide-eyed and still whispering. "Do you want to see them now?"

Them?

"Please."

"Okay, but close your eyes first."

I obey, and as my eyes are closed I hear excited whisperings and the rasp of a zipper opening. Then I feel something soft plopped into my lap.

"You can open your eyes now," Nikki says.

I do that, and then I look down and see a black velvet pouch bag.

"May I open it?"

"Yes!" They giggle and squeal and jump up and down in anticipation.

I stick two fingers down in the bag and push the sides of it back and then I turn it upside down, dumping the contents into my lap.

"Oh, my God," I whisper.

The girls are besides themselves with delight at my reaction.

There are seven wedding and engagement rings in my lap.

There are two sets of women's engagement and wedding rings and three that look like wedding bands for a man. With the one that the crime scene unit found on the day of the murder and the one that Jenny gave me earlier, that makes nine rings found at the scene of a murder. I might have expected many things, but never this, not even after Jenny's telltale slip of the tongue.

"Where were they?" I ask the girls, letting them see how impressed I am.

"In the tower," Jenny answers proudly. Then it sinks in that they're not going to get to keep them. "Are you going to take them?"

"I have to, girls. They may be evidence in a murder case."

They nod, sadly understanding. But

their material loss is greatly ameliorated by the fact that each has got her best friend back.

"Nikki," I say, "I thought you didn't go up into the tower."

"Oh, I didn't! Jenny gave them to me."

What a generous gesture, I'm thinking, for Jenny to keep the boring old boat bag with its mundane contents and to give the glamorous, glittery rings to her pal. But canny Jenny quickly dashes any such idealization of herself.

"Yeah. I was afraid my mom would find out."

"My mom would never search my room," Nikki says.

"She must trust you a lot," I surmise.

Nikki, the quiet, timid one, grins. "I don't know. But I always keep it clean so she won't have any excuse to mess with my stuff."

The girls giggle, and I am left with the impression that in my manuscript I made Nikki Modesto a little too good to be true. Like everybody else, I fell for those big brown innocent eyes that are now dancing with even more mischievous glee than Jenny Carmichael's blue eyes are.

"You two are a pair," I inform them.

They fling themselves at me, and I get

sandwiched in a furious hug.

"How did you end up with one ring, Jenny?" I ask her.

"Oh, when I found them?" she says. "I took two of them out and put them on, but one of them dropped off my finger. Nikki let me keep the other one, since I let her have all the rest."

"Wait a minute. Are you saying this pouch was in the canvas bag?"

"Oh, yeah," she says, confidentially. "It was all there."

My heart gives a lurch at that moment, because I am thinking: *What's Artemis going to think when she opens the bag and her rings aren't there? And, more urgently, what's she going to do?*

It's great, it's sweet that the girls are back together. But now I'm left with their strange and mysterious treasure. Nine rings. Just like in J.R.R. Tolkien's classic trilogy of fantasy novels with its famous poem with that ominous last line . . . *"One ring to find them all, and in the darkness bind them."*

It strikes me that the rings provide me with the perfect bait to go fishing again, but not so carelessly as last time. In fact, forget fishing. This time I will set something more like a bear trap. And nobody's going to get hurt. It's just my reputation that may take a beating.

"Deb?" Using my cell phone in my car, I catch her at work, at the Bahia Beach newspaper offices. "How would you like to have an exclusive story about a murder that happened in this city last Friday night?"

Susanna

14

There are several interviews left on the tape in my car's stereo, and so, on my way to meet Deb at the *Sun-Journal*, I play the next one. It begins with me asking defense attorney Tammi Golding the same question I asked her client, Bob Wing.

"Why Steven Orbach, Tammi? Out of all the killers on death row, why would you and Bob and the church pick him to save?"

Her answer is more practical, if not necessarily any more convincing than Bob Wing's was. "Because it was a rush to judgment, Marie. Consider: a young woman gets killed. There's a known murderer on the premises. The cops are over-eager, especially since the victim is related to one of their own. Voilà: they've got their man."

"Well, lord, they'd be remiss if they *didn't* suspect him, Tammi," I hear myself say on the tape. "Wouldn't they?"

"Sure, any reasonable person might have

suspected Stevie, but strange things do happen, you know. It is possible to have a convicted murderer on the premises of a crime he didn't do. And last I checked, in this country you still aren't supposed to be convicted for a crime you didn't do, no matter how numerous or heinous the previous ones you did do. And every citizen ought to be grateful for that. Or some time when they're in Kmart they could find themselves arrested for a crime just because they happened to be standing there when one is committed, and the cops run them through the computer and find out they have a previous arrest on a parking ticket. 'Ah-ha,' the cops say, 'here's a proven criminal, let's arrest her for this one, too.' That's not the way it's supposed to be. There is, theoretically, a presumption of innocence until proven guilty."

"Didn't they prove that Stevie killed her?"

"They may think they did. We don't."

"So, basically, you think Stevie Orbach is in jail because he killed his mother," I say slowly, trying to understand what she's telling me. "You think that because he did that, his guilt in Allison's death was just assumed. And that since they couldn't keep him in prison on the one murder, because he was a juvenile at the time, they'd just keep him on the other charge. Well, Tammi, a lot of people wouldn't object to that very much; that'd be just fine with them. A guy kills his mother, he shouldn't get out anyway. That's how their thinking goes. He gets arrested and sentenced to death for a later murder he didn't commit . . . so what?"

"I hope these are rhetorical questions, Marie." On the tape, I can hear a wry smile in her voice. " 'So *what*,' you ask? So is this still America or not?"

"I believe it is, even here in Florida. But, Tammi, it's also true that in America, if you've got the evidence, you'll likely win the case. Regardless of whether the cops rushed it . . . didn't they prove it, ultimately?"

"Reasonable people could disagree."

"Wasn't it his semen?"

"Yes, it was."

"So he raped her."

"Not necessarily, Marie. I will stipulate that they certainly had sex."

"She was drunk, Tammi. You call that consent?"

"I'm not calling it anything, including rape. We have semen, but no sign of struggle or injury."

"But his hair and fiber —"

"All over her. Yes. That happens when people have sex," she says, dryly. "But they never found any of his hair or any fiber in her apartment, and that's where she died."

"Really? Not in his rooms?"

"No. Really."

"How'd the prosecution get around that, Tammi?"

"They didn't have to. He had some screwy defense attorney who allowed Stevie to allude to his previous conviction, so then the prosecution could pounce on it."

"But he did it as a juvenile. Can that be revealed in court?"

"That's been one of our grounds for appeal, but we always get turned down on that, because the higher courts say it didn't turn the verdict. They say the preponderance of the evidence would have convicted him anyway."

"Tammi, my mind registers what you're saying, but I'm still snagged back there on the dead mother. Stevie is one hell of an unsympathetic cause célèbre."

"American justice is built on protecting the least among us."

"That's what your minister told me, too, in his way."

Again, I hear a smile in her voice. "In his way, yes."

"But what about Allison's poor parents, Tammi? They just want Stevie to get what they believe he justly has coming to him. This crusade of yours just kills them."

Her tone is acid. "I hear that crap all the time in death-penalty cases. People whine, 'But what about the family? They'll feel better when he's dead.' My answer to that is — okay, then let's kill him today. And then we discover tomorrow that he didn't do it. So how is that going to make the family feel, hm? Where's their vaunted peace of mind *then?* Where's the comfort in knowing that they pressed for the execution of an innocent man . . . *and* . . . that whoever really killed their loved one is still at large. I'd like somebody to explain to me how *that* will make a family feel better."

"Stevie's no innocent, not really."

"Let me tell you something, Marie. I know of a study done of kids who've killed a parent. In the cases that were analyzed of kids up to their late teens, they couldn't find a single incident that wasn't preceded by years of severe child abuse. Not one, unless there were drugs involved, or the kid was older. You think young kids kill their parents for fun? Casually? For no reason? Kids *love* their parents, in spite of everything; they're dependent on their parents and they'll defend their parents; they'll fight to go back to bad parents, just because that's the only mom or dad they've got. It has to be horrible at home before a kid will murder a parent, Marie. Listen, Stevie was fourteen when he killed his mother. She was a known abuser in a big way. Maybe he's a monster as a result of that, although I personally don't think so. I think he's a young man who killed the sadistic guard of his own personal prison camp. Lots of prisoners of war might have killed their guards if they'd had a chance, and we'd throw them a ticker-tape parade. We know they're not a danger to anybody else in society. So maybe Stevie didn't kill Allison, and wouldn't ever have killed anybody but his mother."

"But the sex . . ."

"She was seventeen and drunk. Stevie was twenty-one, and he'd also been drinking that night. It makes them young and horny and stupid, but it doesn't mean he killed her."

"Okay, then who killed her?"

"*That* is what the cops were supposed to find out."

"What does Bob's arrest do to your efforts on Stevie's behalf?"

She sighs, and it's quite audible on the tape. It's an uncharacteristic gesture of discouragement on the part of this normally indefatigable attorney. "It's over. We haven't quite exhausted all of our legal appeals, but we're out of money in our defense fund. I'm working nearly for free, but there are a lot of other expenses. Artie would throw in some money, but her husband says they've got her legal defense to pay for. I can't argue with that, since I'm one of the ones they're paying. Plus, the death-penalty committee at the church voted to divert the funds away from Steve to Bob. Against Bob's furious objections, I might add. Before this happened, Bob was supposed to see the governor to plead our case for Stevie, but that's dead, too. Name me a governor — a politician — who would even be seen shaking his hand now and I'll show you somebody who'll lose his next election. Or hers."

"What about the other death-penalty projects in the country?"

"They've got their own backlog of cases."

"So it's over for Stevie?"

"Notwithstanding a miracle, yes."

"Please forgive me for asking an infuriating question, Tammi, but how do you feel about that?"

She doesn't snap at me as she might do. "I feel . . ." She stops, then starts again. "I feel guilty. Guiltier than Stevie, that's for damned sure. And as a citizen of this state, so should you."

"If some supporter of the death penalty had thought this up, and murdered Susanna, and framed Bob, they could hardly have come up with a better way to shut you down, could they, Tammi?"

The tape plays her bitter laughter. "Don't think I haven't lain awake considering that possibility, Marie. In one of my more desperate moments when I was preparing for trial I even thought about floating that in front of the jury."

"Just out of a general philosophical curiosity, what's it going to take to end the death penalty in this country, do you think? The death of a provably innocent person?"

"That's what they say, but personally I think it will take more than that. I think most people don't care if an evil person gets killed by mistake. They're just glad he's dead and that he can't hurt anybody anymore. Justice be damned, they'll say, this is a higher justice at work. So if Ted

Bundy, say, had *not* been guilty of the murders for which we killed him, who gives a shit? He killed plenty of other girls. He's better off dead and we're better off with him dead. Oh, there's the question of the *real* killer, but that's another story.

"No," she said, "the kind of case I think we need — God forgive me — is the execution of a person who never did anything wrong. And as crummy as this sounds, it's probably going to have to be a white person, probably a white man, specifically. A good white man would be the ideal innocent person to execute by mistake. *That* would change things."

"Like Bob Wing?"

"God help us, yes. When we inject our three different chemicals into him on the day he dies, we *will* be executing an innocent man, Marie. Trust me on that. But it won't make any difference if I can't prove it."

"If somebody else confessed to the crime," I suggest.

"Which is going to happen any day now," she retorts, "I'm sure."

"Well, at least you got one of your clients off."

There's a silence on the tape and in my car all those months later, I think I remember a certain guarded look on the lawyer's face. Even at the time, I wondered if she really believed in Artie's innocence as much as she believed in Bob's. "I'll be honest, Marie. It's not so much that I got her off as it is that without any physical evidence Tony Delano didn't get it on."

"You're glad she was acquitted, though."

"Of course!" It comes so quickly that it sounds forced. "You know what they say about half a loaf . . ." She leaves the rest unspoken . . . *is better than none.*

"Tammi, the evidence against Bob is so strong. And yet I get the impression that you really do believe he didn't do it. What is it that convinces you in the face of all that evidence?"

"I believe him," she says, simply but with conviction ringing in her voice. "I believe that they weren't having an affair, I believe that he didn't place that baseball bat in his house, I believe he didn't rape or kill his wife. I know him and I know he couldn't ever do those things."

Well, lawyers have been known to be wrong about their clients.

"Tammi, why don't you sound as convincing when you talk about her innocence as when you talk about his?"

"I don't?" She sighs. "Oh, dear. Off the

record? Maybe it's because, going into the case, I didn't know her very well, and you know what? I still don't. She didn't cooperate very well, Marie. If you can describe a woman as the strong, silent type, that's her, even though everybody says she used to be the life of the party. Well, she's not anymore, let me tell you. I think she's hiding something, and she may go to her grave with it before anybody finds out what it is."

I have pulled up into the newspaper's parking lot several minutes ago, but I've been sitting here in the sun so I could hear the whole interview. I didn't interview Stevie Orbach for my book because it wasn't his story and I didn't need him in it. It was just one chapter, after all. But now I'm feeling an urge to interview him, too. Maybe I could add a scene to my book, something about what it's been like for him to have people devoted to saving him, and to have his "savior" end up there on death row with him. It might give me an unusual glimpse into Bob Wing's soul; maybe even the key to his passion for his lover, whom he may never see again. I'll have to do this interview myself, though. Deb's too young and inexperienced to be sent off to chat up rapists.

Then it hits me: barring a reprieve, Orbach will be dead in five days.

If I'm going to see him, I've got to do it now.

"Mr. and Mrs. Tobias have agreed to see me at eight o'clock tomorrow night," Deb tells me before she interviews me. She has on a godawful dotted skirt-and-blouse combination today, with the same clunky shoes. "I'm going up there tomorrow night, but I'm not so sure anymore that it's a good idea."

"Why not?"

She makes a grimace of sadness. "I think she's lost it. All the trauma and grief, or Alzheimer's, or whatever it is, she doesn't seem to have her mental faculties about her anymore. I told her that I wanted to find out about the note she left and about the cake tin, if she didn't mind, and she said I could see them if I wanted to! Like that's even possible. I didn't say anything, but it kind of shocked me, you know?"

"I can imagine," I say, sympathetically.

"When he got on the phone he practically told me she's crazy."

"You don't have to do this, Deb."

"No, I still want to. Maybe he'll know something."

It sounds like a wild-goose chase to me, but then, that's often the nature of this work.

Deborah's editor is excited about the story I'm giving them and tells us it will run in tomorrow morning's paper. It won't use Artie McGregor's name, because I haven't given it to them. It won't say, specifically, that I have seven of the nine rings, the other two being in the possession of the police department, because I haven't given that information to them, either. What I'm pretty sure it will say is that George and I planted in the house some property that belonged to somebody who might have been involved in the murder of Susanna Wing, and that we wanted to see who might show up to collect it. I'm leaving Bennie's name out of it. If Deb wants to bring in the name of Artemis McGregor on her own, that's her choice. I'm sure she'll quote me as saying, something like, "We don't know if the person who killed George is the same person who took the bag, but the bag did disappear from the house. They didn't get everything that was originally in it, though." If Deb had followed up by asking what that was, I'd probably have told her. But she didn't ask. Some other time, I'd better give her a few tips about interviewing techniques.

★ ★ ★

By late afternoon, Franklin DeWeese, in his role as state attorney for Howard County, has arranged for me to interview Stevie Orbach tomorrow, pulling some very high strings to get me in on short notice. I am aware this should have required a month of requests, in triplicate, working their way through multiple layers of bureaucracy. I'm not questioning his means, I'm just grabbing this chance he has opened up for me.

"May I see you tonight?" Franklin asks me.

If it's Franklin, it must be Monday. This morning he drove his kids to their preschools and now he's a bachelor again.

"Sure," I tell him.

"You want to eat out?"

My heart leaps at this unexpected capitulation. "Great. What time? Which restaurant?"

"I meant out on your patio," he says, smoothly. "I could bring over some steaks. We could fire up the grill."

And I could throw you on it, I'm thinking as I repeat, "Sure."

His own work keeps him at his office late, and I don't want to stay up late, because I have a long way to travel tomorrow and I have to get up early to do it. So we settle for leftovers in the kitchen, saving the rest of what little time we have together for the bedroom. This is fine with me, as I am in need of the comfort of his body against mine. Not only that, but I want to keep my vow: if these are our last nights together, they'll be memorable, by God. But as luck would have it, afterward he's the one who goes right to sleep and I am left staring at the ceiling, until I quietly get up and go outside.

The night air is nearly as comforting as he was.

I stretch out in a chaise lounge, melting into it.

Like nowhere else I've ever been, the air in South Florida is soft, so soft. After my last book tour, riding home from the airport late of a winter's night, I opened a window in the backseat, closed my eyes and felt the soft air pat my face like a lover. It's always like that: when I return from other places, Florida whispers to me, *Welcome home, Marie.*

It had been a long tour, that one. Sixteen cities in two weeks. Hard air in all of them. But then, riding home . . . and now, sitting here by myself in the starlit darkness, the air is soft as a caress. On that tour, I was in cities north and south, east and west, and everywhere I went I compared it to here. I couldn't help it, I always do. "We have nicer palm trees than you do, California," I'd think, in my chauvinistic way. Theirs are spindly, the leaves are sparse. Ours are thick with fronds, thick as shrubs, magnificent if you like palms. Not everybody does. Not everybody likes South Florida. I love it, love it. I don't care what other people say. I am unabashedly its lover and it is mine, always here for me, always soft, receptive, listening, murmuring to me.

There's a cushioned porch chair across from me, the one where Deborah Dancer sat, and it looks starkly empty in the moonlight, as if to remind me of the obvious — that while I may have a lover in my bed tonight, I am mostly alone. I don't feel lonely, though, except lately when Franklin is with me.

"I think it's over," I tell the empty chair.

I came out here, my Florida, because I couldn't sleep.

But only a few minutes with you, my Florida, and now I can lean into this air, this soft air, and sleep for days. I want my bed now. I want my open windows. I want to be sleeping naked and alone between clean sheets if I cannot walk into the daylight with the man who sleeps there now.

Susanna

15

When I drive past the guardhouse at the entrance to my residential enclave, my heart aches. There is a stranger there now, a young man who doesn't know me. We wave good morning at each other and I'm glad he can't see my eyes behind my sunglasses.

It will feel good to get on the road and drive a long way today.

Florida stockpiles all of its male death-row inmates at the Union Correctional Institute in Raiford and at the Florida State Prison Main Unit in a town aptly named Starke. Both Bob Wing and Stevie Orbach are in FSP, where the death chamber also happens to be. Starke is thirty-five miles north of Gainesville, so I have about five hours of driving from Bahia. To get there in plenty of time for my 2:00 p.m. interview, I leave home at seven in the morning, with the sun and the ocean to my right. By the time I get home tonight, only one of them will still be there.

He still looks exactly like Allison Tobias's grieving dad described him: a big, muscular guy, though now he's got a prison pallor. He is by no means the first condemned man I've ever met with just before his execution. I always find it beyond strange to look at, to talk to, a completely healthy, alert human being who knows he will be dead in a few days.

This man now has less than four days to live.

There are pickets outside the prison, there is a murmur of protest in the world over his impending death, but no more than there is over the execution of any American prisoner at any time. As reported in the media, and as I observed it outside, it seems merely reflexive, the usual response of people who are opposed to the death penalty as a matter of principle, no matter the crime, the victim, the killer. It feels to me as if everybody knows that this man's execution is a foregone conclusion.

We're separated by bulletproof Plexiglas in a stark, gray clean booth, and just as it was in my interviews with Bob Wing, there is a perforated metal circle between us through which we can converse. His muscular arms rest on the counter that hides him below the waist; his long, blunt fingers are entwined with each other, his wrists are in handcuffs. His hair is cropped so close he looks near-bald. His face has that sculpted look that some athletes get, and he looks scrupulously clean. Death-row inmates are allowed showers every other day; he appears to take regular advantage of the opportunity.

I don't underrate the self-discipline it has taken for this man to keep himself in this condition on death row, where the men rarely get out of their six-by-nine-foot cells. There are windows just across the corridor from the men's cells, letting in some daylight. Orbach doesn't have any extra freedom of movement. And he's not popular. I've asked. He engenders a certain fear, or call it respect. Looking at him now — at his strength, at his careful expressionless face with its wary watchful eyes — I know I would never mess with him. I can understand why neither guards nor inmates want to, either.

"Thank you for seeing me," I say carefully.

He nods, watching me, waiting, even more wary than I. I know that, like me, he's been up since before dawn; on death row, breakfast is served at five; he'll get his third and last meal of the day between four and four-thirty.

"I was going to ask you if I can call you Stevie, but that name doesn't fit you, does it? What do you prefer?"

"Steve."

"May I ask you questions for my book?"

He lifts an eyebrow, lowers a corner of his mouth, shrugs almost imperceptibly.

"You look athletic. Did you play sports?"

"I wanted to." His voice is firm, a businesslike tone between baritone and bass. "Football."

Sometimes, interviewing killers, there'll be a moment that catches me off guard and I am struck by the "if only" of their lives. Call it sentimental, but there can be a sadness about it that catches me unawares. I have one of those moments now, realizing he was a boy who finished high school in prison, whose life story is a diary of pain, both his own and that which he inflicted on others. For just a moment, I have to look down; I can't continue. I don't let on to anybody that killers can break my heart as much as their victims do. It's not politically correct to say that, or to feel that. But I know, as no one else can, that I couldn't do what I do, write what I write, without some feeling for them. Sure, I know: it's easy to feel that when they're caged. My sympathy would vanish if any one of them came after me or somebody I loved.

I remember Allison Tobias and look back up at him.

If he noticed my lapse, he doesn't let on. One by one, I go down my list.

"Did you kill your mother?"

"Yes."

"Why?"

"It was her or me."

"Did she abuse you?"

He shrugs his massive shoulders. "Who cares? I took care of it."

"Did you ask anybody for help, before you killed her?"

"What do *you* think?" he asks, with a hard edge of sarcasm.

Having read the literature, I say, "I'd guess that you did. Teachers, maybe a social worker or two, possibly a cop, or a neighbor, maybe some relatives. Right?"

He nods, and I see in his eyes that I've won a small point here. Still going by the literature, I say, "And either they didn't believe you, or they tried to help and it made things worse, or they were too timid to do anything. I suppose you tried running away, but they caught you and either punished you by placing you in a juvenile center, or they just took you back to her . . ."

His only movement is a slight twitching of his eyelids. I could go on summarizing the probable childhood of this man I've never met before, but I'm not here to talk about his torturer of a mother.

"Did you kill Allison?"

"No."

"Did you rape her?"

He hesitates. "Maybe. She was drunk and I took advantage. Is that rape?"

"If you have to ask, then it probably is."

He nods, though I don't get any sense of agreement.

"You want to say anything else about that, Steve?"

I watch him as he thinks. "She cried afterward and she said she shouldn't have done it. She got up and got dressed and left and I never saw her again."

"You didn't follow her upstairs."

"No."

"Did you hear anybody who did?"

"No. I heard a lot of people — the other tenants — going up and down at weird hours all the time, every night almost. So I didn't pay attention that night. Besides, I was out cold. Asleep after that."

"Who do you think killed her?"

"I've thought about that." For the first time the slightest hint of a smile reaches his eyes and mouth. "I've thought about that a lot. Whoever it was, she had to let them in. Either that, or they were already inside her room. Like I said, she was drunk and she was crying. One of the other tenants or the landlord, they could have asked her what was wrong, pretended to comfort her, got inside her apartment, like that. I don't think she felt real attractive. A girl like that, she might have let anybody in."

I hadn't expected him to talk this much. Or, rather, I hadn't known what to expect. In an odd way, he's almost easier to talk to than Bob Wing is, because there's no charm to confuse things. He speaks in a cold, clear, simple manner. My sense is that he's pent-up with words to explain himself. This may even be a kind of release for him.

I feel as if I'm seeing — hearing — the inside of his thoughts and fantasies. Are they merely justifications that he's made up to cover his own guilt? Or are these his ideas of the truth?

"If you ever got out of here," I say, feeling cruel, "what would you do?"

His eyelids twitch again, small muscles he can't quite control.

"I don't care to say," he says.

"You get to talk much to Bob Wing?"

He quirks the side of his mouth, giving himself a sarcastic expression. "Yeah, we talk about 'justice.' "

"What's he like?"

"What's he *like?* Look at him, for Christ's sake, listen to him. Look at the work he's done for sons a bitches like me. He's a righteous man. And an innocent one. He shouldn't be in here, neither one of us should."

"What about Mrs. McGregor?"

"What *about* her?"

"Is she guilty?"

"No way."

"Does he miss her?"

That gets me a cold stare. "He misses all of his friends."

"How's he doing in here?"

"If you want to know, ask him yourself. Listen, you trying to get me to tell you stuff about him, I'll tell you one thing. If they execute Bob, then you can blame that murder on me." For the first time, I see a hint of passion in his expression. His jaw and his lips have tightened. "He should have left my case alone, I've told him that. From the beginning, I told him, don't be a fool, stay the fuck away from me. I'm death for anybody who touches me. I told him. I warned him. He can't say I didn't. And now he's in here because of me." Suddenly he leans forward and whispers intensely at me. "You write that in your book. That they went after him, that they framed him, to keep him from springing me. He's here because of me and he's going to die because of me. You tell those bastards that, you tell them that I know, even if nobody else does."

"What is it you know, Steve?"

"What I just said."

"But why would they do that?"

He looks contemptuous. "Because somebody killed that cop's niece. They weren't going to stop till they pinned it on somebody, and I was available, wasn't I? I was a cockroach down in the basement, that's all I was to them. They didn't look any further. Why look for anybody else when they already had a real live killer right there on the premises. And they're going to go after anybody who gets in the way of executing me. That's the way it works. Welcome to the real world. Bob Wing was a pain in the ass to everybody who wants me dead, so when they got a chance to get rid of him, they did it the easy way, just like they did to me."

"Do you think he killed his wife?"

"Yeah, he killed her like I killed Allison."

And what am I to make of that statement? Take it as pure sarcasm, or as a disguised confession of truth?

"Fuck it," he says, turning his body away from me. "Nobody gives a damn, nobody ever will. I'm a piece of trash to the world and so is he. Just a couple of sacks of garbage they're going to set out at the curb. Fuck it. Forget it."

But those aren't Steve Orbach's last words to me.

Before he leaves the cubicle, he leans close one last time to breathe into the circle these words: "Watch your step. People who get involved in my life get dead in their own life. If you get hurt it's your own fault. I'm not taking responsibility for it. Stay away from this, let it die. Let them kill me. That's what Bob should have done, and he didn't, and now they're going to kill him, too."

I stay seated a little while after he has gone, pretending to finish my notes. The truth is, I'm too disturbed to get up and leave yet. He accused law enforcement of framing Bob Wing — and, indirectly, Artie McGregor — in order to halt the effort on Orbach's death-penalty appeals. It's the

Howard County Sheriff's Department, the Lauderdale Pines Police Department, and the Bahia Beach Police Department that he's talking about. God knows he wouldn't be the first convict to yell "frame-up," and it used to be that nobody paid any attention. But lately in this country there have been so many publicized and proven cases of that very thing in the criminal so-called justice system that it's much harder to deny and ignore them.

There's no denying the cops hate Bob Wing and Steve Orbach.

In Bahia, they even keep a poster counting down the days until Steven Orbach's execution. They're not interested in any late evidence that might suggest the presence of somebody else in the mansion where Susanna Wing was killed. And the police chief is eager to get his hands on my book before it's in print. Is that to please his wife, as he claimed? Or is it to make sure that I tell these stories the way the cops want them told?

It's true that when Bob was arrested, the campaign to save Steve Orbach hit a wall, and they were his last, best, only hope.

So, is this a condemned man who'll say anything to save himself? But even if he is, it's still possible the cops "rushed to judgment," as Tammi said. They might have been honest, but prejudiced. What if they *were* too quick to grab Orbach just because he was a natural suspect? What if they didn't frame Bob Wing but were just a little too quick to arrest him, too?

"No," I say out loud. No. Even if you discount the baseball bat, even if you claim somebody else put it there; even if you claim that he and Artemis were telling the truth about their infamous two-hour drive in her car, there's no way around that telephone conversation the women overheard. The minister was screwing around on his wife. And she had a million-dollar life insurance policy on her life and he'd nearly gone through all the money he'd inherited from his first wife's death and how was he going to continue to look like the local saint if he didn't have money to spend on his pet causes?

No, he did it; he had to have done it.

Because if he didn't, who did? Not just a stranger, no way. It wasn't a stranger who used that baseball bat to kill her and then put it back in their hallway. It was either Bob Wing, or somebody close to them. But it had to be Bob Wing. It has to be, because of the affair, because of the money, and because the evidence points to him and to nobody else, except possibly her.

Orbach's desperate, that's all, and grabbing at straws.

I do know one thing: I will never again think of him as "Stevie."

Upon leaving a prison — any prison — the sunshine always feels so good on my face, and so does the fresh air. I savor the comparative quiet, the taste of freedom on my tongue and the muscularity of it in my body as I stride away from all those locked doors. Sometimes it makes me feel as if I just want to keep walking, just to prove I can and that nobody can stop me.

Today, as I step outside, the sun stabs my eyes, but who cares?

As I traverse the parking lot, I glance back over my shoulder at the red brick administration building, wondering if we were taped or monitored. I've asked before, at this and other prisons, and I've never quite believed it when they told me no.

I take my keys out to unlock my car, trying not to touch the door, because it's stinging hot. As I stand there, the key half in and half out of the lock, I am struck, as if by lightning, by two of the wildest, most appalling thoughts I've ever had. Maybe it's the influence of what Orbach said to me in there, but whatever it is, I am momentarily paralyzed with the shock of my own epiphanies, if that's what they are. The next second, I'm frantic to get inside my car, to my cell phone, and I turn all thumbs doing it. Finally, I'm in and dialing Deb Dancer's work number at the newspaper.

"Deb's out for the whole day," I'm told, "on a story."

"Can I reach her?"

"You could leave a message on her voicemail."

I do that, saying, with as much urgency as I can force into my voice, "Deb, it's Marie. Do not go to see Ben and Lucy Tobias without talking to me first. Even if you have to miss the appointment. Don't do it until you've checked with me. I think it could be dangerous. I'm not kidding. Don't go."

Then I call her pager and hope she will either call in for her messages or call me back when she sees the page, and that she'll do it in plenty of time.

Then I act on my second insane thought, by calling Tammi Golding at her law firm. When she says hello, I say, "Tammi, when I interviewed you several months ago, you said you thought the death penalty in this country wouldn't be abolished until a provably upstanding, innocent person gets executed. You believe that Bob Wing is innocent. I don't know about that, because even if you could account for the evidence against him, even if you went so far as to say it was planted by somebody else, there's still not one single thing that points to another killer. Not unless it's Artie herself, and why would she set Bob up when it meant she would be arrested, too? But let's assume you're right. Let's say that he's innocent. What I do believe is that I've never met anybody who cares as passionately about abolishing the death penalty as he does. We both know he's probably going to be executed. So, Tammi . . ."

I take a breath, then just say it.

"Tammi, if he knew of exonerating evidence, would he say so?"

There's a silence. And then she gasps. "Oh, my God in heaven, Marie."

"Would he sacrifice himself for the sake of the cause?"

"Sweet Jesus, he might. But the world would have to find out that he really was innocent."

"Yes, after he died. Might he leave that evidence somewhere it could be found after his execution?"

"Not at the church," she says, sounding as frantic as I felt a few minutes ago. "Too many people going through his things there. His home. His private papers, that's where it would be if it does exist. Marie, could you meet me there? Will you help me look?"

"Why don't you just ask him?"

"If he's really planning something like this, he'll never tell me so."

"Give me that address again and tell me when to meet you."

"Shit, I've got to be in court the rest of this afternoon. How about tomorrow morning, Marie? Early, like around six, is that too awful for you?"

"No, I'll be there."

"Jesus, Marie," she says, and laughs a little, "I don't know whether to hope you're right or you're wrong. If you're wrong, he dies. If you're right, I can get him off, but I've got a lunatic for a client."

"I wouldn't be a lawyer for anything," I tell her.

"You're wise," she says and hangs up.

Only then do I leave the parking lot. As I drive out, under the arching sign with the capital letters that spell out Florida State Prison, I feel dizzy from the heat and from my own precipitous actions.

The rest of the long drive home I am anxiously waiting for Deborah to call me. Periodically I try calling her again but never raise her. I call Information and get her home phone, try that, leave a message, get nowhere with it. Why doesn't she answer her page? Isn't that what the damned things are for? When she doesn't, with every hour I drive south, a fear builds in me that brings back all the worst moments of the night that George Pullen died. Oh, Lord, please, don't make me responsible for another death of somebody who is only trying to help me. Finally, and only as a last resort, I place a call to Detective Lyle Karnacki at the Bahia Beach Police Department, but what I have to suggest to him makes him so angry that he slams his phone down in my ear.

I can't think of another cop who will want to hear what I have to say.

When I call Franklin and lay it out for him, he says exactly what I'd expect a prosecutor to say. "You're dreaming, Marie." He's not offensive or condescending when he says it, not at all. But just as Tammi Golding is convinced of her man's innocence, so Franklin takes for granted that his side is almost always right. "Stevie's guilty as sin."

"But what if — just what if — he isn't, Franklin? What would you advise me to do?"

"I'd say be careful and I'd tell you to protect the evidence. But I still say you're dreaming up a little extra plot for your book."

"I hear you."

It doesn't offend me. You can't blame him for sounding unconcerned. He trusts the system, because it's his system. But I'm not like him. I'm an outsider, constantly looking in at that system he loves so much, and not everything I see in it — nor everyone — inspires my trust.

So I can't get a cop to help me, and my very own personal prosecutor thinks I'm dreaming. But that isn't going to stop me. Maybe nobody's life depends on whether or not I persevere, but maybe — just maybe — it does.

Susanna

16

Ben and Lucy don't live in the same house where they raised their daughter. By the time I interviewed them for my book, they had taken some of the money from their various lawsuits and bought themselves a much larger home on the water. It's not on the ocean but rather, on one of the narrow dredged canals that stripe South Florida. This house is painted pink; it's big but not pretty, being all angles and juttings that translate into high ceilings in the interior of it. Lucy has furnished the rooms with over-stuffed, upholstered pieces so that even the largest of the spaces feels cramped. Ben has a pool table in the family room, but it stays covered most of the time. He told me he never plays. She told me that's because he'd rather watch television with her than waste his time playing a stupid game with beer-drinking men.

When I met them, they didn't seem heartbroken so much as incendiary.

"Our daughter would still be alive," Lucy declared to me, growing red-faced as she spoke, "if it weren't for those criminally negligent landlords. They should have been charged with some crime, we tried to get the police to charge them with something, but nobody listened to us."

"Nobody cares about the victim's family," Ben chimed in.

"You did win your civil suit against them," I observed.

"That's nothing," she said, dismissing with two words the valuable property in which we sat, not to mention the livelihood of the landlords, who lost almost everything as a result of the suit. "It's our daughter we're talking about, my own flesh and blood. Isn't she worth more than a house? They should have gone to jail, but that's never going to happen."

"I think the wife's dead now," I pointed out.

"Well, *he's* still alive," Lucy snapped. "And our daughter isn't. He's still walking around, enjoying life, and hers got cut off before I even had a chance to hold my grandchildren."

"I'm not sure I'd say that he enjoys life, Mrs. Tobias."

Ordinarily, I don't argue with the people

I interview, but there was something about this woman and her husband that got my back up at almost everything they said. I tried to make myself stop, for fear I'd alienate them so much that they wouldn't talk to me, but I soon discovered there wasn't any danger of that. Lucy Tobias was on a roll, with a rare captive audience to hear her out. After a while I realized she probably wasn't really hearing me, anyway.

"They should have had a foolproof security system, for one thing. Why, I walked right in there with a key and nobody stopped me or so much as asked me what I was doing there."

"But that didn't contribute to her death, did it?"

"No, but it just goes to show how careless they were with other people's property. And, imagine, hiring a known ex-convict, a murderer, a person who had killed his own mother. It is simply beyond my comprehension. I cannot understand how any human being could behave so irresponsibly."

"They should have checked his background," Ben said.

"I believe they did, Mr. Tobias. They thought they were doing a good thing, giving a young man a second chance —"

"A second chance to commit murder," Lucy interrupted. "They were as good as accessories to my daughter's murder. They ought to be charged, just like him. They ought to be in jail for the rest of their lives. And those so-called friends of Allison's. Those immoral, drunken girls, Emily and Gretchen."

"Whores," her husband called them.

"They killed her. Poured alcohol down a girl who had never had a drink in her life and then abandoned her so she could get attacked and killed by that horrible boy. If I had my way, they'd all get the death penalty, all of those people who killed my daughter."

"You don't think she ever drank before, Mrs. Tobias?"

"Heavens, no. She knew what I'd do if I caught her."

"What would you have done?"

She never answered that, except to repeat, "She knew what I'd do."

Neither of them were what you'd call well-adjusted, but she, especially, seemed unbalanced to me when I met them. So I can't say that it surprises me to hear that she may have slipped further off the deep end. Lucy Tobias has been "unbalanced" all along. That was always simmering beneath the words I wrote about them, when I was trying to bend over backwards to be kind to this couple — and not to libel them — who had lost their daughter so horribly. It was obvious, too, in what Emily Rubeck said in her interview, as well as in the extreme financial vengeance that Lucy and Ben wreaked on the hapless landlords. By the end of my first meeting with them, I knew that this was a woman I would never want to cross, because she had already shown me she would stop at almost nothing to satisfy her compulsion for revenge. And for punishment. She had always punished Allison far beyond the pale of ordinary discipline. The slightest infraction of her impossible rules seemed to propel her into uncontrollable rage and cruelty.

Now I worry: At the outer limits of her fury, how far would she go? What sort of punishment would she lay on a daughter who had moved out over her objections, who disobeyed, who didn't call, who got drunk, who had sex with a stranger?

If there was any truth at all in Lucy's offer to show Deb the actual note and the cake tin, then Steven Orbach didn't kill Allison. *"Whoever it was, she had to let them in,"* he said to me today. And then he said,

"Or they were already inside her room."

And who, besides the landlords, had a key? Her mother.

By the time I turn off the highway into the Lauderdale Pines, it is dark. I can just barely remember the Tobias address and how to get there, but eventually the ugly house rears up in front of me.

Deb's little red car is parked in front. She told me her appointment was for 8:00, and it's now 8:15. What I want to do is to race to the front door, pound on it and shout for them to let me in, but I make myself sit and think what to do next, and how to do it calmly and rationally. There may be nothing at all amiss here. My concern may be wildly misplaced. It may be that I am the crazy one, not Lucy. This could all be a product of my imagination, fired into feverish delusion by listening to Steve Orbach's fantasies, and by the guilt I feel over George Pullen's murder.

Forcing myself to calm down, I decide that I have two immediate goals, and they're urgent: I want to draw Deb safely out of that ugly house, but I also want to know if there's any evidence that could keep Orbach out of the electric chair in three and a half days. That's it.

"Be careful. Protect the evidence," Franklin said.

I stare at the house and see lights on downstairs. They're probably all three sitting in there, having one of the weird conversations the Tobiases have with people, probably the only kind they do have. Deb's asking her questions. Lucy's acting batty. Ben is agreeing with everything his wife says, even when it's completely nuts. And everything's fine, if you don't object to a bit of insanity, megalomania, narcissism, or early senility.

Okay, I think I know how I'm going to handle this.

I have to make sure that Deb's young presence, her pointed questions, don't trigger this unstable woman's wrath, and I have to find out if there really is any incriminating evidence to worry about.

I get out of my car, shutting the door softly behind me.

This one's for you, George.

I walk quickly up to the front door, ring the bell, and then move back down off the steps. After a couple of endless moments, I hear movement on the other side, sense somebody looking through the peephole, and then hear and see that person slowly opening the door to me.

"Yes?" Ben Tobias asks, from behind the screen door.

He looks the same as before — a short, stocky, nondescript man of sixty or so.

"Do you remember me, Mr. Tobias? I'm Marie Lightfoot?"

"Hello. Yes. What is it?"

"I believe my assistant is here. I need to see her."

"Oh." He pushes the screen door open and I back a little further away from it. "Well, come on in, then."

"No, thank you. I'll wait here."

My plan, feeble though it is, is to get Deb out here so I know she's okay, and then ask her if she's actually seen any sign of the note or the cake tin.

From inside, Lucy Tobias yells, "Who's at the door, Ben?"

"Nobody, Lucy!" he calls back, then says to me, "She wouldn't understand. I'll go get your assistant, but you ought to come in." He glances over my shoulder at something and then gets a puzzled expression on his face. "Lyle? What are you doing here?"

I turn to find his policeman brother-in-law at my shoulder.

In a deep, gentle voice that matches his

appearance, Lyle Karnacki says, "We'll all go in." He puts a hand at my back and nudges me forward up the steps, through the open doorway and into the foyer of the Tobias home.

"I thought —" I start to say to him.

"And I had second thoughts," he says to me, sounding infinitely sad.

"Wait a minute, Lyle," Ben protests, trying to stop us from progressing into the living room. His brother-in-law steps in front of me, takes Ben firmly by one arm and walks him into the cavernous living room. "Lyle, it's not what you think," Ben says, sounding aggrieved. I follow along behind. In the space between them I see Deb seated on a huge, overstuffed white sofa. Lucy is seated in an armchair; her hair's an uncombed mess and she's wearing wrinkled, mismatched clothing with a pair of old-fashioned high heels. But her face lights up with pleasure at the sight of her brother coming toward her.

On a coffee table in between them Lucy has laid out dessert.

There are fancy plates with gold rims, and silver dessert forks and coffee spoons. There are demitasse cups and saucers, and matching silver creamer and sugar holder. And there is a cake, a white cake with lemon icing, that sits on the bottom half of a battered old cake tin, the top of which sits on the table, too. Deborah is eating a piece of cake. In her lap, there is a small, folded piece of yellow paper.

"Lyle," Lucy beams. "Want some white cake, sweetheart?"

"Sure," he says, his voice cracking like a boy's. "That was Allie's favorite, wasn't it? White cake with lemon icing. Isn't that the same kind of cake you carried over to her apartment that night?"

"Um-hm," Lucy says, moving toward the cake knife.

"Did you take it in that same cake tin, Lucy?"

"Um-hm," she says, picking up the knife and slicing into the cake.

"And you brought it home with you later, after she was dead?"

"That's right," Lucy says, sliding his piece of cake onto a plate.

Lyle goes to Deborah and plucks the note out of her lap. He opens it and reads it, and then says, "And you brought the note home with you, too."

"Um-hm, you have to clean up after yourself, dear."

She advances on her brother, the cake in one hand and the knife in the other.

"Lucy," her husband says, sounding weak and frightened. "Don't."

Lyle lets her get close and then he simply reaches for her wrist that holds the knife and clasps her so that she cannot do any harm to him, or to anyone else. She doesn't even struggle, but only looks confused, as does Deborah, seated on the couch.

"Marie?" Deb asks. "What's going on?"

"Why don't you answer your pager?" I ask her.

"Oh, I'm always turning it off and putting it in my purse and forgetting about it. Why? Did you try to reach me?"

"You don't understand," Ben Tobias says to Lyle.

"What don't I understand, Ben? Didn't she kill Allison?"

"You don't understand that I didn't know what she did, not until a long time afterward. And I never knew she still had the note and the tin. Not until she brought them out tonight. She never would have" — he throws a venomous glance at my assistant — "if this woman hadn't asked her about them. Nobody had ever asked about them before. It's all her fault."

"It's always somebody else's fault, isn't it, Ben?"

Lyle has taken the knife away from Lucy and led her to a chair to sit down again. When he looks back up at us, it is not with sadness but with revulsion on his face that he inquires of his brother-in-law, "Were you just going to let us execute that boy, Ben? Were you going to let us kill him in her place?"

"He deserved to die. He had sex with my daughter. He killed his own mother."

"But he didn't kill Allison, did he, Ben?"

As Lyle makes the phone calls he has to make, and as he draws out of his sister and brother-in-law the story he needs to hear, I start taking notes, because I'm a writer and that's what writers do.

Eventually, these notes will become a new chapter . . .

Anything to Be Together
By Marie Lightfoot

CHAPTER 8

Ben was snoring beside her, which didn't usually keep Lucy awake, but on this night she couldn't sleep. Their daughter still had not called to tell them she'd returned to her new apartment, back safe from wherever it was that she had been this first night on her own.

Horrible fantasies played in Lucy's mind as the minutes ticked by.

In some of her imaginings, her daughter had been kidnapped, raped, and killed; in others she had run away with a man. In none of them did Allie's mom envision her daughter simply out having fun with her friends as a normal graduating senior might do: a few drinks, a little flirting, lots of laughter, and some tears as they recalled the memories of their school years together.

With every minute Lucy's fury grew.

When Allie lived at home — only last night! — there were strict curfews and unyielding punishments for breaking them. It didn't matter if the girl was an hour late or a minute, she knew the rules: a week's grounding for every minute past curfew. Grounding meant no telephone, no television — of which there was not much allowed anyway — no visitors or visiting, homework and dinner in her room, never leaving it from the moment she got home after school to when she left for school the next morning. Once Allison was fifteen minutes late because the friend's mother who was giving her a ride was late, but the punishment held, because a rule is a rule. For fifteen weeks, a third of her freshman year in high school, she spent every nonschool hour in her room. It never happened again, because Allie never again relied on anyone else to take her places. The only way to be sure of making curfew was to go where her parents took her and for them to pick her up again. There were many rules and many punishments, all of them appropriate, in her mother's view.

In the Tobias household there was only one view: Lucy's.

On this evening, what had begun as anger had quickly turned into fury.

She was enraged at her husband, too, for sleeping through it.

All right, Lucy thought, *if you won't help, if you don't care, I'll take this into my own hands.* She'd show them both. Forget the car. The apartment was an easy walk. Lucy quietly arose from bed, got dressed, and let herself out of the small house. Keeping to shadows, she paced the sidewalks between home and the Hibiscus Avenue rooming house.

At the back door of it, she saw the note was missing.

She's here. She read my note. She didn't call me.

Allison's mother used her duplicate key to enter the back door.

Quietly, she climbed the back steps.

From one of the rented rooms on the second floor, music was playing softly. The cake tin still sat, undisturbed, beside Allison's door. *She doesn't even care enough about me to take my cake inside!* Her fingers trembling with fury, Lucy used her other duplicate key to let herself into her daughter's room, expecting to find the girl already asleep — or awake and reading. She flipped the wall switch, intending to wake Allie up, to hurt her eyes with the sudden light, to shock her, frighten her with the fact of her sin against her parents. But the light showed the room was empty.

She took my note and left again. Probably with a boy.

Her daughter was a whore, that was clear. Out all night at the first opportunity. Doing God knows what. Lucy had tried, she had tried so hard to mold the girl into a decent woman, a daughter of whom one could be proud, but it was clear that Allison had failed her.

Lucy turned back and picked up the cake tin.

For an hour she sat on the edge of her daughter's bed, holding the cake in its tin, in her lap, waiting. She would wait all night if she had to. She would be there when the slut got back and she would punish her as no girl had ever been punished before.

When the door to the room finally opened, Allison saw her mother.

What her mother saw was that her daughter's blouse was buttoned askew, that her face was swollen, her lips were swollen. Lucy smelled liquor, she caught the scent of sex.

Allison, still drunk, came into the room, started to say, "Moth—"

Lucy carefully set the cake tin on the

bed. Advancing silently toward her daughter, she drew back her right arm and brought it forward into the side of Allison's head with all of her might. The girl staggered, fell to her knees. Her hands flew out to catch herself, but she fell all the way to the carpet. Allison moaned, and started to cry, "Mom, Mom." Something inside Lucy, some fragment of "sanity" that wanted to preserve her own safety, realized that no one must hear this. Quickly she grabbed the pillow off the bed and pushed it into her daughter's face, pushing down, down, harder, harder, and holding it there until the girl was still. The note on the yellow paper had fallen out of Allison's pocket and Lucy scooped it up and took it away with her.

Lucy carried the cake in its container on her walk back home.

She didn't tell her husband the truth until much later, after the trial, after the lawsuits, when one day he uncharacteristically opened her kitchen cabinets to look for something. That's when Ben Tobias saw the cake tin that was supposed to have disappeared, and that's when he also realized the truth. Like his wife, from that day forward he chose to believe it was everyone else's fault: his daughter's for bringing discredit to their family; the landlords' for hiring the boy who lived in the basement; Allison's friends for getting her drunk; Lucy's brother, Lyle, for not checking the tenants thoroughly enough; society; the media; the world. Lucy was driven to do what she did; it was everybody else's fault, and it was all so terribly unfair.

"They will believe that forever," her brother, Lieutenant Lyle Karnacki said after they were taken into custody. "My sister will now blame *me* for everything, from Allie's death to her own execution, if that's what it comes to. She's always been right and the rest of the world has always been wrong. She'll never change."

Maybe not, but Lucy Tobias is going to have a long, long time to think about rules and punishments, although in her increasingly confused state of mind, it is possible that she will eventually forget she even had a daughter, much less that she murdered her.

Susanna

17

That night, I insist on sleeping over at Franklin's condominium, because he's got the hot tub. After a long, naked soak in his bubbling spa, he whispers four perfect things in my ear: he tells me he was wrong; he says that I am brave; he says that I may have saved my assistant's life, and certainly Steven Orbach's; and he tells me he's never had better sex in his life than we've had the last few times we've been together. Like tonight. As he carries my sleepy body off to his bed, I wonder if I ought to remind him that he now has less than a one-month reprieve himself.

The morning will come too soon. I hurry into sleep to greet it.

"What's funny?" Tammi Golding asks me, in Bob and Susanna Wing's living room the next morning. "What'd you find over there?"

"Nothing. I just remembered something." She knows, and is jubilant, about

Orbach's impending freedom, but she doesn't know every detail of how he got it. "Last night when we finally left the Tobias house, my assistant says to me, 'So, did I do a good thing, wanting to know about the note and the cake tin?' "

Tammi smiles at that, too. "I hope you said yes."

"Are you kidding? I gave her a raise on the spot, and she hasn't even worked for me long enough to collect her first paycheck." I stand in the middle of the living room and look around it, imagining it filled with church members on that long-ago Saturday morning when they were looking for Susanna. "Maybe we need her here. You and I don't know what we're looking for, Tammi."

"I have a theory about that." She's dressed for court, in a blue silk suit with a demure ivory blouse, while I'm slopping around in writer clothes: sandals, shorts, and T-shirt, with my hair pulled back in a ponytail. Trying not to yawn, I listen carefully to her. We're both tired and neither of us quite believes this possibility, in the bright light of early day. But we're going ahead with this search-and-rescue mission, just in case. "This evidence that Bob is innocent, if there is any, will be plain as day.

We'll know it when we see it. I think it has to be that conclusive and that obvious, or he wouldn't have used it."

"If he has actually done this thing we think he may have done."

"Yes. If. Okay, you're a writer, follow me in a little suspension of disbelief. Let's say it's the day after his execution, all right? Yesterday they killed him and today, as his lawyer, I have come to his house as he once asked me to —"

"*Did* he, Tammi?"

"Yes, actually. Before he entered prison, I told him to turn all of his important personal and professional documents over to me for safekeeping. His will, tax papers, everything. He gave me a pile of stuff. But he also said, 'Tammi, there are a few things I didn't have time to gather up. Go over to my house right afterwards and go through the drawers in my desk —' "

"That's where it is, then."

" '— and take anything that you'll need to clean up my affairs.' "

"That must have been a terrible conversation to have with him."

"It was."

Drawer by drawer, file folder by file folder, we look through everything.

"Look at this, Tammi," I say, drawing her

attention to a file labeled "Susanna." Inside is her birth certificate, a list of names and addresses, and a single photograph of her as a teenager. She's seated on the wide stone railing of a porch, beside a teenage boy, and there's a white cat walking away from them. While Tammi exclaims over how attractive Susanna was then — "sexy little thing!" — I am frowning over the birth certificate. "Wait a minute. I have in my book that she was born in California. This says Denver, Colorado. Everybody told me she spent her entire life on the West Coast, until she married her first husband. I'm really glad I found this. I don't like to put mistakes like that in print. That can happen when I don't get to talk to a person myself. Especially with victims, I have to rely on other people's memories and impressions of them."

Tammi hands the photo back to me, with the single comment, "Sad," and I slip it back in the file and set the whole thing aside for perusal later.

"Why haven't you done anything with this house, Tammi?" I inquire a little later, as we're working our way through papers and odds and ends. "Doesn't the church own it? How can they afford to keep it like this for Bob?"

"I know," she sighs. "They haven't had

the heart to hire a new minister, so there's nobody else to live here. And they refuse to sell it, because they want to keep the faith."

When we're almost through and still haven't found anything that leaps out at us, Tammi says, sounding worried, "If it's so obvious, why can't we find it?" And then, a little later, with her hands hanging limp in the last drawer, she sighs, "It's not here."

"There was always the possibility that this was nonsense," I admit. "But let's not give up so soon. Maybe he wanted to make it look as if he didn't do this on purpose."

She brightens up a little. "Yeah."

"Maybe he wants you to trip over it accidentally, so no one will suspect that he planned things this way."

We both get to our feet again and start putting drawers back in the desk. Then we split up to cruise the small house, looking for we know not what. Fifteen minutes later, I hear a jubilant cry from the direction of the kitchen. "What?" I yelled back.

"It's here!" Tammi shouts, and then comes running into the bathroom, where I'm standing in the middle of the room. She waves a small piece of paper at me and keeps shouting, even though I'm only a couple of feet away from her. "It was posted to the door of the refrigerator with a magnet. Look, it's a receipt from a filling station! They *were* at a garage! The date and the time is here, and it's perfect! It's right in the middle of the time when Susanna was getting killed. Marie, they couldn't have gotten to the address on this station — and got gas — and driven back in time to do it! This is the alibi, Marie. This is it! I'll get witnesses from the station and this receipt and take them to a judge and I'll try to get him out of there."

"He's going to be disappointed," I say, a bit wryly.

"Tough. He's going to be alive. What's the matter?"

She has noticed that I am not responding with as much enthusiasm as I might. But that's because I'm transfixed by my own discovery. In front of me, on a rack, are two hand towels, one of them blue and the other one orange. There are matching bath towels above the bathtub and extra towels in the same colors on shelves above the toilet.

They are identical to the bath towel and washcloth in the canvas bag.

In my mind's eye, I see Bob Wing grabbing them out of the linen closet and stuffing them into the boat bag.

A little numb, I pick up one of the towels and hand it to her.

"Tammi, they may not have killed her, but they were having an affair."

"Let's go see Artie," Tammi suggests, holding the towel away from her as if it's something dangerous that might bite.

"Artie . . ." Tammi doesn't say anymore than that as she hands the precious filling-station receipt to the other woman.

Artemis Hornung McGregor, when she sees what it is, leans heavily back into the sofa, where she's sitting in her own family room, and then she begins to sob, saying, "Thank God, oh, thank God somebody found it."

She wants to get out of her house to talk about it, so we walk, the three of us, down to her dock. Artie, with her cheeks still wet from tears, unties a sweet little motorboat and we help each other into it. It's easy for me, since I'm in shorts and sandals, but it takes both Artie and me to help Tammi, in her snug suit and stylish shoes, to get in and get settled. Without complaint, the lawyer takes off her jacket, turns it so the lining side is up, and folds it in her lap. Her skirt may soon be ruined by splashing water, but I doubt very much that Tammi cares about that.

Artie sits at the stern, so she can steer.

Under her commands, I unhook us from the final cleat and we're off.

With a minimum of noise and wake, we glide into the residential canal on which she and Stuart live. Their house is a huge, modern one, but it's one of the rare examples that's beautiful. That's due, in part, to artful landscaping that all but hides the house — no mean feat — amid dozens of palm and fruit trees, vast flowering shrubs, and winding hedges. It's easy to forget, because she has been hidden and silent since her arrest, that in her other married life Artemis was one-half of an extraordinarily successful business team. There's something in the unhesitating, confident manner in which she captains this small craft that brings that other, earlier, image home to me.

"Sound carries across water," she comments as her hair blows about in the soft, warm breeze. We're swiftly moving toward the much larger, much choppier Intracoastal, where this little boat will be a minnow among whales. I check the location of the life jackets on board, count enough for all of us, and then just grab a railing and relax. I love boats, love to be on the water, have many times been in much rougher water, in even smaller boats than this. "I'll take us where nobody can hear us talk."

Tammi and I exchange glances: Are we alone together on a wide body of water in a small boat with a murderer? Apparently neither of us believes so.

"I have to be in court by one-thirty," Tammi calls to her.

"No problem," Artie responds.

We moor in a backwater canal where signs warn boaters to go slow to avoid hitting manatees, the lovable, ugly "sea cows" of Florida, with their propellers. Artie tosses me a line and I tie us up to a hanging mangrove root while she jockeys the boat into position to secure another line to hold us steady so we won't float into the rat-infested mass of mangrove roots that lie all around us. We haven't seen a house or a boat or another human for at least a couple of miles. You don't have to travel far in these parts to get the feeling you have returned to old Florida and left noisy, glittering new Florida far behind. Jets leave contrails in the sky above us, but apart from that and our own boat, this could be another century.

Seated in the stern, facing us, she finally speaks.

"The day that Susanna died went just the way we said it did, Tammi. We set out to visit the nursing homes, as usual. We really did have car trouble, but I managed to glide us into a filling station. We ran out of gas, if you can believe that." She shakes her head in a kind of wonder at the vagaries of her fate that day. "That's all it was. Stuart had used my car last and he forgot to tell me it was on empty, and I didn't notice until it was too late. By the time the warning light came on, we were on the highway. We thought it was a miracle when we managed to drive a while, get off an exit ramp, and coast into the filling station."

She looks up at me. "Maybe it *was* a miracle, after all."

"Why haven't either of you told me all this before?" Tammi demands, sounding as infuriated as she has every right to feel. "Why didn't you produce that receipt to establish your alibi?"

But that, it seems, was where their story took a darker, secret turn.

"We were shocked when Bob was suspected, then arrested," Artie tells us, looking as if she still feels that way. "And we were even more shocked when I was." For the first time, there's anger in her face. She adds, in a tone caustic enough to eat through steel, "I guess we hadn't heard the rumors."

"Were you having an affair with Bob?" I ask her, since Tammi doesn't.

"No! We were both married, for heaven's sake. I respect and admire and love Bob, but I don't *love* him."

"And he feels about you . . . how?"

"The same, I think."

Tammi says, "Pat Danner thought you two were immediately attracted to each other the day you met."

"Oh, he's handsome," Artie concedes. "I could hardly miss that. And he's charming as all get-out. But he's my *minister*, and he's married. I would never do that. Never."

"What *did* you talk about in the car the day that Susanna died?"

"Our marriages," she says. "We told you the truth about that, and I still think that's private, Tammi. Why should I have to divulge everything we ever said to each other? We're innocent. We shouldn't have to do that. But if you just have to know, I started it, by telling him that sometimes I worried that I rushed into marriage too soon after my divorce. I didn't feel as if I knew Stuart very well, because it all happened so fast. And he — just being nice, probably — told me that sometimes he felt the same way about Susanna, that they had rushed it."

It is dawning on me that Artie McGregor may actually *be* the tremendously decent person she was once considered to be. Either that or she's a tremendously good actress. None of this explains the phone call that the church women say they overheard, however.

"How do you account for that?" I ask her.

"They lied," she declares, looking straight at me.

But why would they? I wonder.

"Go on," Tammi urges her.

"We were hit out of the blue with everything that happened, Tammi. But then Bob realized that God was giving him a chance to do something important for the world . . . to let himself be wrongfully convicted and to be executed, so that the people in this country would finally see that under our system of laws it is possible for an entirely innocent person to be put to death for a crime he didn't do. He intended you to go through every legal maneuver, Tammi. That was very important, so that nobody could say later that you hadn't exhausted every appeal and every avenue to free him."

"My God," their lawyer says, looking as appalled as she sounds. "But what about you? You may have been acquitted, but everybody thinks you're guilty. Your reputation, your name is completely ruined."

"My name was ruined by the rumors and the arrest," she retorts. "I had nothing left to lose. I'd lost my friends, my church, my good name. Whatever I said, there would always be people who thought the worst of me. Even people who don't think I'm a murderer think I was having an affair with him, and they probably always will think that. You know how it is, how it *still* is: when it comes to sexual misconduct, people are still inclined to blame the woman more than the man."

"But still —" Tammi says.

"Why did I go along with his martyrdom? Because my minister, my spiritual counselor, asked me to, Tammi. I could have said no, of course. But I didn't, because some things are bigger and more important than my reputation or any individual life."

"And yet," I say to her, "when we showed the receipt from the gas station —"

"I burst into tears and said thank God." With a single nod she acknowledges the contradiction. "The longer it has gone on, the longer he's been on death row, the closer he gets to actual execution, the more doubt I have about this plan of ours. I think this is a wrong thing for him — for me — to do. I can't help to murder him. And that's what it would be. It's absurd. It may even be wicked. It's all built on a lie — that we can't prove our innocence. But we can. If you hadn't come to me with this receipt, I was about to come to you, Tammi."

I see her clearly now — her beauty, her own great personal charisma — and I see why people once adored her on sight, why even her ex-husband had only praise for her. Once again, it was all hidden in plain sight in my own research and manuscript, but like the police, I was too blinded by my assumptions to see it. Except, except, the telephone conversation and the blue and orange towels . . .

"You'll get him off now, won't you, Tammi?" she pleads.

"Let's hope that I can."

Artie and I both stare at the lawyer.

"Hope?" Artie repeats. "But surely with the proof of that receipt —"

"Ladies," Tammi says, looking somber, "many a man has remained in prison his whole life long in spite of better exonerating evidence than that. Some have even gone to the death chamber in spite of somebody else confessing to the crime, in spite of new witnesses coming forward, in spite of everything short of DNA. Can I get Bob off? I'll tell you the truth, Artie. Marie. I don't know."

In the stern, Artie's face goes pale, while I feel a little sick myself.

It's obvious that this dreadful possibility never occurred to Artie, but I wonder if Bob has been so naïve. Far from being the exonerating evidence it looks like, that gas receipt could be his "fail-safe" mechanism for demonstrating in a horrible way that the system failed to protect an innocent man. If Tammi can't get him freed on the basis of it, if he dies in spite of it, that will prove his point, most tragically.

"There has to be something else," I blurt.

They turn to stare at me, but Tammi catches on instantly, and snaps her fingers. "Of course," she says. "Bob knows the law of capital punishment cases better than I do. If he has set things up so that he will be proved innocent only after his death, then

there has to be something absolutely in-
controvertible that we haven't found yet.
The problem is, he's so damned smart, he
may have hidden it in a way that guarantees that we *can't* find it until he's dead.
Artie, what is it?"

"I don't know of anything else! I'd tell
you if I did, Tammi."

"We have to find it," Tammi says intensely. "Can you talk him into telling us?"

"Are you kidding?" Artie looks at her
lawyer as if Tammi still hasn't quite gotten
it yet. "This is a holy crusade to him, as it
was to me."

On the way back in to Artie's home,
Tammi asks her about her husband's role
in all this: "How much does Stuart know?"

"Everything."

"My God, Artie, he let you —"

"Let?" I see another hint of the successful businesswoman in the fiery look
that Artie gives to her lawyer. "That wasn't
his choice to make. Oh, he could have
stopped us, for his own sake. I would have
agreed to that in a minute. It isn't pleasant
to be married to a woman who goes on
trial for adultery and murder, let me tell
you. He knows that people think he's a fool
to stay with me and to believe in me.

364

Stuart has been a saint about all this. But you've got to understand, he's a man of high principle, too. We all chose freely to make our own sacrifices for this cause."

It's the most amazing pact that I have ever heard of. And the frightening thing of it is, it still might work. If the receipt alone, and Artie's testimony, don't suffice to get Bob off, and if we never find any other exonerating evidence, he *will* die for his cause.

Stuart McGregor meets us at the dock and helps us tie up.

I have a feeling that Tammi and I both are looking at this tall blond man with the youthful face with much greater feelings of respect than we ever did before. We may personally think that the pact the three friends made is lunacy, that it's a horrible sacrifice of several lives, but there's no denying the high conscience of it, or the courage of these people.

Tammi strikes just the right tone as Stuart gives her a hand up out of the boat. With utter casualness, she says to him, "Did you get my letter about reversing the power of attorney? Now that we know for sure that Artie's not going to prison for the rest of her life, you won't be needing that."

She looks back over her shoulder at his wife. "Just sign the papers and mail them back to me."

"I didn't see them, Tammi."

"I've got them, honey," Stuart tells her, and then he explains to me, "When we were afraid that Artie might be convicted, Tammi suggested that I get power of attorney so I could handle Artie's affairs in her absence. Thank God we won't be needing that."

"Who's got Bob's power of attorney?" I ask them.

"I do," Tammi tells me. "Stuart, let's go in the house. We have something to tell you. And we need to enlist your help in searching for something."

When I run all of this past Franklin, he rather surprises me by being willing to consider that it might be the truth. But he's pessimistic that the receipt alone will do the trick.

"It still looks as if they were having an affair, no matter what she says."

"I know," I agree, feeling anxious about that myself.

"And," the prosecutor adds, "if they didn't do it, who did?"

I have Tammi Golding's go-ahead to be

telling this story; if we can get prosecutorial or police cooperation, we'll take it, gratefully. But Franklin warns me not to expect much sympathy from Tony Delano, and he turns out to be right about that. "It's all her word," Tony complains to me, over the phone. "And you already know how I feel about *that* lady."

Detective Carl Chamblin does not surprise me with his reaction to the same story.

"I don't buy this for a fucking minute."

"So I guess we can't count on the cops to help us look for new evidence?"

"You can count on me to hold the stopwatch till his time runs down."

"But, Carl, you were wrong about Steven Orbach."

There's a long pause, and then he says, true to character, "Maybe he didn't kill Lyle's niece, but he was still a killer and he deserved to die." But then Carl says something that does surprise me: "You actually saw her? Artie? She look depressed to you? Her husband told me she tried to kill herself after we questioned her about George Pullen's murder. He said she drove out to the old mansion and was going to throw herself out of the tower, but he stopped her. I wanted to ask him why the fuck he bothered. I say, next time let her jump."

Part of me can't believe this, because it seems so at odds with the intensely alive woman who took us out in the boat today. But that was after we told her we'd found the gas receipt. Before that, the woman who met us at the door was guarded, quiet, withdrawn. God knows, it would be understandable if she had been depressed to a point approaching suicidal despair, especially if she felt she was conspiring in an act that was tantamount to killing Bob Wing.

"You're all heart, Carl," I tell him.

He laughs and hangs up.

Susanna

18

Two weeks have gone by and although Spring Break is cresting, nothing else has broken through. When Tammi Golding tries to talk to Bob Wing about his plot to save the country's soul, she gets nowhere. He pretends to be astonished she would even suspect him of attempting such a thing. Nor has our search for any other evidence proved fruitful, and Tammi's attempts to get him a new trial — much less get him set free — on the basis of the gas receipt and Artemis's new testimony are falling on deaf ears in the justice system.

"It doesn't help that my client won't cooperate," she says with wry anger. "If he weren't already sentenced to death, I think I might strangle him myself."

Nor has any bear stepped into my trap with its shiny bait of rings.

The edited manuscript comes back to me, however, and I set to work to add the new ending on the Allison Tobias murder. Trying to figure out what to say now about Susanna's death is more problematic. I don't know what to do — what to write — about the turns in the story.

One thing I can do is correct simple things like her place of birth.

And so on a gorgeous day on which I have no intention of moving from my own sunny patio, I open the folder labeled "Susanna." There's the birth certificate. And there's the photo of a teenage Susanna on a front porch with a blond boy and a white cat. And there's the list I didn't pay much attention to when Tammi and I were going through Bob Wing's belongings. The only thing I remember noticing about the list is that it seemed to be a list of names and addresses.

And that's what it is, all right.

But when I turn it over, I see handwriting that looks immature, unskilled. The words "My home sweet homes" are scrawled across it in pencil and underlined. Underneath there is a poorly executed sketch of a fist, but its meaning is very clear: the third finger is raised, pointing angrily up at the word "home." It appears to me that I have in my hands a list of the various foster and group homes where

Susanna lived when she was young. She didn't live in California at all, it seems, but always in Denver. And who can blame her for not wanting anybody to be able to track her sad history. If she wanted to say she was from California, if she wanted to pretend that all of the records of her pitiable childhood were destroyed in a flood, then let her.

Suddenly, the researcher in me kicks in. I cannot just reprint this list, I need to actually see some of these houses, take some photos, see if I can interview anybody still alive who will talk to me about her.

Almost before I know it, I'm on a plane heading to Denver. In the luggage rack I've stashed an overnight case that's big enough for boots, coat, gloves, and hat.

My first stop is at the house in the photograph, which is easy to match to Susanna's list because I can see the numbers of the street address in the picture. It looks much the same as in the photograph: a medium-sized brick house with a front porch made of field stone; two second-story gables; and painted wood everywhere there isn't brick or stone. There is a small front yard with a slight incline and cement steps leading up to the porch. It's all under fresh snow. The steps have not been cleared, so I leave the first footprints going up to the house. I don't even see mailman footprints. What doesn't show from the photograph — and may not even have been there then — is a chain-link-fenced backyard and a detached garage.

The woman who answers the doorbell is elderly.

"Yes?" she asks, guardedly through a locked screen door, wrapping a housecoat around her for warmth from the cold air my visit is letting into her house.

I hold up the photograph for her to see. "I'm looking for information about this girl who may have lived here at one time."

The old lady unlatches the door and reaches out a hand for it.

I place the photo into her palm, which she draws back inside again, though she doesn't relatch the screen.

"Who are you?" she demands, as she holds the picture up to examine it. But before I can tell her my name, she exclaims in an emotional voice, "Oh, where did you get this picture? I don't even have a picture of her myself. It's been so long since I've seen her —"

When she looks at me, her eyes are wet.

"You know the girl?" I ask her.

"The girl? Oh, yes, I knew the girl, but it's the cat I'm talking about. My precious Snowy. Sweetest cat I ever had. She was poisoned not long after this picture was taken." With obvious reluctance she handed the photo back to me. "I could cry just thinking about her again. But I wouldn't want *that* picture of her, not with who else is in it. That child was not one of my favorites."

"You knew her?"

"Of course. She lived here for a good year and a half. Wouldn't have been so long, except that midway through her parents died. Awful thing. Must have been drunk. One of them, probably him, left the car running in their garage one night. Asphyxiated them sure as somebody'd put a pillow over their faces and smothered them." She gives me a hard look. "What became of the girl?"

"She's dead."

"I'm not surprised, she was bound to go young."

"Murdered," I say brutally to this hard old bat.

"I'm not surprised by that, either. Most people get what they have coming to them. Some people think they don't, they think there's no justice in the universe, but I know there is, because I've seen it go to work time and again. Who killed her?"

"Her husband's on death row for it."

"Really. Now that's a surprise. He was wild for Carly."

"Carly? Did you call her Carly? Her name's Susanna."

"Well, maybe it was when you knew her, but when she lived here, it was Carly."

"Why was she staying with you when her parents were still living?"

"Why? Because they wouldn't admit the truth about their own family, so somebody wiser had to take her away from them before something worse happened."

"Worse than what?"

"Worse than Carly killing her baby sister."

"What?"

"Parents claimed it was crib death, but little Carly bragged about it to her school friends. Carly — why am I calling her that? That's not what we knew her as. Carly Shugarz. We called her Sugar for short. Was there ever a child so badly misnamed as that? I'm trying to remember the name of this boy. Her boyfriend, the one she married when they were both too young. He was as bad as she was, if not worse. Lived in that group home for delinquents down the street. What was his name, started with an S . . .

"Stuart!" the old woman says. "That was it, Stuart and Sugar."

For the rest of that day and the next morning, I pay visits to other homes where Susanna stayed, as well as dropping by the Denver police and the courthouse. Amazing, isn't it, how much easier it is to find things out about someone when you know their real name? On my way back to the airport, I glimpse a billboard advertisement for the Denver Broncos. It's bright with their team colors: blue and orange.

Blue and orange bath towels and washcloths . . .

You never know what will lodge in a person's subconscious, as the colors of the hometown football team may have stuck in hers.

Susanna/Carly/Sugar killed her baby sister. Did she kill her parents, too?

Susanna has known Stuart since they were young teenagers. Married him way back then. When they "met" in Bahia Beach, at the Sands Gospel Church, they pretended not to know each other. She told everyone that her first husband died in a rock-climbing accident, leaving her rich. Maybe it wasn't an accident. Stuart told everybody that his rich wife had died, too. Maybe that wasn't an accident, either. Stuart and Susanna both showed up at the grief group at about the same time, and they both found themselves new, rich, lonely spouses. How many times have they married and murdered?

My god, I know how many: all I have to do is count their trophies.

Nine rings. That number must hold the key to their killings.

I feel more chilled than a mere coat could ever warm.

And then, when I'm belted into my seat and the airplane's taking off, I remember Carl Chamblin's offhand, mocking remarks: "You met Artie? Did she seem depressed, to you? Her husband says she tried to throw herself out of the tower . . ."

Stuart McGregor has Artie's power of attorney, giving him legal control over everything she owns. It is entirely possible that he has been spending it all along, but what will happen when he wants it all? When he tires of this game? It appears that he is already setting the stage for her "suicide."

I cannot reach for the phone in the back of the seat fast enough.

"Tammi, it's Marie. Please listen to me —"

By the time I get into my car at the Bahia Beach International Airport, my cell phone is already ringing and the caller ID says it's "Tamara Golding."

"I'm back," I say into it.

"Thank God. Marie, I can't find them. Remember when you went up to the Tobiases' house, and all you wanted to do was get your assistant out safely? That's all I've been trying to do first, get Artie away from him, make sure she's safe before we do anything else."

"No cops?"

"Oh, we've got cops on it, all right. I can be damned convincing when I have to, but they're not finding them, either."

"Where have you looked?"

"There aren't many places *to* look, Marie. Their house. The church. All of her work was volunteer, and so was his, although I found out that he has quietly dropped out of all church activity since the murder. I guess he was only doing that to make himself look genuine. The fact that he doesn't consider that to be essential anymore tells me that he doesn't consider *her* to be essential anymore. He's going to kill her, make it look like a suicide, and cut and run, Marie. How could we all have been so blind?"

"Tammi, that was their talent and their skill, and they were good at it."

"Why do you think he killed Susanna?"

"I don't know."

"And we don't care right now, I suppose. It doesn't matter."

"Tammi, did you check the old house?"

"Of course! That's where he claimed she was going to kill herself, so that's the first place we checked when we found out they weren't at home. Marie, the truth is, they could be out grocery shopping. They could be doing something perfectly ordinary, because she doesn't know who he is and what he wants, and he doesn't know that we're looking for him."

"What are you going to do?"

"I'm going to park where I can keep an eye on their house. What about you, Marie?"

"I'm going to go home. I don't know what else to do."

"I'll call you if anything happens."

"Yes, do. Thanks, Tammi."

"How could we have been so stupid?" she wails, just before hanging up. "It was there to see, all along."

"Tammi," I say, trying to make her feel better, "it's a lot harder to read between the lines than most people realize." And I

should know, since the lines it was all between are the ones I wrote in my own
book.

I'm exhausted, worried, fearful for Artemis, frustrated.

And glad to be back to the heat, the humidity, the soft, heavy air. I can't wait to
walk into my own home. But on the way, I
pull into Bayfield, the housing development where Bob Wing lived first with
Donna and then with Susanna. We've been
tearing it apart — Tammi, Artie, and I —
in our futile search for the elusive exonerating evidence, and by now, by necessity,
we've all got our own keys to it. It's not
just the house we've searched, either, but
the garage, the two cars, the crawl space
above the house and the tool shed behind
it. It has become an obsession with us. We
know it may be crazy, but once started, we
can't seem to give up on it, because giving
up means giving up on a man's life.

As usual, there are cars parked all up
and down the streets, because these homes
hold growing families with multiple vehicles. There's a snappy green sports car
parked in front of the Wings, and a van,
and I wonder which neighbor owns them.
My own car I park right in the driveway.

Then I walk up the front path and take out my key and put it in the lock.

As usual, the door opens without resistance and I am here again.

This is where I've put the pouch of rings that nobody seems to be interested in. Once I learned that Artie wasn't the person who would be looking for them, I realized I didn't know enough about what — or who — I was playing with. I had thought she might try to contact me about them, trying to disguise her identity. I didn't want to endanger myself by keeping them at my house, and when I told Tammi about it, she suggested leaving them here, where nobody would think to look. But now that I know they were trophies of crimes, I want them closer to me, so I can hand them over as evidence of Stuart and Susanna's crimes.

Picking them up now seems like the responsible thing to do.

I walk through the living room, toward the kitchen, where I have stored them in a container that holds artificial sugar packets.

As I am reaching for the jar, I hear a click.

The hair rises on the back of my neck as I realize what it is: the turning of the dead bolt on the front door.

Without even stopping to think about it, I drop my purse and move as quickly as I can toward the back door in the kitchen. As I reach to unlock that door, a man's hand comes down upon my wrist and Stuart McGregor turns me around violently to face him.

"Where are the rings, Marie?"

"Where is Artemis, Stuart?"

"That's right. A lot of people are looking for her right now, aren't they? And whose fault is that, I wonder? Could it be yours, Marie? Nosy little Marie. You had to go to Denver, didn't you? Had to check things out. And now there's nothing left for me to do but clean up here and go so far away that nobody will ever find me."

How in heaven's name does he know all this?

He is at least ten inches taller than I and more than a hundred pounds heavier. It takes very little pressure of his body on mine to get me to move in the direction he wants me to go — out of the kitchen, which I scan frantically for potential weapons, and down the hallway, toward the bathroom. He pushes me into it, where I see Artemis crouched on the floor of the shower stall, her mouth taped, her hands and feet taped, her eyes wide and terrified when she sees us. He has wrapped an electric cord around her neck and flung it up over the shower head. All it will take is for him to lift her a little higher, just high enough to keep her from getting a grip with her bound feet or hands.

I put all of my sympathy for her into my eyes, which he can't see.

"You won't make anybody think she killed herself," I tell him, keeping my voice as cool as I can make it, hoping there's no tremor in it.

"Maybe not, but I can confuse them long enough to distract them. And you, Marie, you're another distraction of a different kind." He turns me to face him, grabs me by my hair, and pulls my face up toward his, intending to force me to kiss him. I let him do it. Let him feel hard resistance at first, then a melting in my lips and my body as I seem to acquiesce to him. As I slip infinitesimally in his grasp, I bring up my hand that holds the keys and attack his face with them, aiming for his eyes.

He yells in pain, releases his grip just enough to let me gouge him harder. I squirm in his arms with all of my strength until I'm managing to kick and shove him.

When his upper arm brushes my mouth, I sink my teeth into him, and he screams and curses me. By now he's desperate to regain control over the demon he meant to rape and kill, but I don't stop. My life and Artie's and Bob Wing's are at stake in these horrible few seconds, and I am a woman infused with power and strength I didn't even know I had. I am only vaguely aware that I am screaming. When I can, I pound him in his groin and only then does he fall back away from me, gagging and clasping himself. I follow him as he stumbles as far as the kitchen, where I grab a long-bladed knife out of a countertop holder.

As he falls backward, I drive the knife into his upper arm, pinning him to the wall of the house. He screams, seems almost to faint, grabs his upper arm and attempts to wrench out the knife, but he can't do it. Stuart stares out at me from eyes that shine with agony and hatred.

I am panting and in pain myself. He slammed me against the bathroom door and doorsill, against the toilet and the sink, and I hardly felt any of it at the time, but now I feel almost as bad as he looks. I'm pretty sure I'm only bruised, though, and that nothing's broken. "Nobody's going to die on my watch today," I tell him as I call 911. "Not even you, if I can help it."

I hurry back to free Artemis.

Together we use the electrical cord to secure him so he can't hurt us, and then we find an extension cord to use as a tourniquet to stop his bleeding. I don't have the stomach to remove the knife from his arm and the wall. So that's how the paramedics find him, when they arrive five minutes later.

And all the while, even in the worst of it, there is a cool, detached part of my brain that is taking notes on everything . . .

Anything to Be Together
By Marie Lightfoot

EPILOGUE

They were a matched pair: evil for evil, no holds barred.

If the devil had split himself into male and female he could hardly have done a better job of creating malevolence.

They felt their attraction instantaneously when they met.

To hear him tell it — finally, and much later — "like" attracted "like" as surely as hydrogen bonds with oxygen. It was like a sharp jolt of electricity that entered through their eyes and traveled at light speed down through their breath, hearts, minds, groins. It was love — or lust — at first sight. What did they see in each other? The devil knows his own. At a dark, submerged depth below the light of consciousness, they recognized each other. Surely there was something ancient, wicked, and intimately familiar for each in the other's eyes.

Before long, they knew they could do any-

thing together, even murder — especially, and most deliciously, murder.

They met when they were both thirteen years old.

The first time Stuart ever saw Susanna was unforgettable for him, as it probably was for her. He was walking past the foster home where she was living at the time in Denver; that's all, just walking past on his way from middle school to his own group home.

When he turned his head, he instantly met the girl's eyes. She was looking at him. He had a feeling she'd been looking at him ever since he came into her line of sight.

Caught by her unwavering stare, the boy stopped walking so suddenly that his backpack shifted, but he didn't pay it any mind. He was a thirteen-year-old boy and had constant sexual fantasies, and one of them was sitting only yards away, staring at him. The girl had on a sleeveless green top that left her stomach bare, and a skirt so short that it rode high up on her perfect little legs, and she wore brown sandals, and one of them was dangling down, hanging by the big toe of her left foot. She was leaning forward with her hands flat on either side of her on the wide concrete porch railing.

Her legs were wide apart. He felt as if he could see all the way to China.

The girl didn't have to say a word to him. His feet took control — or was it another part of him? — and they turned him to face her, and then they walked him up to the foot of the steps leading up to the porch, and to her. She looked his age but he'd never seen her at his school, and he knew he would have noticed a girl like this, this girl.

She spoke first, establishing the pattern that would hold until the end. Her first words were completely ordinary, but they were the sexiest words he'd ever heard.

"You live around here?"

If he'd been a grown man, he might have laughed at that, at himself, for hearing promise and poetry in those four banal words.

"Yeah."

They both lived "around here," if here was an invisible metaphysical location where evil bred and grew. She — who killed her sister, who murdered her own parents though nobody knew that yet, who would one day slay the cat who slinked around the side of the house — she lived exactly in the realm that this boy inhabited, too.

"Fucked, isn't it?" she said, her dark eyes challenging him.

"Totally."

He would rarely disagree with her, not until the very end, and then, having no practice in denying her anything she wanted, he would take his argument to its fatal, melodramatic, logical extreme. He would one day go too far, even with her, because he had never learned to stop before he got there.

The day that Susanna sat on the front porch of her foster home watching the blond boy slouch down her street by himself, she drew her own death to her. The boy came just as eagerly, ignorantly, almost innocently to his fate, too.

They became inseparable almost immediately. No foster parents or group homes, no detention centers, courts, cops, or judges, no social workers or shrinks could deny them one another. She was pregnant at fourteen, at fifteen, at twenty, and maybe more often than that. The pair of them sired at least three living children they would never see, or want to. They didn't seem interested in abortion, found pregnancy sexy, delivery climactic, abandonment a thrill. At twenty-two, however, over her objections he got a vasectomy, which he never reversed. She should have noted that early mutiny; it hinted at a strand of independence in him.

Her autopsy revealed that her own reproductive organs were battle-scarred but functional, hence the condoms in the canvas bag. She tired of getting pregnant and never fully trusted his vasectomy. Besides, forcing him to use condoms — to his intense annoyance — was a way to punish him for getting it. It's only natural to wonder, where are the children they bred? Certain studies have demonstrated a genetic predisposition for criminal behavior ranging from burglary to homicide. It may not be true. But if it is, the question assumes the urgency of self-interest: for our sakes, where are Stuart and Susanna's children now?

"We're just alike," she told her blond-haired boy. "I killed my parents and you want to kill yours."

"Fuck, yes."

"I could help you do it, I know how."

"I don't know."

"Come on. Why not?"

"What do we get out of it?" This wasn't rebellion on his part, this was a certain innate business sense that she would learn to appreciate. A killer needs a good business manager. "I can walk out anytime I want to, I don't have to kill them to do it."

"But they deserve it."

"Yeah, well who doesn't? Except us. Look, they're only worth what we could get in a garage sale of their stuff, their furniture and crap. They're not worth it."

"But I want to."

"God." He turned and took her in his arms and began to kiss her and make love to her. Nothing, nothing turned him on like her talk of killing people. God, she'd actually done it. Three times. His girlfriend was a triple killer. God, it set him on fire, melted his brain, reduced him to skin and nerves and hands and mouth and penis. "What was it like?"

"You *know*," she teased.

"Tell me again."

How long, one wonders, did it take for them to cook up their first murderous scheme? Who thought of it first? Did either of them need to be persuaded by the other? Who was the instigator, who the organizer? Was one more ruthless than the other, or were they truly an almost perfectly matched set?

It feels right, somehow, to think Susanna spoke first.

"We could each find somebody with money."

"How would we do that?"

"It's easy. I could look for an old, senile guy with a lot of loot. You could sweet-talk some rich old lady."

"How would we find them?"

"Obituaries, to see whose husband or wife has just died in a rich part of town. On the Web. Through dating services. Whatever."

"And just wait for them to die?"

"Oh, no. We don't want to wait."

There are so many places in this world to find lonely people who have money to lose — maybe a lot of it — to somebody smooth who courts and caresses them.

"Why do they have to be old?"

"I guess they don't have to be."

"I want somebody younger than that. I don't think I could do it with an old broad."

"Not even for a million dollars?"

"Maybe, but why should we if we can do better?"

"I don't want to think of you with somebody younger, prettier or richer than me."

"Nobody's prettier than you. And when

we get through, we'll be the richest ones."

"We'll have to marry them."

"Life insurance?"

"Yeah, and their wills."

"Better find people with no families, right?"

"Good idea, baby."

They drew up their "rules of engagement," a phrase that sounded hilarious to them:

1. Must be worth a minimum of $100,000.
2. Must be younger than fifty.
3. Attractive.
4. Can be single, or divorced, or widowed, just so there's money.
5. No kids.
6. It's good if their parents are both dead, even better if they don't have brothers or sisters or any family who cares about them.

They found their first pair of victims in Newark, New Jersey, by dedicating themselves to studying the obituaries and then using the Internet to check credit ratings and so forth. It was quick work: spot a promising obituary on a Thursday, check it out over the next twenty-four hours, show up at the funeral as an acquaintance or admirer of the deceased.

"I didn't know him well, but I thought he was a great guy. So intelligent. I'll always remember his kindness to me. And I liked the way he talked about his wife . . . about you. I can see why he thought you were so great."

Making up stories, insinuating themselves, flattering, consoling, comforting, offering help that they made a point of delivering promptly and sympathetically while other people fell away . . .

"Your wife blessed us, by bringing us together."

"Your husband can rest easy, knowing you're being taken care of now."

There were twin courtships. Twin marriages. Twin murders. Twin inheritances. Nine rings altogether: the rings from four marriages, plus the "real" rings from the symbolic marriage that Susanna and Stuart staged for themselves, alone.

After their first successful campaign in New Jersey, they moved south. Raleigh, North Carolina, was their next murderous stop. There they honed their developing skills of hunting and killing, and after that they drifted still further down the coast, to Bahia Beach.

★ ★ ★

It might have gone on forever, except that Susanna picked wrong.

She married the Reverend Robert F. Wing knowing he had collected on a policy on his late wife — but not knowing he intended to spend it all unselfishly on causes of conscience. When she saw how fast the money was going, she told Stuart, at one of their Friday trysts in the old tower, "I don't want to wait on the money I'll get from the policy on his life. I want what's left of her estate, too. We have to kill him now."

But Stuart didn't want to. It was too soon, he said. Too risky.

"What's the real reason, Stuart? Are you telling me you like her? Cute little Artie? You like being married to rich, cute little Artie? Maybe you don't want to kill her anymore and split her money with me? Maybe you want to stay with her and keep her money all to yourself?"

That would happen over her dead body, Susanna warned him.

When he made that prophecy come true, he unleashed within himself a rage he didn't know he felt. It wasn't only a rage against the woman who had controlled his life for so many years; it was a rage against life itself.

394

And the funny thing was, Stuart was as surprised as anybody when his own wife was arrested for the murder of Susanna. For a while, he even half-believed the rumors about an affair between Artemis and Bob Wing. But then he came to his senses. No woman who was married to Stuart McGregor would ever look at another man. Stuart was irresistible to lonely, vulnerable women. Hadn't Susanna always told him so?

Why did he want possession of the canvas bag but not the rings? To him, the bag seemed like incriminating evidence, but the rings were only a woman's silly souvenirs.

Stuart thought he had the last laugh on Bob Wing, on Artie, on Susanna, on everybody. The last time he visited Bob in jail — before the minister was sent to death row — Bob told him a secret for safekeeping.

"Stuart, you're the only person I'm trusting with this information. Please keep it until after I'm dead. You know the filling station where your wife and I got gas? While Artie was paying for it, I walked around the corner to an ATM to get some cash to pay her back. When the time is right, tell the authorities that my face will be on the videotape of that transaction. That will be the ultimate proof that Tammi will need to clear my name."

Susanna

19

It's a sunny, perfect Sunday morning when Tammi Golding and I take Steven Orbach to church. He was released from prison twenty-four hours before his scheduled execution. Now Sands Gospel has set him up with a small apartment and a little cash, and they're on the lookout for a job for him.

In the sanctuary, he stands up, looking uncomfortable as Bob Wing introduces him. The preacher is back in fine form, raising the rafters with his sermons about the justice system. He is regarded as a fool by some and a saint by others for his willingness to sacrifice his own life so that others might live.

Bob steps back from the pulpit to allow Steve to take center stage. Steve is dressed in new clothes the church has furnished him. He looks sternly handsome as he says his thank-yous. They seem to be sincere, if not altogether effusive. There are tears among the congregation, a standing ovation; heartfelt hymns are sung, and a vow is renewed among them to continue to work for the abolition of the death penalty.

Artemis is not a member of Sands Gospel anymore. And who can blame her?

Afterwards, Tammi wants to take the four of us to brunch, but Bob Wing can't go. He has hands to shake after church, and nursing homes to visit with gifts of flowers from the sanctuary. There are some people — Tammi and me, for instance, two incurable romantics — who kind of hope that one day he'll stop by Artie's small, elegant new house and ask her if she'd like to go along with him. We know of at least one old man whose face will light up at the sight of her.

"Brunch?" Steve repeats as if it's a foreign word. "Sure . . . brunch."

"Eggs Benedict" is what Tammi orders for Steve, who's never had it before.

This strange interlude was all his lawyer's idea. I feel uncomfortable with it, though I'm going along because I'm a carnivorous writer and these people are the meat for my plate. Tammi, high from this victory, is animated, wanting to relive my "adventure" for Steve as if we're kids who can't get enough of ourselves.

"The note," she says. "Tell him how you thought of that, Marie."

"I didn't. My assistant did." I glance up at him. "You probably don't even know that there was a note from Lucy on the front door that night. It said that Allie was to call her the minute she got in. Well, that note wasn't on the inventory-of-evidence list, and it wasn't among the stuff the medical examiner turned over. So where was it? It should have been there, either in your rooms or in Allie's room, or even someplace on the stairs if she had dropped it. Her friends said she'd stuffed it in her pocket, so where was it? My assistant even called Lyle Karnacki to ask if he knew."

"He told her nobody had ever come across it," Tammi interjects, as she passes the salt and pepper to me.

"He told Deb — my assistant — that he had thrown a fit until the crime-scene unit collected everything that was anyplace that Allison had been in that house that night. If she had walked on the stairs, he wanted those stairs vacuumed and the debris collected and examined. He was a bastard, he said, because he was so determined to make sure they had all the evidence they needed to —"

"Convict me," Steve says, looking at his plate with a blank expression.

"Yes," I agree. "The medical examiner listed the contents of her pockets. No note."

Steve is being fairly patient with this nonsense. At least I guess it's patience. I don't know if he's patient, or kind. I don't know anything about him, really, except that he killed his mother and he didn't kill Allison Tobias. I don't know if he is, at heart, a decent or possibly a rehabilitated person. I don't know what the years have wrought in him. If he's angry, bitter, vengeful, he doesn't let on to us. He doesn't show much of anything. Forbearance, maybe.

He picks at the hollandaise sauce as if it's distasteful to him.

I'm sitting next to Steve in a booth. It feels to me as if neither of us is all that comfortable with the proximity. I'm scooched way over toward the window, he's seated about as close to the aisle as he can get. We're careful not to touch, even accidentally. Tammi's across from us, looking pleased to provide something nice for her long-imprisoned client. She helps me tell my story. "So, when Marie found out the note never popped up anywhere,

400

she realized that might be important."

Not meeting Steve's eyes, I say, "There was only one person who could have had that note if it wasn't anywhere Allison had been in the house. And if that person had the note, then she had to have been in the house that night with Allison, because Allison's two friends saw her put it in her pocket. And if it was in her pocket, that meant it wasn't right out in sight, so somebody would have had to look for it, and the only reason for them to do that was if it would incriminate them in her murder. So it had to be one of her parents."

Looking back, I feel breathless at the leap of intuition I took. My God, it was so little, really, on which to accuse Lucy Tobias to her own brother. But it wasn't only that; in interviewing people, I heard those unflattering stories about the Tobiases. And suddenly I had realized that their character had always been revealed in my chapter about them; but like everyone else, I had my attention on the wrong suspect, and so I ignored what was written between my own lines.

"I called Lyle," I continue, "and told him what I was thinking. It offended him so much that he hung up on me. But afterwards, after I called, he said he couldn't stop thinking about it, and about his sister, as he knew her. He decided that as much as he hated the idea, there was the slim possibility I might be right."

Tammi's cell phone rings. Steve looks startled and I wonder if he has ever heard or seen one before. He watches closely as she takes it out, looks at the caller ID, then takes the call. Five quick sentences and she hangs up, and says to us, "I'm sorry. That's a client. I hate to do this, but I've got to go. Marie, take care of the bill, will you, and I'll pay you back. Steven, call if you need anything, okay?"

She gets out of the booth, and hurries to the door.

It doesn't take Steve two seconds to move over to the other side of the booth. Am I happy to be left alone with him? I am not.

He doesn't ask me to continue my story, and I don't volunteer it. We hadn't even gotten to the cake tin yet, and somehow it doesn't seem important.

"What are you going to do next?" I ask him after a few minutes.

"Finish my eggs."

We eat in silence again until I say, "Are you going to sue anybody?"

"Lauderdale Pines. Bahia. Sheriff's Department. Prosecutors," he says, as cool as if I had asked about the weather. "Tammi's taking care of it."

"Any individuals?"

"Every one of them."

"Lyle, too?"

Steve Orbach's cold, appraising eyes glance up at me. "Yes," he says, and then he shovels in the last of his meal.

"But he set you free."

"No." He looks at me. "You did that. He was going to let me rot, just like every other cop."

I have run out of questions.

When I reach for the bill, he beats me to it.

"But Steve, Tammi wants —"

"No. I'll get it." He insists on buying, even though it's expensive. The truth is, I'm afraid to argue with him over it. I'm afraid of him, period, guilty or not. But I don't want him to sense that, so I smile and say, "Thank you."

"How much tip?" he asks me.

"Twenty percent."

"It was fifteen the last time I was out."

We part on the street, after he refuses my offer of a lift to his apartment. I'm happy for him. And glad he doesn't want to ride with me. I don't know what we've done to the world by springing Steve Orbach on it, but he is finally free as justice demands that he be. Whether this has been a good deed or not remains to be seen, however. And I will probably never know, unless some day I read his name in a newspaper again.

I watch him disappear into the crowd and hope that never happens.

This same Sunday is the last day of the month I've given Franklin.

Normally I wouldn't see him on a Sunday, but he called just a little while ago to ask if he could drop by. Maybe he's going to plead for an extension. I'm not inclined to grant one.

"You've violated your parole, Mr. Prosecutor."

For this bittersweet occasion I've taken particular care in dressing, putting on my makeup just so, arranging my hair in a way that suits me, choosing the prettiest colors in my closet.

I want him to miss me, dammit, because I'm sure going to miss him.

What's that sound? Is that my doorbell?

Isn't this where I came in? But this time, it won't be Jenny and her mom, and this time I check a mirror before I open the door.

"Hi, Marie."

It's Franklin, smiling at me in a tentative way, as if he's not quite sure of his welcome today. But I see he has brought some insurance with him. Two small children.

My heart rolls over in my chest and I am awash in relief and gratitude. He didn't have to go this far — I never expected this, or would have asked for it — but how very good of him to make his statement in this particular way.

Feeling desperately shy, I smile at the children. "Hi."

Their dad places one of his big hands on each of their small heads. First he introduces the little girl. "This is Back-Flip Bertha —"

"Dad!" his beautiful six-year-old daughter protests.

"And this is Soccer Head."

His three-year-old son giggles up at me.

"AKA Diana and Arthur," I say.

They're the budding gymnast and the boy who can't wait to play soccer.

"What's hay kay hay?" little Arthur asks. He's so cute I want to scoop him up and embarrass him with kisses. No wonder Franklin wants to devote his entire weekends to them. I don't know how he can bear to leave them on Monday mornings and be so loving and uncomplaining to me by Monday night.

"AKA is 'also known as —'" Franklin stops when he sees that's too much for the child to grasp. "It'll make more sense after you know your alphabet."

"I know my alpabet! A, B—" Arthur's still reciting letters as the three of them troop past me. Diane looks watchful, suspicious of me, of why her dad has brought her to see this strange woman they've never met before. This woman who is not her mother.

"We're going out to supper," Franklin tells me, "and I wondered if you'd like to join us."

His daughter looks as if she wants nothing to do with this idea. Arthur, meanwhile, up to his XBZ's, is racing for one of the sliding glass doors, which he throws himself against with a thud that sends us all hurrying after him to make sure he survived.

"Oooo," he exclaims, pointing to the bridge.

His dad shakes his head, then looks at me, waiting for my answer.

"Thank you," I say directly to him. But then to Diana I say, "But this is your time together. I think you should have it all to yourselves. May I take a rain check?"

"It's not raining," Arthur explains to me.

His sister looks up at her dad to see if he'll insist that I go with them.

"I really want you to go," Franklin says to me.

"I appreciate that," I say. My tone of voice is light and casual, but I hope the look in my eyes tells him how intensely I mean those words. "But I have a compromise idea. Stick around long enough for some pink lemonade. And then you guys go off on your own, because I've really got to work tonight."

Diana's whole little body relaxes.

Franklin smiles at her, and then at me. "I think we could take a few minutes for lemonade, if that's okay with you kids."

"Mo-nade!" Arthur yells.

"Yes, please," his sister says, happy enough now to join him at the glass and to exclaim over the view.

I went out to lunch with Antonio Delano last week — not on a date, just to talk about the Wing case — but it wasn't much fun. He spent most of the meal bitching about the trials, pardon the pun, of being a prosecutor. The man in my living room at this moment will never do that; he's doing what he was born to do. Does it conflict too much with what I was born to do?

Maybe not if we do it out in the open, in the sunlight of public opinion. That should keep us honest. Not only that, but he's willing to put up with a writer who goes underground for weeks at a time and who looks like Medusa when she surfaces. There's a lot to be said for a man like that. And, anyway, there's nothing wrong with Franklin DeWeese — or with me — that a few movie dates and some pink lemonade won't cure.

I believe I'll pick up some vacation travel brochures tomorrow.